* * * * *

FINDING

AN

ECHO

by

JACK FRANKS

KDP PUBLISHING

For Ethan

*****

PASTURES OLD

I

Helmand Province, Afghanistan

THE town was eerily quiet and the retreating sun left long black shadows dancing at their feet. The men's black boots, steel capped and stiff, pounded along the unforgiving, arid, sandy floor. Each step kicked up a small puff of dust that bellowed in a silent zephyr and waltzed round the camouflaged troop. Each man had his own heavy duty rucksack and regulation desert camouflage for the mission ahead. Their helmets were equipped with microphones and receivers but the soldiers were mute, focused only on the sounds and movements all around them.

A man's scream pierced the stillness, a deathly echo mocking them, as the scream reverberated into the distance. The shriek from their comrade rang through their headsets from his microphone, but it was distorted by the pitch of his screams, which only served as a chorus behind the live screaming from him just a few feet away.

It was Private Singh that had fallen. A man at his physical peak capable of running a mile in under five minutes and someone who often proudly boasted of once running twenty-five marathons in ten months. His party trick in the barracks was to challenge any man to a one-handed push up competition, whilst smoking a cigarette, and those who witnessed it could attest he once smoked two cigarettes in a row to beat an American marine.

His screams rang louder but instinct took over. No one ran to Singh's aid. He was left on the ground clutching what was left of his leg. It was a textbook sniper manoeuvre: shoot one soldier in the head and the rest will hide; shoot one soldier in the leg and the rest will come to his aid, then you can pick them off one by one. However, these men were war conditioned now, and every one of them darted in separate directions to their nearest hard cover.

"Everyone stay where you are, do not approach him. Sniper in position far left tower," shouted John.

"If we wait too long the sniper will kill him and move," replied Private Denning.

Singh's screaming was relentless. The high velocity sniper bullet, almost 3 inches long, had gone straight through his thigh above the knee, obliterating the bone. His leg hung on by only skin and sinew. His comrades knew that he would pass out soon and they would only have minutes to stem the bleeding.

"I'm gonna move and take this fucker out. On my call, one of you has to put yourself out there and reveal his position," shouted John.

"I'll do it boss," replied Private Danny Blake.

It was difficult to hear one another over the screaming.

The town was deserted. The small two-story town houses were a monolithic, dirty-white but lacked any individual character or life. Towards the centre of town ran a dusty road which was occluded by a tall bell tower with a clock at its summit. Even the houses seem to frown with overwhelming ennui. There wasn't a person in sight: no vehicles, no stalls, no shops open, a venerable ghost town: a perfect ambush.

John darted from behind the low brick wall from which he had taken cover and round the back of a row of town houses, keeping his head low as he ran, moving quickly, zig-zagging his run. He was met by a row of backyards with six foot high walls between each of the thirteen domiciles laid out in front of him. He threw his gun over his shoulder and ran and vaulted the first garden wall. It was easy enough, just twelve more to go. He ran, jumped, ran, vaulted, ran, climbed, ran, and sprawled: it reminded him of his time as a junior recruit completing his PT drills to make the grade as a soldier. As he vaulted the final wall along the row of houses his arms ached and his hands and knees had been cut by the coarse brickwork. His fingers and hands bled a sandy crimson which struggled to flow over his callous hands. He could see the church tower ahead of him now.

"Okay, go, go, go!" barked John over his headset.

Private Blake received the muffled response from John and sprang into action. He ran out from cover just metres from Singh who was now lying silently still, cradling his own leg as he lay there peacefully. Blake ran and jumped over Singh and continued forward to cover on the other side. A sniper round was fired in the distance which moments later whistled across the floor by Blake's feet.

"Mine," said John, as he witnessed the sniper's rifle peeking out on the third floor of the clock tower.

Fearing the sniper would take umbrage at being duped and decide to shoot Singh fatally, John barked another order, "Start firing, I need sound cover!"

A hail of bullets rained on the bell tower. John set off, running at full speed from the end of the row of town houses towards the base of the tower. He ran through the door and listened intently for footsteps or voices. He noticed a staircase to his right inside the old building and ran towards them. The sounds of gunfire drowned out his pounding feet ascending the staircase. He counted the floors off in his head: *one, two, three*.

He slowed now to a crawl as he reached the landing of the third floor. The sound of someone panicking in the room to his left could be heard; the sounds of metal being packed away and the unscrewing of a sniper sight. John was now breathing heavily and his heart raced as he felt his muscles pulsate under the skin. He bent down low behind the door to the third floor room. Most men would just walk away from the gun but resources were tight for the rebels and he'd have to pack it to take with him. John knew it was time. With a sangfroid motion, he withdrew his pistol slowly from the holder on his thigh and entered the room with a mouse's patience. The sniper was looking down packing his equipment as bullets ricocheted off the tower walls.

"Cease fire," John said over the headset.

As the sniper turned, John placed the barrel against his cheek, a kiss of death, and shot once into the face of the tanned man. The sniper, a son, a brother to five siblings, and father of three, died instantly. Singh died before he reached the medical bay.

FINDING AN ECHO

*****

II

CARGO

GALBRAITH strode along the pavement with celerity and purpose. It was not the workload she was nervous about, or the task ahead, but the reaction from those who would soon be deemed her colleagues. She knew women found her intimidating, and men failed to look past her alluring dimensions. All the attention was a curse. In school, she had been singled out by the other girls; jealousy often precedes hate. She maintained her brisk pace, marching along the grey pavement, while the wind brushed her white hair against her frosty, pale cheeks. Gravity pulled her head down but pride kept her chin held high. Rush hour morning traffic queued, as she segued through the small gaps to cross the road, zig-zagging through the cars. Somebody sounded their horn over the new album she had playing in her ears - *Choruses From The Cherokee*, and a cyclist threw her a censorious look.

Having crossed the road, she began counting the small numbers along the building line. The sky cast a grey filter over number 221 and a large nimbo-stratus was spitting out a distasteful sun. She had reached her destination, arriving early of course, in time to pass through the office unnoticed to await the perfunctory dressing down from her new inspector. She had planned well for today: she was wearing minimal make-up, but depending on the office demographic, she could apply more. Her hair was freshly cut, bobbed to just above the shoulders; her suit wasn't new or ostentatious, and mostly unrevealing; her shoes were flat and her nails bare. As she approached the opaque glass of the front door, she caught her reflection, dark and unrecognisable.

A friendly man whose nametag read Ernie greeted her at the front desk with a bright smile and showed her the way to the CID office.

"You must be Imogen? I'm Inspector Walsh," she said extending a hand.

A thousand thoughts raced through her mind. She hadn't had a female boss for a while and was glad to have toned down her appearance. The inspector had not given her first name causing Galbraith to immediately grasp who held the power. Walsh firmly shook her hand and their eyes met for the first time. Galbraith was smart enough not to wait for the inspector to break the stare. She noticed her expensive earrings, ringed fingers, red designer suit and the cleavage highlighted by a gold pendant hanging slightly too low. The pair exchanged pleasantries and walked into the inspector's office, closing the door behind them.

Galbraith followed the standard procedure, nodding politely and keeping her attention focused. Inspector Walsh asked about her level of service and what she wanted in terms of her career. But mostly, the inspector discussed her own vocational exploits and what she expected of Galbraith as part of her team. Her pedagogical musings began to tire Galbraith after the first fifteen minutes. Once the inspector had finished her introduction ad nauseam, she stood up and opened the door offering her a sparkly hand out of the mire. Galbraith felt the first pang of nerves. Walsh led her into the office where faces began to pop up over desks like meerkats rising over paper hills.

"Team," she began, "can I have your attention please? We have a new member joining us today. This is Detective Constable Imogen

Galbraith and she has come from the lovely borough of Kensington and Chelsea to work with you reprobates so please make her feel welcome-"

"Apologies," said a latecomer who walked between the two women stood at the front of the office. He made his way to the far corner as Walsh's eyes followed him like a spotlight on a stage. He reached his desk and Galbraith noticed how the stranger, unlike the other men, appeared indifferent to her presence.

"As I was saying, Imogen is a brand new detective who has been posted to our squalid hellhole. She informs me that she is unfamiliar with the area so I will pair her up with one of you until she finds her feet. I know you will all make her feel very welcome. She will be joining Martin's sub-team. Be nice."

Galbraith saw the same faces she had seen ever since joining the police service; men with mouths beaming wide, surveying eyes and wandering minds. Walsh then glanced over to the latecomer and said, "Forrest, my office please."

"I'm not interested, Ma'am."

The inspector replied, "John, I've looked out for you for a long time now. How many times have I looked past your tardiness, your poor dress standards, and the fact that you seem to be growing more unstable every day? Do you know what those people out there say about you? They think —"

"I don't really care what they think," he said, sitting with his hands interlocked at his chest. He appeared to be very calm, almost halcyon.

"And that's your problem. This is a disciplined service, John. I think you need some time off. Why don't you just take —"

"I told you, with all due respect Ma'am, I'm not interested in taking any time off. And I don't care what people say. I've never let you down, and you know that." He spoke without any animation or physical gestures.

The inspector paused before speaking, "Okay, if that's how you want it to be. I've been thinking, the new girl needs someone who knows their way around and you need a friend. I'm pairing you both up." John opened his mouth. "And don't even think about saying no," she continued, "this could be a good opportunity for you, for both of you."

Beads of sweat ran across his leathery skin, as he sat, cooking under a barren sun. His heart no longer red was tinged a dark crimson, blackened but not yet black, immolated by time and experience. The melancholy Forrest was unable to see the end of his torment. His arms tucked into his body, he leant forward to get a closer glimpse of the gravelled tarmac. Straining to think positively, he tried to smile his way out of the despair. But the smile was false, his eyes gave it away, and one corner of his mouth soon subsided. Forrest threw the cigarette away to the ground and crushed it with his boot. He stood up slowly, turned and headed back into the office, blowing out the last of the smoke.

The building was too hot and the heating ran all year round. The walls were grey, plain and oozed institutional. The occasional notice board gave outdated information, and news clippings of old glories littered the halls; *you were only as good as your last job*, thought Forrest. The fire retardant doors were heavy and the corridors were devoid of sunlight. He passed a familiar face, but not one that would engage him in eye contact.

He strolled into the office and headed to the corner desk that had been his nook for the past four years. The weathered detective removed his jacket and rolled up his sleeves before sitting down; a tattoo of an eagle's wing peeked out of his shirt. Galbraith sat opposite him looking sheepish. He could tell she was reluctant to break the ice, but serendipitously, it was the radio that broke the frosty barrier.

"*All units, immediate response required, any units free to attend the ExCel London Centre. Reports of a suspicious death. CID required...*" *said the female operator.*

"Get your coat, kid," Forrest muttered.

Galbraith stood up swiftly.

"I'm Imogen by the way," she said as she looked at him with eyebrows raised, wondering whether to extend a hand.

"Good for you," he replied, still not making eye contact. "Let's go."

Forrest drove through the busy London traffic with aplomb. Galbraith noticed his calm efficiency and his ability to read the other vehicles like a savant. At one point he broke away from the in-built Satnav's verbal orders to turn right. He noticed Galbraith's head turn towards him, so he muttered to her, "Crane in the distance." She did not quite understand and dwelled on the thought. The siren whistled above their heads and inside they could hear the revolutions of the warning lights. Galbraith was pondering her tattooed chauffeur. *Why was he so aloof?* It was as though she never existed. They did not speak and neither party showed an interest in doing so. She knew better than to take this personally. She had seen the other officers' reactions towards him when he appeared late for work. She had noticed the inspector's disapproving stare, and that he had not ironed his shirt; she even wondered if he had slept the night before, or was sober, or even mentally stable.

The two officers arrived at the ExCel London, a large convention centre on the River Thames. Huge signs hung over the façade of the building announcing *London's Biggest Car Show* to be held there at the weekend. Uniformed police were already on scene and had surrounded an articulated lorry with its rear trailer doors pinned open. A small crowd of workmen in high visibility jackets had gathered to watch the commotion. Forrest pulled in front of the artic and got out of the car without saying a word to her. Galbraith busily searched for her notebook and pen, took the radio, her cuffs and her coat. The lorry driver was speaking with two officers at the side of the road whilst another two were stood at the rear of the lorry with torches in hand.

"Wait!" shouted Forrest. "Don't go inside that lorry!"

One officer, who had already placed a foot on the rear step of the artic, quickly retreated. Forrest then made his way over to the driver. A sergeant who was stood by him turned and opened his notebook to brief the approaching Forrest, but he dismissed him, and looking only at driver, said "Tell me everything."

"I come from Italy. I got tyres in there..."

The lorry driver explained in an Italian accent that he had driven from Florence on a delivery to the ExCel. He said the vehicle was stocked with expensive tyres for sale at the car exhibition and he had a breakdown of the goods on a manifesto. He said he collected the lorry but was not present when it was loaded and had no idea of how it had happened. He explained that he had left Italy twenty-five hours ago, travelling through Switzerland, into France, across the Channel from Calais and on to London. He spoke about taking a break in Dijon where he slept in his cab overnight. After waking up, he went to his cargo and checked the seals on the load were not broken. Having done so, he set off for England.

When he arrived at the ExCel, he made his way to the depot and spoke with the delivery controller. At this point, he opened the rear doors and was almost knocked off-balance by the smell. An effluvium of death lingered in the back of the trailer. Forrest listened intently. The driver explained that he had seen this once before, and without hesitation, he called the police.

"Constable, can you take Mr Bargasso to your car and provide him with a seat?" said Forrest.

The constable escorted the lorry driver towards a marked police car parked at the edge of the road.

"You two, set up a cordon around the lorry and then speak to the on-looking workmen."

The two officers nodded; one took cordon tape from his vehicle and began securing the scene; the other officer approached the group of onlookers and began recording their details.   Forrest then met with the uniform sergeant on scene. It was a difficult balance to strike. The sergeant outranked him, but this was a CID matter, and Detective Forrest had overall control.   "Sergeant, I need you to question the delivery controller for the depot. I want to know who made the order for the tyres and to confirm the driver's story with the logistics company."

He nodded bashfully in reply. Forrest then made his way back to his car and pulled two packages from the boot. He returned and threw one of them at Galbraith.

"Put that on, kid. You won't need any of that other stuff."

He was looking at her coat and notebook cradled in her hands as he spoke.

Galbraith appeared concerned. "Shouldn't we wait for the Scenes of Crime Officer to get here?"

"Why?" he replied. "I don't need a forensic expert to tell me what a dead person looks like."

The reality of the situation dawned on Galbraith. She had seen a dead body before, taking the report of an old man who had passed away whilst living alone, dying comfortably in his sleep. She had also seen a post-mortem as part of her initial training, and she never forgot the sucking sound that precedes the human skull being removed from the brain. But this would be different.

Galbraith opened the package he had thrown at her revealing a forensic suit packed tightly inside. Forrest and Galbraith began dressing at the roadside. They donned the white paper suits, taped their gloves to the sleeves, put plastic covers on their feet, pulled the hoods up over their heads and finally placed masks over their mouths. Both officers held torches and Forrest entered the rear of the lorry first. The eighteen-wheeled beast stood 14ft high and the cargo was packed almost to the brim. The tyres had been exposed from their wrapping which lay scattered around the trailer. Forrest climbed up the rubbery row of tyres at the entrance to the trailer and vaulted on to the top. He was able to see into the depths of the lorry: it was dark and the loose wrapping made it even harder to see clearly. The smell of rotting flesh pierced his face mask and the hood made his journey even more cumbersome; he ventured further into the hold. Suddenly, a face appeared in the light of the torch and its eyes glowed in the dark. Forrest stared at him through the beam. The face swelled with tears and the mouth cried a foreign lament. It brought memories back to Forrest which he cared not to relive.

Eight people had begun that journey, but only two had survived. Forrest helped them both from the hold and out into the light. The six remaining bodies were left in situ and forensic teams were brought in. A coroner would establish the cause of death but foul play was not expected. The lorry driver would be formally interviewed and his history researched, but most likely he had been an innocent party in the travellers' quest for a better life. There would be no media jeremiad and the exhibition at the centre would continue on as planned.

Galbraith had a quiet moment with Forrest in the station later that night.

"What will happen to the two survivors found inside the trailer?" she asked with an almost childlike curiosity.

"They will be sent back home," he casually remarked whilst sucking on a cigarette.

Home, she thought, *what a funny word*.

FINDING AN ECHO

*****

III

HOME

GALBRAITH lifted one leg out from the foamy sheen and watched the bubbles pop as she wriggled her toes. She saw the colours of a rainbow swirling in each small bubble nestling on her glabrous skin. Closing her eyes, she concentrated on freeing her mind from all thoughts, worry and doubt. She focused on being truly in the present, letting go of the day's events and the augur of tomorrow. She felt the warm water hugging her neck as she drifted lower into the tub. Sinking, the water caressed her head and face, as her mouth became an island on a soapy ocean. She breathed deeply, in for seven seconds, and out for eleven; the tension in her shoulders loosened with every breath. The water lightly bobbed around her breasts with each inhalation, as she watched her mind non-judgmentally and observed its deliberations.

Her mind hopped on Lilly-pads of thoughts: the new job... her boss... the journey to work... this evening's yoga class... was Masterchef on television tonight... she needed to call her mother... the water felt warm... John Forrest. Each thought lasted just a moment, like the bubbles popping on her skin, drifting in and out of her consciousness, disappearing as quickly as they came. Galbraith had meditated most of her adult life and had visited retreats in Nepal and Thailand. She was well versed in Mindfulness techniques and visited Amaravati Monastery in Buckinghamshire at least once a month. Neither her friends nor her fiancé shared this passion, but she found deep refuge in escaping the concrete clad capital, whenever possible.

John Forrest. Her mind stuttered, then fired incessant questions at her. *How did he end up like that? Were the rumours true? Could he endanger my career?* She hoped that tomorrow could provide the answers. She then climbed out of the cast iron bathtub and stepped on to the heated floor tiles. Making her way to the master bedroom she picked out a red silk nightdress.

"Sweetie, you won't believe the day I've had," he said, looking over his copy of a *Bill Bryson* book. "Those bloody Americans spent an hour talking about themselves and then dismiss your proposals as an afterthought. Word is that they have another bidder. So Andy's being pessimistic about the acquisition and wants us in on Saturday to work on the presentation. Sorry about that Poppet."

He put his book down on the bedside table.

"No, it's fine darling. It looks like I'll be busy for the next couple of weeks with this new job anyway," she replied

"How'd it go by the way?"

Galbraith climbed into bed.

"Today was pretty distressing actually. We found six people dead inside a lorry trailer. It was so sad. Two of them were still alive in there, too. They said they'd come over from North Africa and had managed to get into the thing before it left Italy. Then the coroner said that that number of deaths was highly unusual and he suspected carbon monoxide poisoning but wouldn't' know until the post-mortem was conducted. Can you imagine how awful that would have been for them being stuck in a lorry trailer, slowly being poisoned? I mean, this guy I was working with today, he barely batted an eyelid."

She looked over at her fiancé who wasn't batting any eyelids either, "Are you sleeping, Matt?"

Galbraith turned off the lamp and settled under the duvet. The super-king size bed sometimes made her feel like she was sleeping alone. She looked over at her fiancé. He still gave her the goose bumps she felt when she first saw him at Alison's 20th birthday, all those years ago. She studied law and he'd read economics. They were the perfect university couple, nominated by their halls as most likely to be the first Nottingham couple to get married. He had many other suitors and, to her great annoyance, she was once again the envy of other women. She watched him as he slept peacefully, before kissing him on the forehead and nodding off by his side, their feet touching at the end of the mattress.

It was gone midnight as she rode him like a horse into battle, swinging her head back and forth in theatrical fashion, she groaned wildly and free. He knew she was over-playing her part in this charade, but it added to the spectacle. He reached up and wrapped her hair round his large fist forcing her to lean forward as he sank his face into her breasts. His hands discovering the body before him; be it alive in lust or cold in death, he felt a sense of familiarity with a naked morsel. She thrusted her hips into his groin as he squeezed her tightly at the waist. Her body began convulsing, her nipples hardened, and her face and breasts swelled a cherry red. He squeezed forcefully as climax drew near and pushed so hard with his thighs that she elevated another foot higher above him. As he came, she clawed at his tattooed chest, raking new lines into old meat. He grunted and sank his head deep into her chest. She climbed off of him, one leg at a time, and slinked off the bed.

The naked woman gathered her black dress and underwear from the red carpeted floor and tottered off towards the en-suite bathroom. He lay still and supine on the white sheets regaining his breath and equanimity. A minute passed before he was able to roll over to the edge and plant his feet on the soft floor. The room was darkly lit by an unshaded orange bulb, and even though the curtains were open, it was a moonless night. To his right, a large mirror covered a wardrobe running alongside the bed. He caught a glimpse of his reflection and recognised a scene he had lived previously. Forrest put on his jeans and reached for his shoes as the bathroom door opened.

"How was that, honey?"

"Great," he said.

Forrest pulled his vest over his head.

"Why don't you stay longer big boy?" She twirled her hair with one hand, "We can do coke and fuck all night."

Forrest looked indifferent as he pulled his trousers up and began fastening his belt.

"Ain't my scene, kid."

"Well you just make sure you come and see your friend Candy again."

He pulled his shirt over his shoulders and began doing up the buttons.

"I'll think about it."

With his shirt done up, he pulled four twenty pound notes from his wallet and paid the woman.

Forrest headed for the door and skulked out of the apartment. He was not embarrassed about sleeping with a prostitute and felt no shame, but being seen by the wrong person was a consideration he bore in mind. Forrest was of the opinion that dating was a waste of time. He surmised that a man could join an online dating website where he would send out fifty messages to acquire one date. That man would meet a woman, and if lucky, she'd be better than average looking. They would go on a number of dates, ranging between 3-5, for which he was likely to spend around £200 to £400 depending on how much he liked her. During this period, the probability of their having a long-term relationship was less than 5%, with sex as a realistic possibility of approximately 33%. Ultimately, Forrest deduced that for an average spend of £300, and at a cost of 80 hours of his time, he would receive sex with a reasonably attractive woman. By hiring a sex worker, he could have equally satisfying sex with an extremely attractive woman for a fraction of the time and financial expense.

It was a cold night so he pulled the collar of his jacket up over his neck. He banged the box twice against his palm and then lit another cigarette from the packet. The walk helped clear his crapulent mind. *Would the new girl become another Georgina?* Forrest got home before 1am and looked in the fridge. It was empty. He finished off a half-drunk can of cider from the night before and tossed it into the bin. He then bypassed the bathroom struggling to walk in a straight line from the vodka headache, and went straight to bed, in his clothes, alone.

As he settled down on his mattress, he rolled to the left and took out a lock knife from a drawer in his bedside cabinet. He pulled the blade out and the cold steel reflected a distorted face back at him. His index finger ran down the edge of the four inch blade, teasing the skin as he tested its sharpness. He then pulled back the duvet revealing the wooden beam running along the side of his bed. Blade in hand, he carved six straight lines into the wood, taking his time to get them all to the same size, length and depth. Once he was done, he lifted his head up and looked across the entire beam. There were 117 lines in total. He folded the knife up and placed it back by his bedside and fell asleep.

*****

IV

MEANS

Nine Years Ago

THE fish tank behind him gurgled and sloshed quietly, his ears were accustomed to the motion of the water and he barely noticed it anymore. An old clock ticked graciously in the corner, humming to itself with delight. The boy, bent double, sat at the wooden table, head in his hand, leaning into the paperwork in front of him. He was kept company by three text books that crept over him like an oppressive aunt.

He pulled his head up from his hand and, with the other, brought the letter closer. He was inconsolable, frozen and yet happy, in a soft, muted way. His mother entered the room with a clip clop as her shoes struck the kitchen floor tiles the way shoes ostentatiously would, drowning out the fish tank and the chirpy clock.

"What is it, darling?" she asked, pausing at the fridge door to look over at him.

"I got in. Leeds Uni have accepted me for Civil Engineering."

His words were slow and solemn. His mother closed the fridge and walked over to him.

"John, you listen to me. You're a wonderful boy. No one in our family has ever been to university. Your father would have been so proud of you, and I, I'm so happy for you."

She leaned over his shoulders and put her head behind him. Tears silently rolled down her face and she wiped each one away before it fell to the floor.

"I know, mum. But I'll be away from you for four years. And I don't know if this is the right time. If I take the army route, I'll be gone from you for so much longer. I'm scared I might leave and never get to see you again."

He was looking up at her as he spoke, the young boy lit brightly by the light bulb glowing over his mother's head. His mother sat down by him and took his hand.

"We've been here before, John. I've beaten cancer once and I'll beat it again. The doctors will do everything they can for me. This has already ruined my life; don't let it ruin yours too. You have to be free to do what you want to do. I couldn't live with myself if I got in your way. You can be the great, fine man I know you're capable of being. You just have to go for it, for me, for you," she said.

"And what if I take the army sponsorship and join them following my graduation?" he asked.

"Darling, we've been over this. You know we can't afford it otherwise. I can't support you and I spend all my time caring for your brother. What with the tuition fees, your rent, and social activities, you'll need to get a job whilst you're out there just to stay afloat. The army isn't a bad thing. Your father did well in the navy and was proud of his achievements. You too will look back one day with pride."

"But mum, I don't want to ever kill someone. I don't think I have it in me."

"Then you just work as hard as you can and you won't ever have to. A fine engineer in the army doesn't have to be responsible for deaths, they can be responsible for saving lives. Work hard and make yourself an asset."

"Thanks mum," he said.

The fish tank began to bubble again behind him and the solitary goldfish bobbed about in his bowl happily oblivious to the outside world.

*****

V

TWITCH

GALBRAITH arrived early at work to make full use of an empty gym. The issue was not access to the equipment; she was equally happy running on a treadmill as she was bench pressing; it was more the prying eyes and distracting smiles that put her off. The emptiness of the gym pertained to more than just the lack of its inhabitants. It was soulless, an echo of the lifeless station built around it, and clad in the same industrial grey and frowning décor – the only difference being this room smelt of stale sweat and shallow dreams of being, of being beautiful.

She boarded the RunTrack 2000 and set her run to level 14 at an incline of 4. *Thirty minutes should do it*, she thought to herself. As she ran, she kept her face forward and mechanically pumped her arms with each stride. She breathed in through her mouth and out through her nose. Her hair, tied back into a small ball, jigged side to side in motion with her shoulder blades. Galbraith's headphones pumped a mix by Electric Ambience, a Swedish house group, into her sweaty head. She managed 10 kilometres before her legs began to wane. She rarely felt enervated and was someone of the opinion that burning energy creates energy. She then slowed to a brisk walk before climbing off the treadmill and wiping her face with a white towel. She contemplated wiping the treadmill too, but why polish a turd when it would only dirty the towel.

After studying the gym, she picked up two 10 kilogram dumbbells and positioned herself ahead of a large mirror bolted on the wall. She watched her biceps grow as each arm slowly curled the weights from waist to shoulder. She had no intention of becoming a muscular woman, but found definition on women rather sexy, in fact, she found the figure of a woman sexier than that of a man; she didn't know why, but if presented with both sexes in naked form, her eyes always drew towards the female. She pushed herself hard for the next thirty minutes; the sweat now glided across her forehead and soaked the hair at the back of her neck. Feeling a little weary, she wrapped her towel round her shoulders and headed to the locker room breathy and a little dazed.

Two uniformed officers were discussing their pensions and moaning about low morale in the Service. One was rather adipose and the other looked older than the number of candles she was burning. Galbraith had heard this wittering from colleagues from the day she'd joined the police and had grown tired of the melancholy canteen culture. She had no idea why anyone would moan so much about their working lives and do nothing to change it. She headed for the showers with her 2-in-1 head and body gel and hung her towel on the rack.

She was not afraid to admit being conceited, but she liked her appearance. Public showers and nudity did not bother her. The body was the one thing that demonstrated hard work and dedication in an unavoidable, tangible format for all to see and she saw no reason to hide that. The dirty walls and weak water pressure made Galbraith rush her shower as she scrubbed herself rapidly. She returned to the changing area and found the two cohorts had since left. Galbraith felt good and a slow smile crept onto her face. There was time for one last look in the mirror at her naked figure before getting dressed. She viewed her obverse and saw how her waist curved in above the hips. She then turned to view her profile and patted her tummy quickly like a drum. She was happy. She put on a tight black skirt with no tights, a purple blouse, black shoes, and wore her hair down.

She was the first into the office and settled into the desk opposite Forrest's. She logged into the crime reporting system and saw Martin had assigned two crimes to her work file: a case of a flasher at a swimming pool and an arson attack on a vehicle. She read both reports and began an investigation strategy. The world of policing had become more about risk analysis than anything else; preventing harm to the victim and the public was the first priority in any crime followed by securing evidence and a conviction. The office was populating piecemeal around her. She began researching her flasher using the Police National Computer and saw he was an immigrant from India that had lived in the country for 6 years and had been granted leave to remain by the Home Office. Within fifteen minutes, she had deduced where and when he would be arrested, how many witnesses she needed to contact, the availability of CCTV, and a suitable time for her victim to provide a statement. She then recorded her risk assessment on the terminal and moved on to the arson attack. She started reading the reporting officer's comments when the smell of stale smoke wafted upon her. She looked up and saw a dizzy looking Forrest leaning over his desk. She pretended not to notice the large blue bruise under his left eye.

"Coffee?" he grumbled.

"I've got an arson to work on John. Sorry."

"Hey kid, if you sit in the office the skipper will just give you more to work on. And I'm guessing Walsh asked you to babysit me, so c'mon, before I throw my toys out of the pram."

The pair got in an unmarked car and headed into town. Galbraith pondered the answers to questions she didn't dare pose. He was an enigma shrouded in an aggressive aloofness that intimidated others and left much room for office condemnation and virile gossip. Her one venture with him created more mystery than it solved. Forrest parked outside a tatty café with flaking paint and a drab sign. As she got closer she saw the stained wooden beams that formed a porch seating area. She wondered if once upon a time this place ever looked inviting or vibrant, perhaps when it first opened, but soon deduced that was unlikely.

"My favourite place," he said, as they entered.

They went inside together and she noticed Forrest made no attempt to quieten his police radio as chatter regarding a traffic collision blurted out from his jacket pocket. The café was sparse and the only person present was a waitress sitting on a stool peering at her phone, inhaling her daily cycle of entertainment news and radiation. Forrest ordered for both of them; a camomile tea and a black coffee. Galbraith saw a moment of kindness in him for buying her the drink without offering her a chance to pay, but this was instantly dulled when he walked straight outside to sit on the porch not enquiring as to whether the cold would be an issue for her. He lit a cigarette and slumped into a chair. She was surprised when he started the conversation.

"Boxing."

"Sorry?" she enquired, coyly.

"You're wondering how I got the black eye. I had a boxing session last night."

"Oh."

Galbraith was able to get a good view of his countenance in the morning light. He looked older than he should - his leather skin aged by stress, cigarettes and fists. He had a fair complexion and his blond hair shone in the light, like a halo atop a sad angel. The cigarettes had wrecked his vocal chords making him sound like a rusty gate. She guessed he was once an attractive man, with friendly eyes and a soft nose, which had now become fused into what an internet dictionary might call an *'eyose'*, where the eyes and nose met in an unplanned fashion, like a jigsaw puzzle incorrectly finished by a restless man.

"So what brings you to this dump?" he continued.

"Oh, I wouldn't call it that" she replied. "I wanted to move somewhere with a bit more character. Kensington is a nice place to work, but it's too quiet, I want to really get my teeth into something juicy."

Forrest's mind jumped briefly to the night before.

"You sound like an estate agent. There is nothing here, kid. It's dark, miserable and lifeless. They don't like us here."

She paused. "I've heard it can be tough, but I like a challenge."

The female detective began rubbing her left arm as unease crept in when Forrest took a long, pauseful drag from his fag.

"It's not the challenge you seek. There are no victims or suspects here, there is no black and white; it's just grey. Every crime you investigate, your victim is just someone else's suspect. Each suspect you arrest has been a victim themselves. They will lie, they will fail to go to court and they will seek revenge. It's a lacuna of allegations that swirls everything in the same ink and is spewed out onto your desk."

He has a strange way of speaking, she thought. Silence fell upon her. She tried to think of something to say to build rapport.

"Well, I guess that makes it even more special when you get a nasty bastard sent down, huh?"

"Good point," he replied.

He gulped his coffee with the same hand that was fingering the cigarette.

"Late one last night?" she asked.

The conversation seemed as stagnant as the smell of smoke coming from his jacket. It was fortunate that the radio intervened, *"Can I have a unit now please, shots fired on the Albany Estate. LAS report one victim has received gunshot wounds. Units to make their way immediately."*

Forrest took a final gulp of his black coffee and replaced it with his radio, "Show Hotel-Tango 5 on way."

The pair headed to their vehicle and shot off in a whirl of blue lights and sirens. They arrived a few minutes later to find an ambulance parked up at the main entry road away from the apparent scene. The London Ambulance Service was obliged to wait until the police have made the area safe. The radio traffic was busy with different officers giving their locations as a rendezvous point was being established. A short time later an armed crew arrived and headed into the estate. They went to the scene and found a young black boy who had been shot in the back. He was lying on the pavement quite still, with one leg buckled underneath him. The armed team updated control on the location of the injured party - one of the four officers remained with him whilst the other three cleared the immediate area of potential gunmen.

They swept through the rabbit runs and tight alleyways of the estate but it was devoid of life. The ambulance crew then made their way to the boy. He had been shot once in the back and they feared the bullet had entered his right lung. They applied an open bandage to his wound so air could escape the lung without blood being sucked inside. The little black boy was given oxygen and his neck was then cradled in a foam noose. He looked so small and fragile, like a bird fallen from its nest, lying still on a hard floor.

Forrest went into auto-pilot; his actions were sharp, decisive and automatous. He directed the officers at scene and got them to form a cordon around the victim. He then noted down all the officers' shoulder numbers in attendance in a small black book which he produced from his pocket. He walked around the area and studied all the vehicles parked up and recorded their indexes in his notebook. He then walked through the estate noting the cameras that may have picked up the incident. His eyes darted about like an animal drinking from a water hole, on high alert for danger.

As he returned to the scene two loud bangs sounded close by. Neither he nor Galbraith flinched. The pair's heads tilted upwards as a red stream emblazoned the sky and the firework fizzled out into a dim ghost.

When the boy had been taken to the ambulance, Forrest told an officer to accompany him to hospital for continuity. The detective then stood near the spot where the boy was shot and turned in a circle checking to see all the windows and premises that overlooked the scene. To the left, the building closest to the scene was a five-floor block of flats. It appeared to be deserted and many of the windows and doors had been bricked over to prevent squatters. Even when a flat had curtains in the windows, they were old and stained and the tower-block appeared neglected. There were no lights on in any of the rooms and Forrest pondered it carefully.

He knew two things: firstly, squats like that were perfect for dealers and gangs to operate from as police would not be able to connect the property to any person, and secondly, if the shooter was not local, he would not suspect anyone in that block to have witnessed the shooting. He walked over to his unmarked car parked nearby and triggered the siren. A loud caterwauling bounced off the decrepit structure for five seconds. Other officers at the scene glared at him with angry consternation, but Forrest kept his eyes on the windows of the building. A curtain twitched at a window of the flat second to the right and Forrest noted it in his book before disengaging the siren.

He then looked for the most likely route a suspect would use to flee from the scene, which was the opposite direction of travel for the bullet and the way the victim was headed. He then called for a dog unit to attend to trace the route of the suspect and marked a new cordon to protect the likely egress route of the shooter. Galbraith stood there, quite otiose in her manner, feeling out of place beside Forrest who operated adroitly on his own. She followed him, like a duckling on a rough tide.

Forrest then gathered together the small number of uniform officers who were available to assist.

"Okay! Listen up! You two," he said pointing his finger at a pair of male officers, "go to that small estate to the north and start knocking on doors. I want to know what people have seen, heard, eaten for breakfast. Get the picture? And you three," again pointing at another black and white trio, "get over to that row of shops within the estate. Start asking questions. If the shop has CCTV, seize it. Don't take 'me not know how to operate it' as an answer. If they refuse, tell them we'll report them to the licencing authority. I'll see you all back here in thirty minutes for a debrief."

The band of uniform officers, alike in appearance and mood, seemed to all frown simultaneously in disgruntlement like one symbiotic entity. Forrest nodded at Galbraith and turned his face towards the window with the curtain that twitched.

Forrest banged on the door repeatedly but got no answer. He then opened the letter box and shouted inside, "I'm giving you three seconds to open this door or I'm kicking it in!"

He counted slowly in his mind. Just as three seconds had passed, he got into position to boot the weak lock when he heard a fumbling behind the door. It opened slowly and a shaggy head appeared in the gap.

"Don't mind if we do," said Forrest as he pushed his way inside.

Galbraith hesitated before joining him.

They walked into the living room of the squat. The room had a mattress on the floor with a uncovered duvet and no sheet or pillow – the mattress had a large round brown stain in the middle and was littered with cigarettes and ash. On the floor was an ashtray containing thirty or more butts, more were scattered across the floor. Yellow Styrofoam containers and cans of fizzy drink decorated the faded red carpet. The only furniture was a small wooden table and a sofa that had a rip exposing the padding. A solitary ceiling light lit the room, dangling there like an uneasy question, making one squint. There were empty beer cans on the wooden table along with tin foil, cellophane and a quantity of lighters.

"Why you lot here, I never did nothing mate," said the hirsute man. He appeared not to have slept for days.

"Let's get a few things straight. Firstly, I'm not your mate. Secondly, you're squatting here illegally. And third, you're abstracting electricity," Forrest said, as he pointed to the ceiling. "Now I can bring you in for this or we can have a nice chat instead."

"What do you want?" he moaned.

"Who's the kid?"

"What kid?"

The gaunt male looked down at the floor and began rubbing the back of his neck.

Forrest's eyes narrowed, "Don't fuck me about," he said, taking a large step towards the scraggy man. "Who's the kid who got shot?"

"Just get out! I've done nothing wrong!" he protested.

"You pissed off are you? Pissed? Well not as fucking pissed off as I am!" As Forrest shouted his head clucked back and forth towards the face of the gaunt man and his voice grew louder as did his rage. "Eyes! Look at my eyes! Who's the fucking kid! Who's fuck kid!" His words were lost to the rage coming from within and became of mesh of swearing, shouting and spittle.

Galbraith's mouth dropped open and she had to remind herself to close it. She saw first-hand how irascible her guide could be. The rumours of his capriciousness were true and she now saw for the first time why he had not been co-opted into the office bonhomie.

"Whoa, man, chill. Okay, I seen him once or twice."

He was leaning back cowering away from Forrest.

"What did you see?"

"I heard the shots, yeah."

"Shots?"

The detective's replies were within milliseconds.

"Yeah, three shots. About half hour ago. I went to the window and saw two lads cycle off. They had their faces covered. Your boy was lying on the floor, yeah."

"Faces covered?"

"Yeah, like green scarves or something."

"And?"

Forrest was still staring at him.

"Another boy ran off in the opposite direction. It looked like he was with your boy."

"You know them, don't you, yeah?" Forrest said sardonically.

"I've scored off him a couple times, that's all. I don't know his fucking name or nothin'. He's just one of the local lads, init."

"Scored what?"

"Some white, some brown. Look, I could get killed just for talking to you!"

The man rubbed his neck again.

Forrest shouted back, "You could get killed taking the bins out! Why was he shot?"

"I don't know!" he said as he raised his arms up pleading to Forrest. "I just fucking score from them, don't I. I don't ask questions, man. That ain't a good thing to do."

"Because?"

"What do you think? 'Cos they're in a gang, init. You don't mess with those guys, yeah."

Forrest and Galbraith left the flat and repaired to their vehicle. Galbraith's initial unease at the scene had been replaced with a strange veneration for her perspicacious counterpart. Only one hour ago, he had been unable to sit at his office desk yet here he was directing the officers who in turn obeyed him like loyal myrmidons. Forrest punched in the address of the Royal London Hospital in Whitechapel and began following the prescribed route. He started to ponder all the facts of the case and built an image in his head of what he knew, what he didn't know, and what he could speculate on. He knew that they shot more than once and the victim was running away. He knew that CCTV did not cover the incident and no witnesses had seen anything. He knew that the victim was local and involved in drugs, and thus, he could speculate that it was very unlikely he would be interested in pursuing a legal charge against the suspects. The suspects used bikes so there would be no leads regarding tracing a vehicle or using the local traffic camera network. He also knew that whenever a purported gang member was shot, local CID would not investigate the incident and it would be passed over to Trident Gang Command to deal.

"What are you thinking, John?" she asked as Forrest turned on to Whitechapel Road.

"I'm thinking... I'm glad Trident are the ones taking over the job. I'm also thinking the only thing we have to go on is the ballistic report. There are over three thousand firearm offences every year, Imogen. The only thing I care about is taking that gun off the street."

"Easier said than done, right?"

"There are ways to speed things up," he remarked, in a lazy and cold fashion, almost like he grunted the words.

The boy had been in theatre for the past two hours; the bullet was successfully removed and his lung closed. Certain hospitals in London specialised in gun and knife wounds and the murder rate had reduced due to this just as much as to the efforts of the dedicated police squads. The Royal London was one such hospital. The boy was taken to Ward 13C. Forrest began initiating the hospital protocol with the ward sister. A private room was designated for the boy and an armed guard stationed outside the door and another at the entrance to the ward. Anyone visiting the boy was to be photographed and their details recorded in a scrapbook. The officer would then take the image to the room and get the boy to confirm the visitor was welcome before allowing the visit to take place. This was also a useful intelligence gathering exercise for the police who could match names to faces and see to whom this boy was connected. They needed permission to seize the boy's clothing and that meant speaking with the family.

"What da fuck are ya doing to protect dem kids. Dis is da third shooting dis year on dat estate... I don't give a fuck if I'm shouting... No, I won't calm down... He's lucky he ain't been killed... Wait 'til his father hears about this!"

The buxom woman was stood outside the ward bedroom waving her arms around like an over-zealous conductor. She had a thick Caribbean accent and she sucked saliva between her teeth after every few words. Forrest was amused by her ability not to look either of them in the eye yet be quite able to be hugely offensive all the while.

Galbraith was struggling to communicate with the boy's mother.

"I understand Ms Williams but-"

"You don't understand nothin'! What am I supposed to do? Keep 'im locked in his bedrum? How can a boy get shot at ten in da morning, huh? Dey takin' da piss!"

Her anger grew with every breath until at last she scowled at the well-dressed Galbraith.

Forrest knew why he had been shot so early in the day. Tuesday was the day the local junkies got paid their benefits. The post-office opened at 9am and the queue was healthy albeit the people were not. Young drug-runners would wait nearby, in alleyways or stairwells, for users to leave the post office with their £60 weekly benefit ready to spend it all on a day's worth of crack. The dealers often tied a sock to the inside of their waistband, filled like a narcotic Santa's stocking with crack and heroin wraps; an area the police had no powers to search. Like rush hour traffic, the morning drug trade was as prominent as the evening. He also knew that he and Galbraith were persona non grata.

At this point, one questions the stereotype of the event. Two cops, neither of whom were of black descent. The young black boy shot in a drug deal, the mother with basic English and seemingly a hatred for authority. I'm aware that this might not sit well with some readers. Alas, a doctor from an ethnic minority may break the illusion – or is this a stereotype too?

"Ms Williams, we simply need to speak to him briefly. It's in his best interests," Galbraith said sotto voce, trying to encourage the inimical mother to speak softer herself.

"Fine, but if he tells you to leave den you leave, all right?"

The two officers and the mother entered room 4. It was a large square room consisting of a single bed that could be adjusted using a keypad, two chairs, a sink, a table stacked with medical supplies, and a private toilet. The boy was a veritable stripling and appeared dwarfed by the large syringe in his arm. The room was a pale blue and smelled of ethanol and disinfectant. The curtains were open and one could see across Whitechapel towards the City that seemed to be looking down on its neighbour from opaque glasses. Forrest stood at the foot of the bed as the boy's mother sat beside her son and took his right hand in hers. She pulled a small blanket over her legs, sat upright in the chair, and then readjusted her wig and the blanket once more; an action which made her look like an old granny taking her seat at church. Galbraith walked to the other side and bent down to the boy's level.

"Hi Kelvin, my name is Imogen. How are you feeling?" she said half-smiling.

"I feel bless, man. Not every day you get shot and live to tell the tale, fam."

Kelvin's happiness at his current state of affairs seemed to cause Forrest's lip to curl for a moment.

"Kelvin, what happened to you was very serious. Someone tried to take your life today. We want to do everything that we possibly can to catch those responsible. Can you tell me what happened?"

She pulled out her pen and opened her notebook. Forrest remained in the distance.

"Nah, I didn't see it. I was just doing my t'ing when some bredder hollers at me. I look round then next thing I see them masked up. He's got his hand in a shoulder bag. Man, I knew what was coming. I turned and bounced quick. Then pop, pop. Only knew I was hit when I fell over. That was it. Nothing more to say, fam."

"Do you know who they were?" asked Galbraith.

"Nah cuz, never saw their faces."

"How many were there?"

"I dunno, I just looked quick."

He started to withdraw.

"Were you alone?" Galbraith continued.

"Yeah, just me," he said looking down at his bare chest and stroking it twice with his left hand, wiping away imaginary dust.

She continued quizzing the boy but he remained defiant that he had no idea who was responsible or why. He refused to make a statement to police citing he felt unwell and refused to allow the police to take his clothing. Galbraith looked at Forrest with a look of surrender and shrugged her shoulders before thanking the boy for his time. As she stood up, the mother did also, releasing her son's hand.

Without warning, Forrest spoke.

"Why were the Harrington Boys on Albany's turf?"

It wasn't the question that was important, it was the reaction. Forrest knew the answer would not be true, but he had spent the last fifteen minutes studying the physiognomy of the young boy's face; the bass line in his voice, the tells, the truth, and the lies. Upon hearing this, the boy's eyebrows shot up at the centre and the eyes widened for a micro second. He then scowled immediately and his face screwed up into an angry ball. Forrest had his answer.

"Mum, tell them to leave. What is this bullshit?"

With that, the mother hurled a tirade of abuse at the officers, following them out of the room as they stepped to a rhetorical beat. They left the angry mother at the doors of the ward and headed for their vehicle. Forrest punched another address on the Satnav and began heading north. Galbraith read the destination as *Purple Shisha Lounge.*

"A shisha lounge?" she enquired.

"The Harrington Boys are a gang from Hackney. They've rivalled the Albany over the sale of drugs for many years. We understood that they had reached some sort of peace agreement as we've had no incidents this year, but old sins carry long shadows. The shisha lounge is their headquarters, so to speak."

"Can you be sure it's them?"

"Yes. They are known for wearing green colours, and his face told me all I needed to know when I mentioned Harrington to him. The shooting occurred at a point where the two territories meet. Don't get me wrong Imogen, I feel for the kid. He doesn't have a choice. None of us do."

Galbraith wasn't sure what he meant.

The Satnav informed her that the venue was only two minutes away and she began to feel nervous. She had seen how pugnacious he could be with a reluctant host and wondered how he would deal with a room full of men who may have just tried to murder a young boy in cold blood. Forrest turned off the High Road and into a residential area with a row of shops overlooking a gloomy 1960s estate. He parked directly outside a premises which looked closed from the outside. They alighted from the car and headed towards the front door of the black building. Outside the shisha lounge, a long wooden porch ran across the length of the venue. As they got closer, they could see a shallow light hanging over a bar and the sounds of chairs being scraped across a hard floor.

The door swung open inwards and Forrest stepped inside. The venue was lit in amber like a traffic light stuck between stop and go. Little sunlight was able to penetrate the tinted, dirty windows. There were black tables and chairs in long rectangular rows on either side of the walkway to the bar. Forrest saw dark faces in dark light staring at him.

"We're closed, man" said a voice behind the bar.

"Oh!" He shouted in hyperbolical fashion. "Is that right, boy?" said Forrest placing a long stress on the letter Y.

"Yo G, you heard the man. Get out or get wet," said a second unlit face at the back.

The two police officers continued walking towards the rear of the bar.

"I just want to have nice little chat with you, where's the harm in that?"

As Forrest ascended two small steps he found himself in the middle of a seating area surrounding the bar. Running along the wall ahead of him and to the right were benches with padded seating. The floor was bare and there were no tables or chairs aside from two stools propped up at the counter. The bar to the left sold lager on tap and the wall behind it advertised the *specials of the day* on a chalkboard, but it hadn't been updated in a while. Sat on the surrounding benches were eight men who appeared to have had their conference rudely interrupted. One of the men stood up and took three paces towards Forrest who was now standing in the centre of the upper deck. He walked straight up to Forrest's face and his cap brushed the top of the officer's hair. Their noses almost touched and the scene resembled two fighters at a weigh-in.

"You heard, get out" whispered the capped man.

"Tough guy, yeah," said Forrest. "Why don't you make me big boy."

The two men were both frozen to the spot. Forrest and he locked eyes on each other, neither wanting to back down. The large man facing Forrest began to push his tongue against his bottom lip causing his chin to take a strange shape. His jaw then protracted and his eyes narrowed. Forrest saw him repeatedly clenching and unclenching his right fist.

Forrest leaned in to the man's ear and whispered to him, "Am I supposed to be scared, tough guy?"

"Sit down, Ricky!" said a voice from behind him.

"Yeah, take a seat, Dick. There's a good boy."

The man did not budge. He could smell the stale smoky breath of Forrest on his face. The man behind him called out again for him to sit down, and he slowly backed away, taking his seat on the bench. One of the men who seemed a little older than the rest and was sat in the middle of both rows of benches then began to talk.

"Look, we don't want no trouble, but you can't come in here without a warrant throwing your weight around. Now I'm nicely asking you to leave." He spoke well and used his hands like a politician to enhance his words. "This is my business and I don't want you here, so please leave."

The spokesman was wearing a purple jacket and white shirt and his hair and beard were immaculate. He wore a diamond ring on his right hand that seemed to bathe in the subdued lighting.

"Now listen up. I'm sure you're all aware that one of the Albany Boys got hit this morning," said Forrest. "Shot by some pond scum coward who belongs to your little boys' and toys' club. And seeing as you regard yourselves as businessmen, I'm going to offer you a trade: either you hand over the kid you manipulated to shoot that boy, and the gun, or I will go and get that warrant I seemed to have forgotten, but I won't be coming back here with it. I'll be kicking each and every one of your fucking doors in at four in the morning, dragging you and your families out of bed and shitting all over anyone who tries to stop me. I'll take your cars, your phones, your tablets, your Playstations, and you won't see any of them again for at least six months. So what will it be fellas?"

Forrest stood with hands on hips looking at all the faces sat staring at him. The man with the rings stood up, and upon seeing this, so did the remaining seven males.

"I said get out."

Forrest turned and nodded to Galbraith and the pair headed for the exit and back into the light. They could hear the murmur of the group as the door swung shut. A few moments later, the entrance to the shisha lounge was heard to lock shut.

Anger built up inside Galbraith. Her heart was clobbering against her chest and her hands vibrated a silent dirge. She felt the urge to scream but Forrest gave her no time and got into the car. She paused at the side of the road, closed her eyes and collected herself. She ran a mantra through her head to prevent the dormant from erupting and then focused on her feelings. She shone the light of consciousness upon the anger and strove to control it. *All anger is from the ego. The ego is a fallacy. It is the unenlightened.* As she concentrated, and began to feel peaceful, she heard a loud discordant car horn sting her ears. She opened her eyes, and saw Forrest looking at her with an eyebrow raised.

"You getting in or what?" he said.

She climbed into the car and the volcano finally exploded.

"Excuse me, but who the bloody hell do you think you are?

"Don't overreact, I had it under control."

"You could have got us killed or at least seriously injured! I'm not here to be part of some dick measuring competition! Don't ever do that to me again! You got that?" she said staring at him.

Forrest started the engine.

"Look, I know guys like that. You weren't ever in danger."

"Rubbish! That was totally unnecessary."

Her anger had not diminished. Forrest turned towards her and put his hand to his chin.

"Have you ever heard the story of the Gordian Knot?"

"What? What are you talking about?"

"The Gordian Knot? Do you know it?"

She was puzzled, but in her puzzlement, her anger had dissipated.

"No, I don't bloody know it."

Forrest sat back in his seat and began, "Midas was king of Phrygia, an area of Asia Minor. Midas erected a shrine to Zeus by binding a wagon to a pole held in place by a knot - the most complicated knot known to man. The ends were not visible and the knot had been hardened by the king's men weaving bark through it. Many had tried to untie the knot but all had failed. It was claimed that whoever could untie it would rule over the whole of Asia. Alexander the Great arrived and attempted to untie the knot but found it was impossible. And with that, he drew his sword and sliced through the knot exposing both ends. The riddle was solved and he went on to become ruler. Sometimes, Imogen, the most complex riddle has the simplest solution; it just takes a bit of force to get there."

"And how does that relate to your nearly getting us a good kicking?"

"Just hear me out for a second. The boy who was shot today will never testify. There are no witnesses, no CCTV and forensics aren't viable. The only lead we have are the ballistics. The gun is most likely a pool gun, used by different gang members whenever the need arises. At some point today, Trident Gang Command will take over the investigation and establish exactly the same thing. They will conduct hours of intelligence to eventually pin the most likely suspects as belonging to the Harrington Boys. They will then get authority from up the ranks to carry out surveillance on that gang, at which point, they're all in hiding and the gun is already secure with one of their ladies.

"You see, I don't care about that boy Imogen. I never did. He's just another unlucky soul growing up in a shit city where his only purpose in life is making money by any means necessary. I care only about getting that gun off the street. Gang members are like anyone else. They want an easy life with no stress. I needed to create panic. I want them to think the police are crawling all over them and warrants will be executed imminently. That I'm some rogue cop who hates their guts. The fact is I don't give a shit about them. If we can make them panic, then they might get rid of the gun themselves, or at least slip up and the surveillance team will catch them moving it tonight."

"So we did all that on a hunch of yours?" she looked at him unamused.

"Call it instinct," he said, putting the car back into drive and pulling away.

*****

VI

CHRONICLE

THE wooden desk was beaten and the room smelt of old books and pine. It was cold and a draft flew through a gap under the door. The visitor sat beside an old cast iron radiator, with only their clothing and thoughts for company. The ceiling lights were bright albeit the cover was lacquered by dust and dead flies could be seen spread across its plastic casing. Dust particles danced in the light like fireflies in mating season.

The visitor sat alone in a room that had been neglected by people and time. Glancing at one of the books on the wall, it read *Police and Criminal Evidence Act 1984 Guidance and Commentary*, dated 1993. The only sound was the low hum of a fan at the rear of their laptop, cooling its insides. White fingers danced on a whiter keyboard tapping out an unfinished symphony of someone's ineptitude, inability, cantankerousness and anger. A scathing rebuke on a computer screen, the typist continued their report on the subordinate protagonist.

Reading it back to themselves, certain phrases jumped out of the page… *has received complaints from fellow colleagues… anger management issues… Late for work… standards of dress failing… likely an alcoholic.* The list went on. The report was printed out, signed and dated. The typist then placed the paperwork into a folder and slipped it into a bag. They then packed the laptop away and left the room closing the door behind them, sending a surge of air that made the dust dance a little faster and ensuring time could stand still once more.

******

VII

MEETINGS

They breathed out a sigh of relief as the finishing touches were applied to the open crime reports. Galbraith was able to catch up on her arson investigation having got hold of the Fire Investigator's report. She then arranged for an arrest team to bring in the flasher the following morning for interview. With her crime reports up to date, she thought about her evening plans. There were a few options for her on a Tuesday but she had not spent any quality time with her fiancé in a while. She hoped that tonight they could eat a meal at their favourite Italian restaurant on Broadway Markey over a glass or three of wine. She pulled her phone out and texted him.

Sweetie, finishing soon. Any chance of making Roselli tonight? xx

She sat back in her chair and closed her eyes. It was a moment of solace following an unnerving day. *Ree-dee-dee* sounded from the table and her phone lit up. She looked at the screen and saw that *Darling* had sent a response.

Soz Muffin damn Japs this time. Gonna be a late1 x

She read it again, and thought about replying but clicked her phone off to prevent herself sending a woeful message. Lying back again, she resolved that her ideal plan wasn't going ahead and decided that she probably deserved a night of having her feet up with tea and television. She closed her eyes once more and took in a deep breath. As she exhaled, she noticed the light on her eyelids had dimmed. She opened her eyes and saw Forrest eclipsing the world above her.

"Any plans tonight, kid? Just wondered if you fancied a quick one?"

"Sorry?"

Galbraith's eyes popped open. Forrest noticed she had misread his gambit.

"A quick beer. It's been a long day so I'm off to see Mr Green for a pint, if you wanna join me?"

"Ummmm…" She groaned, tilting her head and squinting her eyes and cheeks.

"Your loss."

Forrest pulled on his duster coat as he turned to leave which made it spin round his body like a bull fighter's cloak, flicking up in the air. He headed for the door when Galbraith called out to him.

"Wait! Um, just give me five minutes, okay?"

They walked along the high street passing rows of shops and cars. One could tell instantly the demographic of the area from the businesses that catered to it. In the space of two minutes, the officers had passed three fried chicken shops, a kebab vendor, two betting shops, a beauty parlour, and a solicitor's firm that specialised in crime and immigration. They reached the junction and turned left into a quiet road lined with trees on one side and bags of rubbish on the other. A large estate on the right overlooked Victorian houses on the left. The tangible division of wealth was evidenced by a small group of teenagers lingered at the entrance to one of the blocks of flats, whilst on the opposite side of the road an aging woman clicked her gate closed and began ascending the stairs up to her front door. Forrest and Galbraith reached the end of the road where *The Green Man* stood proudly on the corner. He flicked his cigarette into the highway and the pair ventured inside.

Forrest asked her to find them a table and he went and bought the drinks. He carried a glass of White Zinfandel and pint of Guinness in his hands to the back of the pub where she had found empty seats away from other people. He kicked a chair out with his leg and put the Guinness in front of her. He then sat down and pretended to drink from the glass of rosé before saying "Whoops" and switching the drinks. A small smile slid across Galbraith's face. They said cheers and clinked their glasses before taking an initial sip of their drinks. Forrest then shuffled from out of his seat to another and positioned himself so that he could face the entire pub.

It was relatively quiet and only local people appeared to be inside; men on their third and fourth drinks at 5pm. A rotund man in jeans missing a belt sent coins into the abyss of a fruit machine. Another older man climbed out from a table with his crutch in his hand and tottered towards the toilets. The pub had not been decorated for what appeared to be decades and the table at which the officers sat had *Gaz woz ere 03* scratched into its top. A radio station played '80s music quietly out of the speakers and a muted television was broadcasting a sports channel.

This was the very pub that had made Galbraith feel uncomfortable growing up. She wasn't cultured in this way of being. She'd not had the parents who talked of pub life or culture; the parents she had had, had the idea of a pub visit being a country stroll and a meal with a glass of wine on a Sunday afternoon. Whereas Forrest was immersed in it, inculcated with stories from his father of the riotous life to be had based on alcohol and all those nights he himself had had since turning eighteen. In essence, the pub represented Forrest: it's appearance was tatty and torn, the inside decrepit, the music outmoded, the décor infra-dig, smoke stained and beer laden, with no future. Any reasonable proprietor would be better off simply knocking it down and starting again in another life. The Green Man was Forrest.

"So do you enjoy your job?" she asked him.

"The job? Yes. I wouldn't do anything else. The people though, are a different matter. Why did you sign up?"

She paused, "I'm still trying to figure that out. I guess it's clichéd but I wanted to make a difference. Sadly, that's becoming harder and harder. I've always lived by the maxim of *'Be the change that you want to see'*."

"Don't ever reduce making a change to cliché. It's the most important thing to an officer," He said somewhat surprisingly. "Anyway, I'd rather be the cash..." he joked.

It was clear that Forrest could be sincere, but rather uncomfortably. Perhaps that's why he drank so much and followed his thoughts with kitsch humour. He sipped his drink as she brushed her white hair out of her eyes with her hand.

"Your turn," she smiled.

"There are two types of officer, kid. There are those that went to university, smoked weed, took drugs, lived off their parents' handouts and after three years graduated. Then one day, they woke up and found out that they had absolutely no idea what they wanted to do with their lives and with their degree in photography or sociology, or whatever, so they joined the Force. The other type had a fascination with the police.

They've always wanted to fight crime, protect the community and lock up bad guys. So which are you?"

She frowned, "Oh, come on John, you can't honestly believe it's that black and white. Nothing is ever black and white. And by the way, I studied Law."

"Sorry, I'm a little bitter. You see, I used to think that you could only be an officer if you had the heart for it, but it is the ones who joined the police for all the right reasons that are now suffocating it. All those that joined with the best intentions to lock up bad people and help the good, they're now disillusioned, miserable bastards. They hate their job, they hate people, and the worst bit is, policing is all they know and all they're qualified to do. They will never leave, so they will carry on for the next ten, twenty or however many years doing a half-arsed job while the public suffer. And I hate them for it."

Galbraith nodded.

"I know what you're saying. This morning two females were chirping away in the locker room moaning about their pensions. One of them didn't look old enough to purchase alcohol."

"Get used to it, kid. Another one?"

"Umm… Okay, but it's my turn," she said standing up. "Guinness, right?"

Forrest nodded. Galbraith took her phone with her and walked to the bar. As he sat waiting, he did not look at his phone or fiddle around. He sat there staring ahead of him, replicating the other solitary men in the bar. When she wasn't checking her phone, she caught glimpses of him from the bar and was surprised by his catatonic look. *What could he be thinking?*

She returned and placed the drinks on the table. He was looking at her left hand.

"So who's the lucky guy?" Forrest said.

She looked down at her ring and rubbed it with her right hand.

"Oh, it's me who's the lucky one. He works in mergers and acquisitions. We're due to get married next June."

"And does Mr Merger have a name?"

"Ha, oh yes, he's called Matt. We met at uni. Sorry, I just meant he wasn't a cop."

"I know," said Forrest, cradling his pint.

"And you? Is there a Mrs Forrest?"

She rubbed the stem of her wine and brushed her hair away from her face, tilting her head slightly exposing her neck. Forrest was adept at spotting flirting and recognised this instantly. He would not read it into though. Many women flirted with men for attention more than lust, but it did make him question their relationship.

"Afraid not. There was someone once, but that was a long time ago."

He saw her looking at his face trying to read between the lines but he was stoic in his response. The wine had given her the courage to ask him.

"Georgina, I take it?"

He laughed loudly.

"You must be kidding? Georgina? Where did you get that information?" he was smiling.

"Oh, I must have overheard it in the office. You know what cops are like."

Forrest put his drink down.

"I guess you'll hear it sooner or later," he said sighing. "She was a great woman. It was a shame she left."

"So the two of you never had a relationship?" she asked.

"Ha, ha, no, never. She did break my heart though."

For the first time in Galbraith's eyes Forrest looked vulnerable.

"What happened?"

"You're not giving up are you?" He said half-jokingly. He sipped his drink and wiped the froth from his stubbled lips using his fingers, stroking them across his face. "Georgina and I worked together for years. As you asked, our relationship was totally platonic and built on mutual respect. She worked hard, played hard and wasn't afraid to throw a few fucks in whenever the situation called for it. We always laughed at the others in the office and their pathetic moaning, their inability to handle pressure; their sycophancy. She was as skilled as any detective you could ever meet. It was never about the money for us. Yeah, it's a tough job, long hours, weekends, nights, blah blah blah, but we never complained. Then one day, she came in, and told me that she was leaving. No discussion whatsoever, no warning, just that she'd taken a job in the City working for a bank on their legal enforcement team and had been offered twice the money to work a nine-to-five. When she left, I never spoke to her again."

Her mouth dropped and her arms locked at right-angles - Galbraith was stunned. She was watching his lips move, hearing his words, but belief had vacated her mind. *Is he for real?* she wondered. Her two eyes caught his, as his lids tightened round the blue glassy sheen of scepticism they propounded. She snapped out of the trance with a shuffle of the head like a beetle wriggling out of sand. Forrest swigged at his drink to the soundtrack of the fruit machine in the distance

"Are you serious? You never spoke to her again because she went and got a better job, for more money, and better hours?"

Her face and his were polar opposites. Forrest took a heavy gulp of his drink titling his head back.

"You don't do this job for the money, Imogen. Only the seat-fillers are here for the money. You do it because you hate criminals. Working for a bank is the equivalent of switching sides. She knew how I'd react and she knew she would lose me. It was her decision, not mine."

Heat crawled over his skin hugging him with unwelcome warmth. He rolled up his sleeves exposing the blue inked centurion on his left forearm. He then stood and Galbraith predicted an exit.

"Another one, kid?"

She looked down at her glass still half-full and cherry pink. Lifting the glass towards him, she uttered that she was fine. He returned a minute later with another Guinness that had already been decapitated. Concern circled Galbraith like a vulture – another question would soon swoon down from the sky of her mind and settle on the resting Forrest below. *Maybe if I leave after this one, he won't keep drinking,* she thought.

"Go easy there tiger," she mocked.

He knew what it meant.

"Maybe you should too?"

Her lack of understanding caused her to feel shame.

"This is only the second glass, silly: I can drink more than that; It's you who can't get in on time," she winked upon finishing the sentence but had immediately realised she had gone too far.

"I wasn't talking about the drink, kid." He looked directly into eyes that oozed confusion and bewilderment. "We all have to escape somehow, so what are you running away from?"

"I'm not running away from anything?" she said, still confused.

"I drink because I like it. You haven't stopped looking at your phone since you booked off at work. And by looking at you, you spend, what, twelve hours a week, maybe more, exercising and running. But what are you running away from, that's the question?"

"Trust me, John, I'm fine. I'd be more concerned about you right now."

A quantum of calm descended upon them and they sat at the table in the grubby pub for the remaining five minutes exchanging small talk. Forrest slowed his drinking to match hers and they finished in tandem. She was going back to the station to get her bicycle and he had a train journey to negotiate. Forrest drew a cigarette at the door and lit it as he passed the threshold. They separated with a simple goodbye and proceeded along different lanes to their respective homes.

Galbraith cycled along a busy highway; her black wheels hugging a blue path. She felt the cool calm air rush past her neck where the hair hung loosely. The paucity of space between her and vehicular traffic was more apparent under the influence of two glasses of wine and at one point she dismounted to pass a roundabout. Nevertheless, the journey was without incident and she arrived home to a house forsaken by her fiancé. She reached for a blanket and snuggled into the sofa, waiting for him to arrive.

Forrest's rolled up sleeves were still wrapped round his biceps as he clung on to a lithe handle in the roof of the carriage. Like wheatgrass in a windy field, the passengers all rocked side to side in motion dancing to different songs playing out of their earphones. The train pulled into Kings Cross station and a seat became free beside where he was stood. He pretended not to notice and waited for the female in front of him to take the place. She hesitated and a man in his thirties adjacent to Forrest took a large stride towards the vacant spot. Instinctively, with his spare tattooed arm, he reached across and blocked the man's path. Looking into his eyes, he muttered "it's not for you" and turned his body offering the man a reply to his back. He looked at the lady and was surprised by her beauty. Catching the coruscant hazel of her eye, he tilted his head towards the empty chair and she smiled and bowed an inch submissively. She sat down but Forrest went back to indifference. One thing he knew, he hated men taking seats on trains whenever a woman was present. Not elderly women, not pregnant women, but any woman.

Train journeys were somewhat strange affairs for Forrest. He remembered his first ever journey, escorted by his grandfather; how he was taught to wait for the passengers to alight before boarding, to allow women on first, and always offer your seat to a lady. This politeness in the detective remained constant over the years as society's genteelness had slowly ebbed away. Fewer and fewer women thanked him when he performed such munificent acts and he often questioned which came first: the death of chivalry or women who cared for it not. On one occasion, he stepped aside to allow a woman to board before him and she accused him of being a pervert. For all of his pleasantry, just as much as he was polite to those indebted, he was cavil at best when someone broke the principles that his father had laid down.

As the train pulled in to Mornington Crescent, he swung like a chimp across the flexible ceiling handles and to the door. The train pulled in to the station and blurred faces silhouetted his reflection in the glass. As the train slowed, those waiting on the platform formed a rock face. The train stopped and Forrest's presence at the doors created a fissure through the people and he passed through the gap with ease. This was not always the case. Forrest would not tolerate anyone blocking him from alighting the train, and should they ever dare to board before he had stepped off, he would barge or even extend a hand and push them back off. He was happy that this wasn't quotidian, albeit more commonplace than previously, and felt no joy in forcing his own standards upon others. When knocking people aside, he was rarely challenged and indifferent whenever he was.

He showed his warrant card to the station attendant who opened the gate for him and exchanged a nod of recognition. He pulled his cigarettes from his coat and lit it in sync with his first step out of the concourse. He closed his eyes on the first pull and breathed the smoke high into the air. A vibrating phone warbled in his pocket but he ignored it. It was quiet on the streets of London as he walked the next three streets home. Forrest felt tired and the cold chill on his ears made him dip his head like a footballer whose team had just conceded a goal. A solitary night walk home in the cold was as close to nirvana as he could grasp; no worries or doubts, or people to bother him. He walked with a curmudgeon sway, his arms swung as much as his shoulders, and his waist not at all. Still pulling his cigarette, he noticed a dark figure coming in his direction up ahead. As the two grew closer, the pavement appeared to narrow. Another principle of Forrest's ran through his mind.

He had a rule for passers-by: he would only ever move 50% out of the way for anyone. If the other person was as considerate as he, then neither would collide and order would be achieved. Conversely, if the person did not move to that extent, then Forrest would pile into them without slanting his body or leaning away. This often resulted in abusive verbiage from women or a stand-off between men. But the one thing he detested most was a person walking along the street staring into their phone. For this person, Forrest did not move an inch. He enjoyed reading but would not be foolish enough to draw a newspaper out and walk along Oxford Street staring at the sports pages and expect people to part the way like Moses before the Red Sea. *It's a matter of principle,* he thought.

As the male came near, Forrest had judged the gap; he had moved the required half-distance to avoid collision. The approaching male had not. He saw the male staring at a phone by his side, seemingly unaware of his advance. He had mentally grasped at the possible repercussions: he may be attacked, stabbed or shot, but principle was all he knew. The two men collided like crashing waves on rock, their bodies spinning round on impact causing them to stand vis-à-vis. It was dark and the street badly lit. Forrest could not make out the stranger's face cast in shadow. The man had a dog with him, the breed was unknown but it was large, hirsute, black and white mutt, and held close to his owner. The two men stood bathed in silence and moonlight, only their breath was audible: in any other context it would have been romantic. He could see the stranger was slim-built and thin necked, his head shaved, and an inch shorter. What surprised Forrest was the lack of response. A stare-down in dusk but no hot breath to scribble on twilight. Time slowed and seconds stalled to individual moments of time. Then the male spoke in sotto voce.

"I haven't got time for this."

He then took one step back and light flickered onto his face. It was only a glimpse but Forrest thought he recognised the stranger. He was not sure where from, too many arrests, too many victims; it could be anyone. His inquisitive mind went into overdrive and he observed the male as he span round and walked off in the direction Forrest had come, his dog beside him. He observed how the male moved: he appeared to walk with timing and balance, and thus, he ruled out the possibility the stranger had been drinking, however, he had a particular sway; the gait of a man concealing a leg injury, concealing weakness perhaps. He saw the man's thick black jacket, black jeans and boots. Too casual for an evening out in the town and the heavy coat meant the man had left his home once the cold of the night had already set in. *I haven't got time for this*, Forrest repeated to himself. *What was he doing with his time?* The man continued along the pavement and turned out of sight.

Forrest reached his door and took a look behind him before pulling out his key, already coveting his bed with his mind.

*****

VIII

DIAGNOSIS

Five Years Ago

THE hospital waiting room consisted of eighteen white, plastic seats. It was easier to clean the blood off such a non-porous surface. The man and woman held hands in the lobby but they weren't a couple. She wasn't crying, not at the moment, but it was clear that her tears were being held back for his benefit. The young man, wiry in stature, head held high and straight, seemed lifeless in the lobby. He stared ahead at a white wall, barely blinking. His lips were pursed and dry, and he breathed softly and deeply through his nostrils.

Her name was called out by an unfamiliar voice and the pair stood up in unison. They were met by a woman in a blue shirt and black jeans wearing a name badge around her neck. She appeared quite young for a doctor, or so he speculated.

They were invited into a small room with a desk; three chairs and a medical bed in the corner. The doctor's chair was able to swivel and was adjusted so she was slightly higher than the two strangers in her room. The doctor was young and still learning the knack for giving people bad news.

The homily didn't take too long. He wasn't annoyed with the doctor, or her constant use of medical argot, although the feeling of déjà vu irked him immensely. He'd been in this room before, not this exact room, but in a similar chamber of bad news. The same doctrinal figure had previously given his mother a moribund message causing her to fulminate like water bursting effusively from a pipe through the cracks in a street. But not this time. This time his mother was calm.

"The important thing is to not give up hope. Yes, the test results show the cancer has begun to grow in your left breast, but the mastectomy performed previously on your right breast was a success, and there is every chance if we remove your left breast we can prevent the cancer from spreading," said the doctor.

"But you said it wouldn't come back. My mother had the option to remove both breasts last time and Doctor Harris said that the cancer wouldn't spread and she didn't need her breast removed. And now you're saying we should," said John tersely.

"I'm sorry but I'm not privy to the information that Dr Harris had available at the time he made his diagnosis. What I do know is that at this time it is important to focus on remaining positive and doing what we can to help your mother. Miriam, I need you to consent to the operation and we need to act as soon as possible. It's a matter of time now and the longer we wait, the more chance there is of it metastasizing through your body."

"Yes, of course doctor. Please, anything," said Miriam Jackson.

"Hang on a second. Doctor Harris said that there was a new drug on the market. Floxa- or Flora- something. He said that it could be used to treat the cancer and that, that it had saved many lives already in Canada," said John.

"I know the drug you're speaking of and I'm afraid we can't get access to that in the UK. It was never passed for use. Now look, we should really-"

"What does that mean!" he blurted out interrupting the doctor. "If it's helping people and saving lives then why can't we have it?"

"Because it's too expensive. A course of Floxaperacin is around eighty-thousand pounds, and there's less than a fifty percent chance of its working. The government wouldn't certify it," said the doctor sheepishly.

"So if my mother was Canadian she'd be okay?"

"John, honey, just leave it. The doctors are doing what they can," said his mother.

"Doctor, I leave for the Middle East in a week. Is there any way the operation can be carried out before then?" asked the son.

"I'm afraid not. The waiting list is a few weeks even for emergencies like this."

As they walked out of the hospital they passed many seated persons in the same waiting area. Another unfamiliar voice called out an unfamiliar name and another couple rose together in the lobby to hear their fate. John looked about him. People in the lobby were staring at his mother, crying on his arm. But he didn't look at that. He looked at the faces of those waiting to be seen.

It was then that he began to realise the changing landscape of his home; how long he had been away. The faces looking back were foreign, clad in different traditions, tongues from other corners and allegiances sworn to far away flags. He saw them, and he detested them. He detested how they sat there in his hospital waiting to see his doctor. He fought against a savage militia from a desert land but all the while they'd crept in to his own country via the back door.

His fists clenched and his jaw became tight as he let the lobby door swing close behind him, his mother by his side.

*****

IX

CRACKER

THE instructor exclaimed, "Exhaling, bring your right to your left and push up into inverted-V."

Galbraith followed her mental checklist as she followed the teacher's instructions: *parallel outer feet, like a capital 'H'; pelvis high, sitting bones open to the sky; inside elbows turned forward; fingers spread, weight distribution equal –*

"And inhaling."

The instructor's voice burst through her inventory, more due to the echo in the yoga hall than the words themselves, which Galbraith knew by heart. She ignored the interruption so as to avoid allowing leeway to potential irritation, and inhaled her left foot forward, keeping perfect balance of her weight between her feet and arms, lower and upper body.

"Anjaneyasana. Stretch up toward the sky, lift and open chest, arms, stare."

Galbraith allowed a trickle of pride to seep into her sinews as she took in not only a measured, calculated inhale but also the success of her sun salutation thus far. They could say what they liked about the true nature of success in yoga, she understood these classes. She had been attending for long enough to teach something to any of the other forty-four beaming advanced session attendees. An image of Forrest taking his own special brand of command over the shooting that day interrupted the shiny serenity of the yoga studio. *Was that his problem: arrogance?* she pondered.

"Exhaling, bring your right to your left."

She lunged her foot forward and instantly shuffled it, in a tiny movement, almost imperceptibly into alignment with the left. *That's what happens*, she reflected, joining forty-four pairs of levitating arms and torsos, *when the mind plays its ego tricks. It's either I'm great and know what I'm doing and thus no one else exists, or I'm meaningless and my existence cannot change a damn thing. Perhaps Forrest wasn't such a mystery, despite the volcanic extremes of his actions.* And the as yet unmatched effect they had on her usually unruffled, professional demeanour. It was her own outburst she was ashamed at. She let the longest exhale of the series guide the smallest movement.

"Hands to prayer position."

She visualised her pride and allowed her perplexed thoughts to sink down through her chest, abdomen, pelvis, legs and feet. She closed her eyes and forced it, with the end of her breath, to bleed into the solid oak varnished studio floors beneath her yoga mat.

"Arms by your sides, step into mountain posture, and breathe."

She opened her eyes, and looked right into them in the mirror. She was always in time before class to slot her mat right at the front, where she could judge her posture and balance better by looking into her own eyes. She pointedly ignored the eighty-eight eyeballs reflected in the mirror.

The purple of her mat beneath her feet seemed to glare with words with which her grandmother had once presented her, "Purple is the colour of independence, Imogen, you don't want to wear too much purple – you won't catch yourself a good man!"

A faint smile flickered into the right corner of her lips as she imagined Forrest bursting into the class, dishevelled and bulldozing questions at people.

"Nice, Imogen!" her attention was brought back as the instructor spoke, "we can all smile now, ladies, can't we – it's Sivasana time!"

He awoke to a headache and sore eyes. Rolling over, he torpidly reached out a searching hand for his phone. A half-glance from a somnolent eye saw that he had no missed calls. *A good sign.* He lay in bed musing on his next actions. With a rub of his chin, he swung his legs over the side of the bed and finished the cheek massage he had unconsciously begun. He realised he had an hour before his shift would commence; *shit, shower and shave*, he thought. He rose from the bed and completed his daily routine on auto-pilot.

The kettle was flicked on and a double-espresso poured. He went into the bathroom and checked his face in the mirror. Age was creeping up on him and he refused to believe that his hair was receding despite conceding it now took longer to wash his face. He showered quickly and without joy and neglected to shampoo himself. He grabbed his toothbrush and began scrubbing his teeth rapidly as he ventured back into his bedroom and searched for a clean shirt in his wardrobe. A flashback: the punch to his head, the pain, the immediate regret.

He spat the last of the paste into the sink and buttoned the shirt hanging loose on his torso. He took a swig of the coffee he had made and left the cup on the kitchen table with the rest. Following a quick look out of his window at the sky to gauge the day, he grabbed his keys, badge, phone and cigarettes and headed out of the door.

The drowsy detective tossed his half-smoked cigarette to the curb and boarded the bus towards the train station. Looking around, he saw how he was surrounded by people of all ages wearing headphones and listening to music, music that was too loud, offensive, rude, and manufactured for profit. He saw those around him staring into their phones a foot from their faces with no idea of their surroundings. Their senses of hearing and vision stupefied. The zombification of the race had already begun. A young man, seventeen years old at most, sat beside him. The teenager had a nervous disposition, always moving, fiddling, and unable to sit still. He was listening to hard house whilst reading a Facebook page. Forrest looked at him with conceit and disapproval.

It was as though the youth of today were afraid of silence, afraid of monotony; afraid that if the mind was not occupied it could wander into the boring now, he pondered. He saw how those around him were obsessed with labels, brands, jewellery; the appearance of wealth. His thought stream ran wild, *a man creates an object from ivory or gold worth more than himself, more than his life was worth, to supply the vox populi's wealth fetishism.*

Forrest became aware that distraction was now normality for sapiens. We've become accustomed to a phone ringing somewhere, the fridge buzzing, the radio speaking, the TV flashing, vehicular traffic crossing the window, and our minds never still. To remove all distraction and find oneself in solitary confinement is a punishment even for those already in prison.

Forrest detested materialism. He rode the bus and took the train despite a healthy bank account. He used an old phone that had no applications and was barely accessible to the internet. He never listened to music and believed it was a distraction. He knew he was depressed, but at least he knew. *Is time now measured by commodity? We live to out-live others in terms of wealth. Our life is constructed by the string of purchases we make, or aim to make,* he thought: *An expensive wedding, followed by a bigger house, a better car, two cars, the promotion at work, two houses, and the final justification to pass it all on to children that happen to have come from your seed, incessantly to the end.*

A recording told him where he was and he alighted at the bus stop for Camden Road tube. He boarded the Northern Line heading south and took a seat on what was a quiet train. People-watching was a hobby of his, and he took joy in reading people's feelings by observing their behaviour. He was able to discern many character traits by simply spending time watching people and their patterns. He was adept at spotting fear, happiness, anxiety, joy, and many other traits no matter how subtle or how disguised. He also knew how to hide 'the tells' transmitted by himself.

He watched another young trendy type board the train at Kings Cross and frowned with contempt when the young man sat opposite him. The male, probably of university age, was the most vacuous of all beings in the eyes of Forrest. A goose amongst poorly informed geese. Waddling from one night spot to another dressed in whatever clothes a magazine had recently promulgated as cool. His hair, cut in the most inconvenient way, tattoos of regret along one arm without meaning or significance, ears stretched to the point of surgical correction, and facial piercings that only served to offend others. Granted, he was the extreme version, but Forrest's hate easily stretched to those at the lower end of the spectrum.

These people would tour the insalubrious urban nightlife of downtrodden pubs, dingy squalid bars and after-parties, which after leaving, most heroin addicts would even feel the need to wipe their feet.

They would snort cocaine cut with a smorgasbord of house products whilst talking about the importance of eating organic food; the types that sit in circles smoking cannabis whilst discussing world inequality and the unfairness of government yet funding the ubiquity of crime through subtle self-indulged means. Forrest pondered, *these people couldn't fall in love unless they'd read a social media post about it.*

Forrest knew he was a grouch, the uncool uncle, a non-fashionable non-liberal, but at least he knew.

He again arrived at work some minutes late and spotted Galbraith typing away at her desk.

"John, we've just had a rape come in. Uniform are down there. I know you're not one to stand on ceremony so shall we get going?" she said.

"My kind of girl."

It was a beautiful building of elegant design that drank light and feasted on the wealthy. There was a smell of lavender in the corridor and the walls had recently been repainted. The pair of officers boarded the lift and both stared straight ahead.

"Let me take the lead on this one, John," she said with purpose.

"All yours, kid."

They exited on the 4th floor to enter a bright and clean hallway. There was no sound and the carpet muffled the clack of Galbraith's heels. She knocked twice on number 404; Forrest spent a second studying the door. A uniformed officer answered; he looked relieved to see the detectives. He stepped aside and allowed the two suits to walk past him, closing the door behind them.

"Hi, I'm Imogen."

"Graham," the officer replied.

"So what do we have?"

"The victim is a Mr Carlos Ramon, aged 22, from America originally but working as a model here in London. He says that he was raped about an hour ago. He came home with the suspect after having a date. The male came on to the victim who rejected his advances. The suspect then anally raped him and made off straight afterwards. He's still pretty upset."

"Where is he now?" said Galbraith.

"In the living room with Smithey, um, Karen, I mean."

"How long have you both been here?" she asked.

"The call was made at one-fifty, and we got here at two."

"Has anything been moved?"

"No," he said looking around, "We've not touched anything."

"Okay, let me see him."

The flat had rustic, lacquered, wooden floors and cream walls with white skirting across the base. A table stood at the corner of the hallway beside the door to the living room that was only large enough to house a bowl of potpourri. The flat was sparse of furniture and it appeared that the tenant must have moved in recently. As she made her way down the corridor, the detective peered up to see three spotlights beaming down upon her. Galbraith took the first left and entered the living room. She saw a female officer and the victim, each sat on a separate sofa astride a table.

The victim had a damp tissue in his hand and his crying had made his eyes bloodshot red. He was wearing a white dressing gown with *Prada Amore* written in gold on the left breast; it was tied loosely at the front revealing a hint of chest hair and muscle. He was coy in his demeanour, his eyes glued to the floor, hands clasped in a ball at the front and the shoulders slumped – the embodiment of grief. It gave Galbraith a chance to stare at the man without raising suspicion. The victim had a tanned complexion, with incredibly neat black facial hair that ran thinly across his refined jaw. His hair was neat, his eyebrows plucked and his figure slight and nimble. He was attractive, and he knew it, but maybe that was all he knew.

There was a rectangular glass table in the centre of the small living room, and two mobile phones were lying on top of a side-table separating the two sofas.

Galbraith spoke softly, "Hello Carlos, I'm Imogen, and this is my colleague, John. Are you okay if we speak to you about what's happened?"

"It's okay."

"Okay Carlos, I know it's hard to go through it all again but please tell me as much as you can about what's happened."

Galbraith took a seat beside the sobbing man and pulled out her notebook and pen.

"Well... I met this guy from the internet," he spoke with a deep voice. "We've been speaking a little while and so we decided we should meet for a drink in town. He seemed like a genuine guy, y'know, sweet and harmless. I had a couple drinks with him in town and he offered to walk me home. We came back here and had one more drink together. Then, then, he came to kiss me. He..." he sobbed and wiped his red eyes again.

"It's okay Carlos, take your time."

"He, his hands were all over me. I pushed him away and he got angry. He shouted at me and called me a cock tease, acting like I was leading him on. The next thing he grabbed my waist and dragged me to the bedroom. I screamed! I told him to stop! I kept saying 'stop, stop'." The victim began crying inconsolably. "Then he threw me on to the bed and put his hand over my mouth. With his weight on me, he took his other hand and forced my trousers off and slid down my underwear."

Forrest had heard enough. He left the room and disappeared down the hall. Galbraith looked at the male officer.

"Graham, can you get some more tissues please," with that the uniformed officer left the room too.

Still sobbing, he continued, "I couldn't move. He was lying on top of me with his hand around my neck. He took out his dick and pushed it into me. I just froze after that. When he finished, he got off me and told me that if I called the police he'd be back. Then he just left like nothing happened. That's when I called 999."

"Well, you're safe now, Carlos."

The male officer returned and handed him a pack of tissues. He took one and thanked him.

Galbraith carried on, "Whenever we got a report like this, we have certain procedures we need to follow. Would you be willing to come along to a centre where specialist medical staff can take swabs from you that will help us catch the person who did this?"

"I don't know. I need time to think about it. I need to let my sister know."

"I know, please take your time. Meanwhile, I'm just going to speak to my colleague, okay."

Galbraith left the victim with the two uniformed officers and went into the hall looking for Forrest. *Where is he?* She walked along the hallway searching for him. The flat had a simple lay out: a separate living room and kitchen, one bedroom, one bathroom. She passed the bedroom to the right and looked inside.

The bed was unmade but the room appeared in order. There was no sign of a struggle and the curtains were open. She left and turned right, heading into the kitchen. She saw Forrest, his long black coat hanging low, studying a bottle of wine. A blue bag lay loosely on the kitchen table. He was wearing gloves and holding the wine bottle with two fingers touching the lid and two fingers at the base to avoid destroying any fingerprints, like forks in a corn-on-the-cob.

"Well, Imogen, what do you think?" he said nonchalantly, without turning around.

Imogen continued walking towards him as her heels tapped loudly on the tiled floor.

"I don't know, there's something not quite right here."

"Go on," he said nodding once.

Galbraith could sense his joy and saw how he was completely in his element. Forrest placed the bottle back inside the blue plastic bag from which it came and rested it back on the kitchen table. He looked at her, his face was relaxed and his brown eyes were heavily dilated like a Disney character.

"I don't think he's going to come to the hospital and give us samples."

"Well, that's not uncommon, is it Imogen: do many victims do that?" he asked rhetorically.

"I know, but then why is a model meeting men off the internet?"

"Again, more common than you think. Not everyone is lucky enough to meet Mr Perfect at university. C'mon, tell me what you see. What's wrong with this picture?" he said.

"Okay, why is he wearing a dressing gown? Wouldn't you think he'd get dressed knowing the police were coming?"

"Maybe, maybe not."

She realised how rusty she had gotten. Every detective knows how to investigate a rape, but admittedly for her, it had been a while. Her anxiety was palpable and he had not missed the cue.

"Okay Imogen, tell me what he does for a living."

"He's a model."

"Okay, what proof do you have for that? Or lack thereof?"

"There isn't any. In fact, it's very odd. I've been to a model's house before, and the walls were coated in self-portraits, portfolio work, that sort of thing – vanity's pride."

"Bingo. So what is his job?"

"Well, we both know the word 'model' is a common pseudonym for 'prostitute.'"

Forrest nodded, "What else corroborates your theory?"

She looked at the table top and saw an unopened letter. The name on the front read *Michael Ramon*. "He's given us the name Carlos, but his real name is Michael. Perhaps Carlos is his 'modelling' name?" Galbraith used her fingers to make air quotes around the word "modelling".

"Indeed. But why would he bother telling the police his false name. What purpose does it serve?"

She paused, and said, "Okay, the guy that was here, he was given the name Carlos. So if we find him, but we accuse him of raping a man named Michael, he won't know what we're talking about. And it'll keep the fact he uses a false name from any statements he needs to make. I suppose, in some respects it was Carlos who was raped, and not Michael."

"Let's not get too metaphysical, kid. Okay, what else did you notice?"

"He has two mobile telephones."

"Yes, he did, on the table," said Forrest. "One was an expensive iPhone and the other an old phone worth, I'm guessing, ten quid?"

"Exactly. Why would a man who wears a Prada dressing gown own such a cheap phone? I'd say the expensive one is his personal phone, and the other-"

"His work phone," he interrupted.

Galbraith continued, "So if we were to look at the old phone, it could show the messages between him and the suspect."

"Okay, four more things," he said.

Galbraith's eyebrows shot up like the headlights on an old sports car and her face was equally glaring.   Forrest   seemed   to   be smiling. He leaned back against a kitchen counter and placed his hands behind himself on to the work surface. He was enjoying the moment.

"Four things, huh? All right, there are no signs of a disturbance in the bedroom?" she said.

Forrest winced, "His story could corroborate that. He said he was dragged there but there isn't much furniture to mess up and he told us that he 'froze'."

She paused. "Okay, his nails."

"Yes…"

"I saw that he gets his nails manicured, they're well-kept and long, especially for a man. Not a single one was broken. If he put up a fight, surely his nails would at least have broken in the struggle." Galbraith suddenly frowned. "This feels weird John. We're in a man's kitchen who says he's just been raped and we're discussing reasons why he might be lying."

"Don't get distracted. The nails are a good point, but not a deal breaker. He had no bruising on his knuckles or his mouth either - the area where he was held down. But there are still three more things."

Galbraith had exhausted her options. She began looking around the kitchen, checking everything over in her mind. She was replaying the incident as the victim described it, trying to visualise the attack. The detective began talking to herself. *The two of them had been in the kitchen when it first began. He said they'd come back from town and were going to have a drink in the flat. The suspect came on to him and he pushed him away. That's when the attack happened.* She looked at the bottle on the kitchen table peeling back the blue plastic bag like a banana skin. *The wine was vintage, eight years old, a French white. It had not been in the fridge, it had not even been removed from the bag.* She then looked in the sink, *no glasses.* She then checked inside the dishwasher, *empty.* She then looked inside the fridge and saw no open bottles of wine or glasses.

"Okay, they came here but they never had a drink like the victim said. The bottle is still in the bag, there are no glasses I can see that have been used or other bottles of wine. He must have made that up."

"Very good," he smiled again, "but what if they drank from the bottle and it's lying in the bin?" Galbraith took a step towards it. "Don't worry, I've checked, there's nothing there. Keep going."

The bins, she thought. She headed out of the kitchen and turned into the bathroom. She looked and saw just one toothbrush in the holder, *definitely lives alone*, she concluded. She saw a small, cylindrical, aluminium bin beside the toilet and pressed down on the foot pedal activating the bin lid to open. *Bingo,* she said to herself. Inside the bin, a condom was lying loosely on top of a ball of tissues and semen filled the ribbed end. A pink condom wrapper, torn open at the end, rested parallel to it.

Galbraith left it in situ and went back inside the bedroom. She checked once more that no one was behind her and opened the man's side-table drawer. It contained paperwork, a mobile phone charger, a key ring, and a pack of twelve condoms. She looked inside the packet and saw nine condoms inside, each with a pink wrapper, and each *'ribbed for her pleasure'* according to the sexist advertising on the box. She delighted at her find and backed out of the bedroom. She could see Forrest was still in the kitchen.

"You're smiling," he said.

"The used condom in the bin matches those in the bedside table. He must have given it to him."

"Indubitably," he said bowing in a sardonic fashion, commending her for her find, "Unless it's from last night. All right kid, one last thing, and this is a little more esoteric."

Galbraith searched the kitchen a second time. She was nervous working in front of him; eager to please and scared to disappoint. She saw nothing of evidential value there and moved on. She peered in the bathroom, but decided not to check it again. She checked back in to the living room and saw the female officer comforting the victim as the male officer made notes in his book.

"Excuse me Carlos, I'll be with you in a moment," she said standing at the living room door.

She came back out of the living room and saw Forrest positioned beside the front door of the flat. He was casual and leaning back against the wall almost inviting her over. Galbraith took her cue and passed-by him, opening the door by a latch above a door-chain. She went outside and he followed her.

"Okay, I think I have it. The victim said he screamed and repeatedly told him to stop, so if we knock on the neighbour's door, they may be able to tell us if they heard anything."

"Nope," he shook his head once swiftly.

"But it's protocol to conduct neighbour enquiries," she said confused.

"Yes, it is protocol. And it's also protocol to view the CCTV we passed in the lift and the main entrance to the building. This is something specific."

She hesitated and breathed a loud sigh of defeat, the kind of sigh that comes from the abdomen and allows the shoulders to drop, reverberating your lips in turn.

"Okay, I give up. What is it?" she said.

She expected him to be gloating, but his face never changed. In a matter of fact tone, he turned and pointing to number 404, said, "There is no spy hole in this door. When you were talking to the man, Officer Graham came into the kitchen looking for tissues. I asked him about when he first arrived on scene. Specifically, if the victim had checked who they were before answering the door, and whether it was double-locked or chained from inside. Graham told me that the chain on the door, the one you've seen, was never pulled across, and the victim answered the door

76

immediately without checking who it was. Does that sound like someone who had just been raped to you?"

"Shit."

Galbraith felt somewhat otiose in the shadow of the perspicacious Forrest. He sensed this but remained silent; he was not the greatest at offering condolences. She had done everything an investigator would be expected to do, but to be supererogatory required more than high scores in exams: it came down to experience, knowledge and reading people. It came down to the desire to do this job when you could have done so many other easier careers, an easier life: being paid more, seeing the world, watching your children grow and having evenings and weekends to yourself, having a routine, a normal sleeping pattern, and a mind – like a broken mirror – shattered to pieces and rebuilt on horrific memories.

Forrest knew that in the police, rank commanded respect, it was handed to you in an instance, and had to be obeyed. In any other industry, respect was earned from hard work and dedication. And for those reasons, he had little respect for rank.

They remained in the hallway.

"Imogen, why do you think he lied?"

She paused.

"Revenge, perhaps? I don't quite know."

"If I was to speculate kid, the bottle of wine has significance here. The wine the suspect brought with him was expensive, bought in order to impress. He's someone with enough money to afford a high-class prostitute and to buy a vintage wine that he isn't bothered about taking with him when he leaves. I'd say he knew our victim, and was probably a regular. Prostitutes know the score: you make a report of rape and the man will always be arrested regardless of how implausible the account may be, for good reason some might say.

"Maybe he hoped our wine connoisseur would become more than a client, and today he told the victim it wasn't going to happen. Maybe he's reporting it because he wants the suspect's family to know what he's been up to. There are many men out there living secret lives, leaving a wife and kids at home whilst fanning their homosexual flames of desire. Or perhaps, he didn't pay him. Or maybe, he was raped. Whatever happens, it'll be one word against another, and in open court all your dirty linen comes out in the wash, but our victim's dishonesty today will not serve him well at the justice launderette."

Galbraith almost smiled; not because Forrest was funny, but because of how he spoke. It amused her and she found his grumpy pomposity endearing.

The two officers went back inside the flat and waited with the man until the SOIT officer arrived. The house was combed over by forensics and the condoms, bedding and clothing all seized for analysis. The investigation was put into place by The Sexual Offences Command who would eventually visually record the victim for his statement, and arrest the suspect to obtain his. Forrest and Galbraith would never meet the client in question, and after leaving the flat, had very little to do with the investigation they had started. They would not be informed of the result and the memory of the case would form another piece of glass in their shattered minds.

*****

X

DRIVE

They left the mansion block and began walking over to their car parked across the street. The sun had set and twilight had fallen upon the city. Forrest pulled a cigarette from the pack and lit it as soon as his feet met the pavement outside the building. The city was alive with commuters rushing, pushing, battling and fighting to get home, in order to relax.

She got into the passenger seat of the navy Ford and waited for him to finish smoking. He leaned over the top of the car and surveyed his environs. The ubiquity of crime sang out to him, he was drawn to it, unable to turn a blind eye. He rubbed his forehead with his hand trying not to see but looked up again and began noting all the offences, ticking them off in his head: *A driver wearing no seatbelt, fineable; another driver sounding their horn whilst stationary, fineable; a drunk male walking with an open can of alcohol, fineable; a male sat begging at the cash machine, arrestable; two youths smoking cannabis, arrestable.*

In the space of sixty seconds, in a salubrious part of London, he had uncovered five offences. He was expected to deal with each in turn; it was part of his inauguration into the police. He still knew off by heart the attestation he swore to the Office of Constable. He repeated it to himself, *I will, to the best of my power, cause the peace to be kept and preserved and prevent all offences against people and property*. He laughed aloud, threw his cigarette to the floor and crushed it with his boot, *littering in the street, fineable.*

They headed back to the station and, strangely for him, Forrest felt an uncomfortable silence. The quietness was bearing down on his mind.

"Hey Imogen."

"Yes?"

"If you could have Bill Gates's fortune, or world peace, what colour would your Lamborghini be?"

He looked over at her as she chuckled but her face soon slipped back into disgruntlement. "You okay?" he asked.

"Um, yes. I, I want you to know that I think you're a great detective," she said.

"Even a stopped clock is right twice a day, kid."

He looked a little embarrassed. There was another long pause.

"Nice watch, kid," he said, glancing over at her.

"Thanks, it was a present from my parents when I joined the police. What do you wear?"

"I don't."

They returned to a busy office of ringing phones, hot coffee and desks cluttered with lunch litter. The room was soulless and bleak. The lighting was ultra-bright and artificial, like a 24 hour newsagent, it was impossible to know if it was day or night. The two windows in the room overlooked an arterial route herding traffic through the urban landscape. Drivers heading out to suburbia were sounding their horns incessantly at the other stationary traffic, unaware that they themselves were equally part of the critical mass clogging the capillaries, and disturbing the tranquillity, of those struggling to live in the city.

She was standing, observing him though the translucent walls of her office, and albeit she was visible, clandestine motives were behind her actions. She was indifferent to whosoever may see her glaring at him. She hated a headache; she hated Forrest. The inspector was at a quandary, chasing the next rank required evidence. Evidencing good work and a reduction of crime figures was difficult. What she needed was a fall guy; evidence that she had handled a difficult situation in a robust and calculated manner, and that situation had become Forrest.

She hated his callous disregard for her title, and that he was different to the other men: sex had no power over him. But mostly, it was because he was dangerous; she received countless reports of his being violent. He had broken a robber's jaw, thrown a burglar down a flight of stairs, and somehow been present when a suspect had set himself on fire, but whatever he did, he always seemed to slip through the net like an oleaginous sea carnivore. She saw her opportunity about to pass the office in flat shoes.

"Imogen, quick word please," said the inspector, poking her head out of the office door as Galbraith walked past.

"Yes, Guv'," she replied.

The pair took a seat either side of the inspector's desk.

"Imogen, you've been working with John over the last few shifts. I just wanted to know how it was going?" she said, sat in a chair with her hands on the desk in the shape of a steeple, resembling a university professor with an undergraduate.

"Oh, I'm really enjoying it Ma'am. I've been learning lots and am really glad to be here. Everyone's been great."

She hoped it did not sound as false as it felt saying it.

"And how about John?"

"Yes, John's been very, um, very studious. He certainly knows his stuff and is giving me opportunities to learn from him."

Walsh looked disappointed. Her eyebrows briefly furrowed as she drummed her fingernails on the desk twice in a rapid motion - her fingernails were long, well kept, and painted red.

"Imogen, you may have heard that John has some issues, but he and I are addressing them. Now I'm happy to keep you both together as it appears that you're getting on well and producing good work. However, I want you to feel you can come and see me whenever you need to discuss anything, anything at all. In fact, I want you to come and meet with me twice a week and keep me abreast of how you're getting along and how he's coping. Is that understood?"

The effrontery! Galbraith thought. *It is not titles that honour people but people that honour titles.*

"Yes, of course Inspector. I'll be glad to do what I can."

Galbraith left the office and felt bile rise in her stomach. She could see through the Machiavellian conspiring of the inspector. How Walsh wished to sink her aculeated nails into the heart of Forrest and make an example of him. Never before had she been asked to spy on a colleague directly for a superior and she was not accustomed to the plastic pantomime of office politics. Wanting to avoid an imbroglio and subjugation by Walsh, she needed to devise a plan to escape the wrath of the inspector. She was glad to have two days' respite.

She returned to her desk opposite Forrest and saw him in his antediluvian nook of a corner desk flicking through paperwork. His de rigueur grey shirt succeeded in blending him further into the office décor.

Galbraith looked at him with sadness, almost pitying him in his halcyon naivety, as he flustered his fingers across the keyboard. If only he knew.

Galbraith thought a lot about what had happened that day at Flat 404. She thought about how a man like Michael ends up a prostitute in London. How someone can reach a stage in life where they are reporting a rape to the authorities and not being believed. She thought about how the man had surrounded himself with material possessions like the Prada gown, and how this would never make him happy. Galbraith checked the time and promised herself to meditate on the matter for twenty minutes before going to sleep to ease her worry and wash away the day's toxins.

Forrest was already asleep. It didn't take him more than a shower to forget such things anymore. He was hardened. In the profession, they call it Compassion Fatigue – when your feelings and care just wither and die through exhaustion. *It's easier that way, it always will be; caring too much will destroy you in the end*, he thought, closing his eyes.

*****

XI

TRANSMOGRIFICATION

HIS dark eyes opened slowly, blinking away the dust of a two hour sleep. He had forgotten what sleep meant and was beginning to feel the age of his body. The lack of sleep gave him a yen for fairy tales and daydreams. He found himself sitting naked in a sunbeam contemplating his life up to this point. The light cut him in two casting him half in shadow and half in blinding light, and neither side was easy to make out in the mirror, judging him dead ahead.

The mirror made him pause. He wondered if he hated himself and wasn't sure, which irritated him further. Looking at his face, he could barely hold it together. Each atom in his countenance seemed to detest the others, each atom knowing in its nucleus, that life is pointless.

He had come to terms with the inevitability of loss and the human fondness for escape. The more he scrutinized his existence, the more he found that lives were now governed by escapism. Entire rooms devoted to the pleasure of making one forget the horrid failings and inadequacies of reality. A living room sofa and its furnishings directed towards a 60inch television mounted on a plinth like a celebrated hero placed on a pedestal within the family home; so large it hides old photos of distant relations, dusty and unkempt.

Forrest realised that his life was a series of human abandonments. Those closest to him inevitably left, departed, never returned. His childhood friend whom he loved as much as children can had migrated to Ireland before they had had a chance to become men together. Even at the age of ten, he had recognised that feeling of great loss. A few years later, having formed a new close friendship, a rarity for him, he was abandoned, for a second time. A better school had a placement and the boy's parents insisted that he took it. The childhood friend joined that school forty miles away, and Forrest never heard from him again. As Forrest grew older and drifted further from his sister, he remained unprotected from the feelings of loss. Then one day, the drifting, non-contiguous sibling telephoned him from out of the blue. "I'm going to Australia," she said. The hammer dropped. Forrest felt the dread roll over him slowly. *The dark ooze*, he named it. That familiar feeling returning once more.

This loss was inevitable. As was the loss of his father. Loss is something the human psyche has had to deal with since evolution spawned consciousness. Countless religions and deities borne to distract the mind from what it faces. From death. Constant reminders in one's life serve to point towards the inevitability of loss. Forrest was accustomed to the sense of it from a young age. The metaphorical plaster was ripped off and the ontological light at the end of the tunnel had grown darker. These abandonments were quick and over in a flash. A phone call, a handshake send off, or the slightly elongated departure that takes place at the airport seeing your loved one walking off into the tunnel of forever.

The death of his father was different. It was one of those events that changes a person. His death was a long, gruelling, laborious, lament involving years of hospital visits, countless doctors and the slow, degrading, unravelling of the human spirit. Forrest's father was diagnosed with multiple sclerosis around the time Forrest first joined the Force. Over the following eleven years his life slowly drifted away. Death loitered in his father's room like an unwanted smell, invisible to the eye but ever-present. Its cold, dark face loomed in the light of Forrest's youth. A slow, gradual slipping away; no plaster to tear off. A warm loving hug, the most beautiful hug you can imagine between father and son, seemingly ever-lasting, and someone slowly prizes them away from you, finger by finger, unfolding you both until one day all contact ceases and a doctor is telling you that it's over.

For all those important men that left Forrest in his lifetime, he had done the same to women. It had never occurred to him that walking away was an issue. It was what he knew. He would leave without an explanation, or merit, or justification, or any dignity intact. One might assume he left them before they had the chance to leave him. But it was more. Forrest dreaded burying them under the avalanche of his inadequacies as a partner. He knew these women viewed him as a coward, but he disagreed. He saw it as a benevolent act, one of offering them an easy way out. Offering them a plaster to be ripped to avoid the inevitability of a long, drawn out, and slow death.

It was a fresh and bright morning without a cloud in the sky. Birds sang in the trees and the world outside his room seemed to come alive. It was a cliché of a wonderful, wintry morning. Sitting on the edge of his bed, he lit a cigarette and breathed the smoke in deeply. As he sat there, inhaling the fumes, an inquisitive squirrel leapt on to a branch of the tree that swept across his view from the open window.

The curious, grey squirrel was an invader to these lands. An immigrant not born in England and one that pushed aside the native red squirrel, pushing it towards extinction. Forrest watched the little squirrel which appeared to be looking out on the world below, contemplating its life in a sunbeam. The officer pulled his silver Walther CP88 competition BB gun from underneath his bed. The gun metal was cold in his hand as he felt the weight of it in his palm. He checked the chamber and saw eight rounds ready to fire. His cigarette was half-smoked and hung loosely from his mouth.

He lifted the gun up to his eye line and aimed out of the window, squeezing the trigger. A single steel ball-bearing pierced the back of the happy squirrel's head. A perfect shot. He wasn't proud. The grey squirrel fell from the branch, which now flexed up and down like a diving board after the diver has vaulted. *Seven rounds*, he reminded himself. His naked body was exposed to the sun, and to the gun. *"Click, click, click"* repeated the gun, over and over. The onomatopoeia of the clicking was mixed in with the sounds of Forrest's grunting and skin shredding. Seven rounds were fired into his chest. Despite the magazine being exhausted he continued to pull the trigger. *"Click click click"*, repeated the gun, but it was now empty.

Chaos suitably sought, he got up and washed the blood off, prizing out the bullets embedded in his chest with tweezers. It was apparent that this wasn't the first time Forrest had done this. *Sometimes you need to scratch yourself to see whether you bleed*, he thought afterwards, lighting another cigarette on the edge of his bed. He wondered whether Death had ever left him, or whether He continued to linger in the corner of his room, awaiting him. His oldest remaining friend. The only one he ever knew would return in the end.

*****

XII

BALANCE

HER fingers splayed like a frog leaping through the air, she pushed out hard and far, all her toes pointing out and her legs vibrating with the depth of the stretch. She yawned the loudest yawn which became high-pitched as it tailed off. She rolled over in the bed and giggled, pulling the covers over her face and then kicking them off her like a child. Matt had gone to work hours ago and she enjoyed a lazy midweek lie in.

The naked Galbraith rolled over and checked her phone: she'd received two text messages, a comment on a photo of her online, and her younger brother Frank had sent her a video link to some people chasing cheese down a hill, which he seemed to think was hilarious.

She got out of bed and headed to the shower, turning it on early to allow the room to heat a little. She repaired to the mirror and stared at her face. It was almost perfectly symmetrical and her nose had a Roman edge to it. She slapped her face with both hands in a playful fashion before turning sideways, still facing the mirror and performing a heavy pout in honour of Marilyn Monroe. She climbed into the shower and sang the words to Disney's *Beauty and the Beast* spending fifteen minutes under the warm spray of the water.

Galbraith stepped out and rubbed her head with towel. The house was empty but for her naked body taking a tour. She checked the weather from her bedroom window and paused for thought. The large nimbo-stratus that escorted her to work on her first day seemed to have re-emerged above her, circling the house like a vulture. *No point in going for a run*, she reasoned.

Her building had its own gym and swimming pool facility, but it was small and she felt she had outgrown it. Seeking to be pushed harder, she packed a costume in her bag and headed for the leisure centre.

Galbraith pushed off the top board ten metres above the pool, completing one revolution and hitting the water with her hands stretched out for an imperfect dive. She resurfaced with a grimace. Two boys in their late teens watched on and one of them appeared to snigger. Not to be outdone, she climbed the two sets of stairs to the top board and dived again, landing flawlessly.

When she was seventeen, she was accused of being gay by her parents; she remembered the embarrassing event well. Upon arriving home, both her mother and father were stood at the door waiting for her, clearly the result of a conversation to which she was not privy. In a sombre tone, they asked for a chat in the lounge and she suspected a death in the family. When her father finally announced that he had no problem if she chose to live her life as a lesbian, Galbraith laughed hysterically. She loved her parents, but their traditionalism and 'best interests' conflicted with her own.

The detective had always dressed more for comfort than pleasure and had worn jeans, baggy jumpers and hats in place of makeup and heels. Boyfriends, few and far between, were never brought home and rarely were her misadventures discussed. Kevin took her virginity at age 16, a boy from her college in the year above. It was not a romantic affair and was the result of three weeks' dating and one night of overindulgence at a party that led to a quick frolic in the one of the host's bedrooms. She never saw him again after that and dated sporadically. Men were simply uninteresting. Galbraith never had an eye for beauty, she never sat gaping at a passing man, or had a crush on a popstar, and never conceived planning her future wedding with a fictional hunk. It wasn't until her second year at university, and her meeting Matt, that she truly settled and found love.

The pool was Olympic in size and subdivided into lanes based on swimming ability. Galbraith spent one evening a week at the pool swimming lengths. She pulled on her swimming cap and googles and dived into the fast lane catapulting herself half the length of the pool under water. She rose and completed the remaining thirty laps without trouble. When she finished, she felt a modicum of listlessness but wished to push herself a little more.

The high board called out to her once again like a clock-tower smiling down on the people below. She climbed to the acme of the board and looked over the precipice. Turning on her heels, she stood with her toes on the edge and her body hanging over the ten metre drop. She had not dived backwards from the high board in several years but something today had spurred her on. The rough board beneath her feet was coarse and felt like a matchbox being rubbed against her soles. The acoustics in the pool were enhanced at the top, echoing round her head in a spiral: the sounds of children playing, splashing and the distant whistle of a lifeguard.

She sucked in one last breath, held it and closed her eyes. She ran through the steps of the dive. *Feet close together, knees bent, arms rotate above the head, and push off with the toes, tuck into a ball and release.* She leapt from the board, the room span and it felt like watching a surreal movie at double speed; all the sounds merged into one, and she forgot to breathe. She hit the water off balance landing on the back of her legs as opposed to her feet causing pain in her behind. *Close enough,* she thought, as she climbed from the pool. It was not conceit that drove her on, but the drive for perfection.

The serenity of the pool calmed her spirit and reminded her of the year she spent in Thailand on the sandy shores of Ko Chang. She spent most evenings reading by the sea, taking in the moonlight and absorbing the sounds of the ocean waves breaking at her feet. It was a solitary year spent apart from Matt but they agreed that if they could survive a year of distance then they would know they were right for each other. She meditated daily and practised yoga with others, soon becoming one of the instructors at the camp. It was a beautiful life-changing experience that made her an adroit swimmer with a supple frame and a clear mind. Galbraith never knew if the exhausting swirl of London's bustling population suited her, but she remained for Matt, and the job kept her spirit refreshed. Yet her mind often wandered back to the shores of the island, sat on the beach staring out at the gentle ocean greeting her.

Having left the swimming pool, she fancied a trip to the shopping centre before heading home and spent time browsing for a new winter coat. She had unknowingly become sybaritic; having found two winter coats in the first hour, she then ate at a coffee shop by herself, and then continued a postprandial tour of the mall. She had returned to the apartment with new shoes, two dresses, a blue cotton shirt for Matt and a print from a scene in the movie *Dirty Dancing*.

Patrick Swayze was hung in the hall and her new clothing stuffed into the wardrobe. She sat down on the sofa in the lounge with a bowl of soup and flicked through the channels on the television. Boredom soon set in. The shopping experience had not been edifying and hadn't improved her already bulging collection of clothes. She blew out hard and her lips quivered amidst her hot, soupy breath. She reached for her phone but Matt had not sent her a reply.

Feeling disconsolate, she opened the lid of her laptop and logged into Facebook. *John Forrest* was typed into the search field: it returned 134 hits, but none were him. She then typed his name into Google: hidden amongst the prosaic ramblings of blogs and websites was a news article on the third page of the feed. The title of the story read *Hero Saves Man From Train Death*. She clicked on the link and the page jumped to a story from four years ago.

Dramatic scenes unfolded yesterday at Kings Cross station as an off-duty police officer was captured on CCTV footage pulling a man from the tracks just moments before an oncoming train raced into the platform.

The man, Raymond Gafferty, is seen on the footage drunkenly stumbling around the platform having consumed a significant amount of alcohol at the Cheltenham Festival earlier that day. There are approximately thirty onlookers, most of whom are trying to avoid Mr Gafferty, who is awaiting the next Northern Line train. The off-duty police officer, who has now been named as Detective John Forrest, is waiting further along the platform. He then proceeds to move towards Mr Gafferty who stumbles closer to the platform edge.

The tunnel begins to light up as the train approaches, and this is the shocking moment when Mr Gafferty falls off the platform edge landing just inches from the live rail. According to witnesses at scene, the man appeared to have been knocked unconscious from the fall. The heroic officer is seen leaping down on to the tracks as onlookers wave at the oncoming train in an effort to notify the driver.

The train pulls into the station at 30mph and the officer is seen on the footage dragging the man underneath the edge of the platform and clear of the train just seconds before it would have almost certainly killed him...

Galbraith read with astonishment. *I never knew about this?* She then heard a key rattling in the door as Matt returned home. He walked in and placed his bag on the table and reached for the fridge. She followed him with her eyes. *No hello, no kiss, no how are you?* Matt grabbed a beer from the fridge and sat beside her.

"What's on?" he said, taking the remote control from her lap.

She overemphasised her feeling of chagrin and stared at him with her mouth agape and eyebrows raised.

He continued, "Sorry, thought you were busy on the laptop, Muffin."

The evening rattled along like most evenings did for her now. They sat watching the television for the next three hours, making compromises on what to view and passing comment on the lackadaisical modern day protagonists. They watched a reality TV show following the lives of unintelligible striplings wandering aimlessly through their youth misdirected by money, fame, and the producers, as they attended parties and were fed enough alcohol so that a controversial event would erupt, perfect for broadcasting.

Next up on the schedule was a game show whereby the contestants had the chance to win a million pounds. This reminded Imogen of the maxim, *'if something is free to use, then you are the product being sold'*. A young couple were the stars being quizzed by an overdressed megalomaniac. They were asked to name which of four celebrity children was the youngest. The old Imogen would have found the amount of babbling and circumlocution to drag the show out for an hour offensive. However, the engaged couple indulged in the show's rapacious antics and guessed incorrectly the answer to the banal question. Imogen even felt disappointment when the quiz host revealed the true ages of the celebrity children and how far off her answers were.

They went to sleep at 22:30 and Matt kissed her on the forehead before turning the sidelight off. This scene had been repeated for many years and both actors knew their lines. She lay there and the image of her parents lying in bed when she was a young girl sprang to mind, but the parents were dressed in the clothes worn by her and Matt. She physically shook her head to wipe the image clear.

He lay there, asleep yet awake, trapped in the exile of somnolence. His body paralysed from the neck down, but his mind burned like a fire flicking wildly and out of control, lighting new realms in the dark channels of his psyche. It had been weeks now. A half-drunk bottle of vodka lay beside him filling the room with a musty odour. He only drank at the end of the day to numb his synapses, not to quench a restless thirst. He had all but given up on sleep, choosing to read into the night, one lone amber bulb illuminating him. He awoke the next morning with no memory of his drift into unconsciousness, with the book beside his face, and the light still shining upon him.

Forrest couldn't tell you why he struggled to sleep. He honestly didn't know. A smart man like himself tries to think his way of the despair, and in doing so, the problem became exacerbated. He read books on insomnia, studied the field, looked at clinical reports, and even once checked into a sleep clinic. He found no fruit for his labour – not even a grape. For all his attempts, from heating milk to buying Valium off the internet, nothing worked. The alcohol helped him doze off, but it didn't hold him there. He'd wake up, three or four times a night, restless, waiting, lying for up to an hour, just to nod off once more. His dreams – they were when he was most alive. Not quite nightmares, but his darkest thoughts played out in his unconsciousness.

He once awoke crying, only the once. The dream itself he doesn't remember, it wasn't important or especially strange. Yet, he continued to cry whilst awake. Emotion overcame him on that night. It was six years ago and he hasn't cried since. It is in these moments that Forrest considers death. Awake but still, he lay on his sweaty mattress staring up at the ceiling and thinking. *Why do they fear death? Religion was created to help those who feared death, but it is also the creator of the fear – the virus and the cure. You simply cease to exist. I didn't exist for 13 billion years. A soul is only something fed to you by the faithful. My soul is dead.*

*****

XIII

RUN

IT was Friday and Imogen's second day off from work. Her living room was warm and comforting. Relaxing on the sofa, the girl decided to unpack her shopping from yesterday. She inspected the new running trainers she had bought and strapped them to her feet, wriggling her toes and extending her foot to test their comfort level. They cost ninety-five pounds and felt light and comfortable, and at the very least, they looked pretty. She stood up and peered down at her outfit, a tight grey vest over her sports bra, black Lycra trousers, and blue socks popping out of the grey trainers.

She grabbed her phone and keys and left her flat, plugging her earphones in and descending in the lift. She waved at the concierge on the way out and headed towards Regent's Park via the canal. Her hair swung from side to side and she realised it had been tied a little too loosely.

It had taken her twenty minutes to complete the two-and-a-half mile journey. On entering the park she bent down to sip from a water fountain. She was breathing heavily but was not tired and only considered this stage a warm-up. Imogen started jogging the circumference of the park and saw a running group coming in the opposite direction. It had occurred to her to join one of these groups but a feeling of aberrance often overcame her when exercising with others, despite the happy glow coming from the group passing-by. She was too competitive, too jealous, and couldn't fit into the groove when exercising as a team.

The run felt more intense today, the wind was stronger than usual and she moiled her way round the park for a second time, pulling the air into her lungs with force. Her top was now sodden with sweat; she paused at the water fountain for a second sip, anointing her forehead, bending her face underneath the arc of water. She rose from the bowl and wiped her eyes with both hands pulling the water down her face. Her face a shimmering hue of ashen white flecked with pink at the cheeks.

She glanced to her left and saw a simulacrum of Forrest moving above a row of hedges foreshadowing a children's playground. The doppelganger had the same scowling physiognomy that Forrest wore. She winced to focus her vision and stared harder... it was Forrest. The figure sailed across the play area, and when, some seconds later, he emerged from behind the shrubs, Galbraith's mouth dropped. He was holding the hand of a small child.

The girl could not have been more than three years of age. Galbraith's breathing had slowed but her face remained contorted, quizzical, trying to understand the scene unfolding before her. She considered moving closer, perhaps saying hello without his approbation. Instead she kept her distance and observed them. She saw Forrest walk the girl to a slide, helping her up its wooden steps and onto the top seat, and then catching her as she slid to the bottom and into his arms. Her conjecture now confirmed; she knew it was his daughter.

The most intriguing aspect of the scenario was how he appeared. Forrest looked relaxed and his cantankerous manner had all but gone. He looked less dishabille in a tee-shirt and jeans and his love for the girl was beautiful to see. It was moments like this that made Galbraith want children of her own. She saw him scoop the girl into his arms and thrust her into the air high above his head while the girl laughed uncontrollably. The play area seemed brighter and the sun less sallow as it pierced the umbriferous, branches bellowing above them.

She sensed her perusing had now become intrusive and it was time to leave. Her run-distance reader showed she had run 6 miles. *That'll do.*

Her keys slept on the wooden table beside the door. Her sweaty robes hung over the stair bannister. She reappeared from the bathroom rubbing her hair with a towel and drying herself off. Donning some comfy clothing, she settled on to the large corner sofa in the living room and opened up a half-read book on the side cabinet. After fifteen minutes, with heavy eyes, sleep took her as a bride.

The waves licked the dark yellow hue of the sand, uniting the secular grains into a religion of water worshippers. The waves hissed as they faded, like the air escaping from a carbonated drink bottle. A tree strained to reach the sun: shaking, as it stretched for more light, more heat. Its solid trunk flexing like a straw from the earth, drinking light, soaking its roots. She sat under its brown curved spine, shaded from the sun; from its light. She sat in darkness, the lee of green leaves protecting her. Staring out to the ocean, watching the vibrant, zoetic waves, cognizant of their power and beauty. As she stared, the tree appeared to bend lower. The large protective leaf that shielded her from the sun now eclipsed the sky. It swooned and stopped lower, coming faster and faster towards her. She flinched when it stopped short of a metre away.

Its long, green, leafy tentacles wrapped her ankles manacling her in   vine   hooks. The branch above her then catapulted to the sky and revealed darkness. And with it, she was flung out into the ocean, hurtling through the air. Invisible: a darkness so black she touched her own face, confused, checking she still existed. A great wind carried her further, across the ocean, before she plunged into it, violently. Hurtling in a spiral, her bones like elastic, her limbs contorting, she smacked the hard surface of the sea.

Her mouth open wide, sweat had run into one of her eyes stinging her pupil; she wiped it away and fought to catch her breath. Her chest bounced like a speaker playing too loudly, vibrating fear to her limbs. The nightmare had ended. The first nightmare she'd had since distant memory could recall. *What's happening to me?*

There was a knock at the door. She climbed off the sofa and released the latch.

"Hey, it's Imogen, right?"

"Yes?" she responded cautiously.

"Name's Dylan, I live at number 62. I think this is yours?"

He held out a small brown box with her name on. Galbraith looked down at the box and then back at her neighbour. He had a certain je ne sais quoi, and on top of that he smelt good. He was wearing a chequered shirt, jeans, and boots. His hair was short and dark, cut recently, but a slight curliness was apparent, and he spoke with a soft Irish accent.

"Oh, thank you," she said taking the package. "So you must have moved in recently?"

He seemed happy to be asked.

"Yeah, just last week. Haven't had a chance to meet anyone from the building or look around yet. Don't suppose you know a good place to eat like?"

Is he asking me out? She took a small step back.

"Well, um, if you walk to the high street, there are many places to choose from. It's only a few minutes away."

"Grand, I'll take a look, thanks. Well it was nice to meet you... Imogen." He pointed and leaned towards her as he said her name, almost relieved to have remembered it, then turned and headed for the lift. He walked with a bounce as though he could feel her eyes on him.

Imogen closed the door and placed the package on the kitchen table. *A handsome man next door*, she thought. She wondered if he was alone. Maybe he could be a new friend for Matt or had a girlfriend she could meet.

Twilight nestled into the branches of the trees lining her street; she gathered her things and headed out to meet two of her friends for dinner, hoping to return in time to catch Matt before he went to sleep. Her night would pass like many other nights had, yet in her visceral core, she felt different, like something fundamentally had changed. She didn't know what, but it was there, and it scared her.

*****

XIV

LETTERS

HE awoke in a cold sweat. Another night, another nightmare. It had been a year now. Four seasons of changing winds, falling leaves, new moons and blooming flowers but still the nightmares persisted. There was no hope of seeking help; he knew that if he sought medical or psychological care, the Service would need to be informed, and his career would be impacted. Forrest was not destined to be stuck behind a desk on medical grounds.

The topography of his mind was unchartered, an inestimable chain of doubts and fears. His unconscious had been marinated for eighteen years in a pool of filth, surrounded by the lowest forms of humanity, slowly soaking up their putridity, like a child subjected to advertisements for too long, it becomes subliminal in the end. A solipsistic hatred for human life grew inside his mind, the prison in his head.

Forrest stared out of his bedroom window through the greying net curtains that hung there, stained, and dotted with holes. In many ways, the unfashionable fabric resembled him. A catcher of flies in the air, allowing one to peer out but not within. He wore this veil wherever he roamed, peering out but not letting others in. The wily officer was used to being alone, accustomed to that feeling of being unwanted. That moment at the airport when you exit the terminal but no one is there waiting for you – that awkwardness; the smiles of those strangers were slits into the heart of this wanderer, once, but no longer.

The feeble morning light caught his naked frame and illuminated his painted physique. He was smothered in tattoos of people, like a skeleton dipped in ink; hard to decipher at first, but each had a distinguishable story. Skulls scattered across his thighs, a Native American on his shoulder blade, a sword down his spine, only his hands and neck seemed blank. He pulled on a shirt running his left arm through the sleeve, covering the tattooed words: *A true warrior seeks a good fight*.

Galbraith scanned the office as Forrest entered. He was a cold breeze to his co-workers whose heads seemed to shrink into their bodies like hermitic crabs when he appeared. No words were exchanged over the next two hours while the officers sat at their desks sorting through the inevitable list of emails accrued over a two day absence.

At 10am, Kirsty, the office manager, sauntered into the CID office carrying a small bag containing more letters than it could manage. She placed it onto a desk in the centre of the room. A package hanging from its mouth vomited out on to the table.

Forrest glanced to his right and locked eyes on the package. Its brown paper wrapping coated in string, neatly bowed like a Christmas present. He shot up from his seat.

"Wait!" he shouted.

Kirsty had three fingers resting on the brown exterior of the parcel.

"What?" she said irritably, leaning back and staring wide-eyed at Forrest who was bounding towards her.

The office fell eerily silent and the phones had magically ceased to ring as he crossed the room.

"Leave that where it is! Do not touch it!" he commanded.

Galbraith's hands were frozen in the air above her keyboard like a pianist finishing a symphony and pausing for rapturous applause. Forrest stood over the mysterious parcel and seemed to stare at it. The curious onlookers watched him like an animal in a zoo enclosure. His eyes followed the edges of the package like a newsreader scanning an autocue, he peered across the front and seemed to read each letter rather than each word written across the front.

He looked at the string and how it was tied. He noted the post mark and how many stamps were used. He scanned the surface and gauged the height. Finally, he touched the package and lifted it with two fingers, just a few inches off the table before placing it back down.

He then looked around the room but whatever it was that he sought, one could tell he was struggling. A lightbulb in his head clicked, and he walked to his drawer and pulled out his ballistic vest. He then returned to the package and placed the vest directly over the A4 size brown box completing eclipsing it in black Kevlar.

"It's a bomb, and although it shouldn't go off on its own, we need to leave, now."

And without another word, he walked out the office and disappeared. It was a surreal moment. The office stopped, eyes searched for other eyes, for confirmation. This hadn't happened before and no automatic response was filed in anyone's memory. Galbraith was the first to stand up.

"Come on!" she said. "What are you waiting for?"

With those seven words, slowly but surely the other workers got up and walked out of the room. As they descended the stairs a familiar voice came over the station's public announcement system.

"This is John Forrest. There is a bomb in the building. Everyone is to leave immediately and reconvene in the yard."

He's serious, she thought. Imogen had forgotten her coat and the cold wind made her cross her arms so tightly her knuckles turned white. There were sixty members of the Service stood in the yard of the police station; all talking and muttering between themselves, on tenterhooks as to what was going on. Some of the crowd wore suits and ties, some were in uniform with their black and white hats on show, there were cleaners in navy blue uniforms, back office civilians in jumpers and overcoats, and a garage mechanic in the distance wiping his hands down with a cloth. Forrest walked through the menagerie gathered in the car park and his duster jacket sailed in the wind. He climbed on to a large bricked air-vent that protruded from a wall and oversaw those below. His apotheosis was complete, each head leaning to one side as they sought the succour of his words.

He looked out to the crowd with utmost confidence: "A postal bomb was discovered in our office just five minutes ago. I am assuming it was intended to kill and maim us, as it has been disguised quite well. Now I need to know if any of you accepted this package today, or signed for it from a deliveryman."

Forrest scanned the crowd but to no avail.

"Speak up if you did. It is very important I hear from you. If you do not wish to do so now, come and find me afterwards."

Again, no one seemed to know anything about receiving the package. In fact, the crowd were bewildered by the whole thing. A voice spoke up from the midst of heads.

"How do you know it really is a bomb," she said, her arms still folded about her.

Galbraith was inviting him to address the crowd. To show off his talent and he did not stutter.

"Well, if you nosey buggers really care to know." Some of the crowd laughed, but most were enraptured by the event unfolding. "Our lovely Kirsty spilt the package on to the desk and it was clearly very heavy from how it dropped and slammed down. I noticed the string on the package too." He watched the crowd and each face was as confused as the next. "The postal service don't use string, they haven't for years. Someone wrapped this themselves. I then looked at the writing on the package and it had been handwritten. Again, not something irregular if you were sending a present to a friend, but the only packages we get are from the laboratory or other cops, not private individuals. Fourthly, it was made out to CID only. No name, no department, just CID. Again, something quite irregular. And how did I know it was a bomb I hear you ask?

"I ran my hands along it and it was bulging and uneven at the top end. The package itself is very heavy, as I mentioned before, yet the postal stamps were completely inaccurate and showed it at least a pound lighter. It wasn't weighed at the post office, it was hand delivered. Lastly, I felt an oleaginous texture to the paper. It's a bomb."

"I cannot command you to stay away from the building, but I've already called out the bomb squad. They'll be here in twenty minutes. It's your call."

Forrest stepped down from his pedestal and joined the subjugated group who lingered in the frosty car park. He pulled his packet of smokes from the duster coat and lit one up behind the shelter of the long lapels at his chest. He was always lonely in a crowd.

"Well done, John, quite entertaining," remarked Galbraith.

"It was nothing, kid."

Forrest felt his mouth going dry.

"Coffee?" he said to her.

He unlocked the navy Ford in the basement and the pair boarded the 5-door saloon. The engine purred like a cat seeking attention from its owner. Its body sleek yet powerful like a panther, a primarily nocturnal beast, set to hunt the prey of the night. They headed into town and Forrest bought the coffees and the pair sat outside, as seemed to be the way.

"So do you like rock music?" she asked.

He blew out a swirl of smoke through his teeth.

"I suppose kid, some Metallica here or Kings of Leon there, but I'm more into classical."

She laughed.

"Seriously?"

"You seem surprised, Imogen?" he said.

"Sorry, it's just the tattoos. It's kind of grunge don't you think?"

He rolled his eyes and peeled back his right forearm.

"What do you see, kid?"

Galbraith studied the detailed landscape inked in black covering the flesh of his lean right arm as he clenched his fist. The scene had an almost patient to doctor feel to it, as Galbraith examined his limb closely.

"Um, okay, I can see a large building, maybe a temple, and a tree, and there's a large figure hovering above it, and then many smaller soldier-like figures at the base of some steps leading into a temple."

"Well observed, but what is it?" His manner reminded her of how alive he was last shift at the crime scene involving Carlos Ramon.

"It reminds me of something Roman. Is it the Senate and a Roman army?"

"Ha ha" he chuckled. "Very close. Have you heard of Valhalla?"

"It rings a bell."

Forrest swigged his coffee and puffed on his cigarette. As he spoke, smoke poured out from his mouth.

"It is a great hall overseen by the Norse god Odin, wherein brave soldiers and other heroes who were slain are received. A hall for the chosen dead. It reminds me to never forget those that lost their lives fighting for what they believed in. Despite my abhorrence for politics, I feel a great love for those who die for what they believe, and all soldiers for that matter, no matter the cause. It is a great honour to check out that way."

Galbraith had to readjust her eyebrows to hide her surprise.

"Even if the cause is flawed?" she asked.

"Yes, even if the cause is flawed. Is there anything you're ready to die for kid?" He paused. "I didn't think so."

"You don't know that. I'm not even sure I do".

"Think about this. If I said to most people, what are you willing to die for? They'd say, 'oh, my kids, my country, freedom.' No one ever says their mobile telephone or a parking space at the supermarket. But you see, in that moment, when someone challenges you, and anger builds up inside, the common man will fight for something petty. A man threatens you with a knife for the contents of your wallet and you find yourself in a fight, a life and death situation, for what? Thirty pounds and the cost of replacing your driving licence".

Imogen pondered; "So you're saying that people will, under pressure, fight for much less?"

"No. I'm saying that if you asked me what I would die for, it's easy. I'd die, right here and now, for principle. No one will ever take so much as a cigarette from me under duress of force. That's because to me, the ability to stand up to tyranny is worth just as much as my country. It is my home. And although some people, in that situation, may choose to fight when provoked, I would choose to provoke a fight."

Galbraith knew that Forrest wanted to prize from her the principles on which she lived and those for which she would die, but Galbraith didn't want to give that to him.

"So what about the rest of your tattoos... How many do you have?"

"Thirty-six in total. Some are recognisable, like the Trojan horse on my shoulder, but some, like this, I doubt many people would know."

Forrest pulled his right trouser leg up and revealed the face of a bearded man wearing a pakol. Underneath the face was the word *LION* in itallics. He was right, Galbraith had no idea to whom the face belonged.

"This is Ahmad Shah Massoud. He represents resistance in the face of conflict."

"And all these people are now dead?" she said.

"Yes."

"Would you like to meet them? Is that why you carry them about you?"

"Kid, I hope you don't think you can be corporeally reassembled after you die. If I ever met my heroes it would surely be a disappointment. A greater man than I once said that."

She paused and repositioned herself in the café chair.

"So, for instance, if you were able to meet this Massoud guy, you wouldn't want to?"

"Ahmad Shah Massoud. And no, if I ever want to meet them, I can: through their words, their teachings, by living the way they lived."

"Can I ask you something, John?"

"Go on."

"I think you're too stressed. How do you relax? I mean, you seem to be serious the whole time. How do you let go? It's so important. Stress is found to be the cause of 80% of common illnesses we get."

Forrest tucked his trouser leg in and lit another cigarette as he spoke.

"I... I guess I mostly let go when I fight. I boxed for many years and I now train in mixed martial arts, jujitsu, wrestling, all sorts."

"John, you're forty-five, why are you still fighting?"

Galbraith sensed she had struck a nerve and took hold of her coffee cup bringing it nervously up to her chin.

"Forty-six actually and age isn't a factor. I enjoy it. What about you?"

"If I get angry, really angry, then I write down what I want to say to that person. It all comes out in the letter. And I then seal that letter in an envelope and leave it in my drawer. The next day or two, I'll consider that letter again, consider whether it should be posted. And do you know how many times I've sent that letter or given it to somebody? Never."

Forrest smiled.

"I've got some stamps if you need them."

She didn't laugh.

"You should write a letter one day, John. You don't have to post it. Just say how you feel and let it all out. Aren't you even curious? Write it and leave it with you for a couple of days, it'll do you good."

He went back inside the coffee shop without speaking to her and she assumed he was using the toilet. A couple of minutes later he re-emerged with another black coffee and peppermint tea.

"So you never send the letters, huh. What was the last one you wrote?"

Galbraith bit her bottom lip and her pupils swung up to the left as she pondered.

"It was to men in general."

"Really? Pray tell," he said.

"Um, it's kind of embarrassing to say, I'm going to sound like a right you-know-what. Okay, basically, I've always struggled with male friends or rather, them with me. I always find, sooner or later, that awkward moment arises when they either fancy me or fall in love with me."

Forrest cringed.

"I told you it was embarrassing. I've had a handful of good male friends, some for years, and then one day they come out of the blue and tell me they want me, or they get drunk and try to kiss me, or tell me they love me. In the end, the friendship fails because of their feelings. I'm not saying it's happened with *all* of my guy friends, but it pretty much sums up a good few of them over the last ten years."

Forrest interjected, "-Tell me about it. I can't stand women throwing themselves at me all the time. I can never catch a break."

He burped loudly and two people sat further along the café looked over.

"Do you have any family, John?" asked Imogen.

He seemed to pause longer than was necessary as though he was tempering his answer.

"My brother Solomon is the only one left alive," he said.

"Oh, are you quite close to him then?"

"No, not really."

"Can I ask why?"

"You don't quit do you?" he said. "I think it's because he was born too close to me. I'm only eleven months older than him. When we were growing up, we didn't have the big brother, little brother relationship. I never had the chance to be his sage, or defend him in fights, or show him how to meet women. Instead, he just wanted to compete with me. We argued and fought about everything. We even shared the same clothes. As we grew up, he had to follow me in everything just to better me. I read law at Bristol University, so he chose law but had to attend Cambridge. I became a cop; he became a barrister. I don't really speak to Sol lest the occasional funeral or family gathering."

"Do you love him?" she asked.

Forrest decided to take a long drag on his cigarette before answering.

"I don't know."

"Are you and he similar?"

"Not really, he's not the happy-go-lucky type that I am." He smiled.

The radio that had lain silent in Forrest's pocket for the past hour soon awoke from its dormancy. In a dulcet tone, the operator calmly announced that a female had been found murdered. Forrest accepted the call.

*****

XV

Claret

THE car screeched to a halt outside the address. This was a part of town Forrest had not often visited in the past four years. The street was lined with trees and hugged by large terraced Victorian homes that soaked up the faded morning sun. Each home had its own front garden partitioned by black iron railings lined up like soldiers along a small white-brick wall.

The salubrious west part of the borough was policed just as much as the east. Money commanded power, the wealthy had to be kept safe, and Bobbies regularly walked the beat there. It was of no appeal to Forrest. He only ventured there when required and happily that was seldom.

Forrest parked up behind two patrol cars already on scene and the two detectives climbed out from their vehicle in a perfunctory manner. The three police cars were amongst the cheapest vehicles on the road. As Galbraith made her way to the front door, she pushed open a wrought-iron gate and ascended eight steps leading up to number 71. The house was egg-shell white, recently painted, and the front door was black with wooden panelling. In the front garden, a small rose bush occupying a circular bed of soil struggled in the winter breeze.

A constable in uniform was standing at the top of the stairs sheltered from the wind by two pillars either side of her. She was clutching a crime scene log in her ashen hands and her lips and face were pale. As they passed her, Forrest said only four words: "Nobody else comes in." He asked Galbraith for the exact time and she replied that it was 11:25am.

He walked past the front door and into a light hallway. Above him was a black chandelier light fitting with eight forks hanging down, each cradling a teardrop light bulb. On the right, a burglar alarm was mounted on the wall with the keypad exposed, and to his left, a mirror beamed back at him. The walls, also eggshell white, were enhanced by deep black skirting boards. As he stepped inside, his boots made a loud clop against the wooden flooring. Galbraith was ahead of him, and two uniform officers were standing a few metres away at the end of the hall.

"Tell me," said Forrest.

A uniformed officer approached him whom he recognised.

"Hello John, how are you?"

"Fine. What do we have Constable Parkes?"

Despite the two officers being the same rank of constable, Forrest let him know who ran the show. The officer opened his notepad. He fiddled nervously. The wide hallway suddenly became cramped and narrow with the introduction of the two suited newcomers.

"Female found dead in the kitchen. Looks like she was stabbed once in the neck. The husband was on scene when we got here maybe two or three minutes after the call was made."

Galbraith jumped in, "The husband is the informant, right?"

"Yeah," he said turning to her, "when we got here the door was ajar. Me and Steph walked in and heard him wailing, so we headed straight for the sound, towards the kitchen. As we came in, we saw him holding her. He was just hugging her, swaying back and forth, crying, and his hands were covered in blood. I've never seen-"

"Has anything been touched since?" barked Forrest.

"Um, no, I don't think so."

The officer shuffled on his feet under the gaze of the male detective.

"I need you to be specific for me Brian. What happened after you went into the kitchen?"

He does remember my name, thought PC Parkes.

"Well, we tried to reassure him really. Steph ran out to get a first aid kit from the car. I walked over and convinced him to let go of the woman so we could treat her."

"Did you tell him that? Did you say you wanted to do first aid?"

"Yes, I remember telling him to let go of her so that we could check her over'."

"And."

"He kept hold of her at first. But when Steph returned, he let go. We laid her flat on the ground and Steph took him into another room as he was being hysterical. I checked her pulse, airway and breathing but got no response. The wound on her neck was very deep. It looks like the knife may have hit the carotid artery. I tried to stem the bleeding but couldn't stop it."

"Okay. Give me their names?" said Forrest, listening intently.

The officer scanned the messy writing in his pocket book for the right details.

"The husband is a Mr Eric Barnes... and... the victim is called Cassandra Pinto-Barnes," he said.

"Where's the husband now?" asked Galbraith.

"He's with Leggie next door in the lounge."

"And what's your name?" she asked of the second officer in the hall.

"Portway. Alan Portway," he said without moving.

"Okay", said Forrest, "here's the plan. I need you three to all wait in the lounge with the husband. Keep talking to him but I want you Brian to record everything he says in your notebook. Just make notes but don't make it obvious. However innocuous his remarks, you will record them."

"Got it," he replied, and the two officers headed into the living room.

Galbraith and Forrest exchanged a look between themselves; "Let's get suited," she said.

The two detectives were now clad in white overalls reminiscent of the first day they worked together. Forrest entered the kitchen first, followed by Galbraith. The kitchen floor was made up of white and black square tiles. A white fridge hummed gently in the corner and a large oak table was positioned to the left side of the room as you entered the kitchen. The walls were as white as the hallway, and just as clean and bright. A spray of bright claret blood shot across the wall adjacent to the table and up on to the ceiling. The floor beneath the body was sodden with blood. Around the neck of the victim, a murky pool had formed. It seemed to be slowly expanding, crawling slowly across the chequered tiles.

She lay there, in a cream woolly V-neck jumper and green skirt, stretched out across the kitchen floor. Her eyes stared up at nothing. Her hair, a mix of blonde and claret, swayed gently in the pool of blood like leaves at a river mouth, the pool itself growing ever so slowly larger.

Forrest pointed to the ground as he spoke.

"We've got to take an alternative route to that of the killer. Follow my path exactly, step by step. We'll mark our route on the log when we leave so the forensic team know where we've been."

He had to pull his face mask down momentarily to get his voice heard and Galbraith nodded in acknowledgement. She was glad he was with her. It was not uncommon during times of austerity and public sector cuts that officer numbers would be reduced to what is termed minimum strength. This meant that at times just one detective would attend such incidents on their own. Unknown to the public, only two detectives need cover an entire London borough at any one point; the term minimum strength had never been so true.

They stepped across and away from the body, hugging the wall to the left and going behind the kitchen table in clockwise fashion. When they got round the other side of the table, away from the door, they huddled together in the corner, avoiding the blood and stared over the body now just a foot away from them.

The wound to her neck was indeed very deep. The knife had penetrated the shoulder through the soft area between collar bone and neck. A gaping hole two inches wide and six deep dribbled red like a bath tap left running. Drip, drip, drip. The victim's jumper had soaked up much of the blood near the wound, but the knife had gone straight through it and into the left subclavian artery. The heart would pump harder as it tried to force blood to the brain, but the artery spat it out across the wall, and all over the floor. Cassandra would have bled out within minutes.

Forrest could tell from the blood spatter that she was murdered here. The pooling, the spatter across the wall, the position of the body. It was clear that she had not been moved.

Forrest kept his back against the left wall and shuffled across to the rear of the kitchen. He positioned himself against the back wall where a rear door had been forced open. He bent over, keeping his feet grounded but bending closer to the door. The kitchen was around 11 feet wide and the door located just off centre at the very rear, leading to a small rear garden. He examined the door, his head shifting side to side within the paper hood. He saw that the window pane built into the wooden door had been smashed from the outside and the door opened using the key left in the lock. The door was still open a tiny margin.

Forrest studied the floor beneath the door and then stepped across taking a huge stride to reach the other side of the room. From there, he slowly pulled the door open and looked outside. He froze there for a moment before stepping out on to the patio. Again, keeping his path irregular, he circled the small rear garden anti-clockwise, examining everything. The garden fence, the flowers growing, the soil, the concrete patio, and then the house itself from behind. He took in whether the windows were open or closed, how much noise he could hear, what smells entered his nostrils and the sounds of the streets far away. As he surveyed his environment, he saw a small robin redbreast perched on the garden fence twittering softly. The robin seemed amused by the large white being shuffling across the garden. Forrest looked at the robin and, taking some bird seed from inside his jacket pocket, threw it over the garden wall and robin flew away. He wondered, *you don't have to change, you only need to grow. A flower grows from a seed, it doesn't take on an alchemical state of swopping properties. One can grow to be the best version of who they are and not as someone else, and therein will lie their beauty.*

Three minutes had passed before he re-entered the kitchen. He closed the door and lunged back over to the other side of the room, landing in the very spot he had leapt from. He looked around the kitchen one last time, searching for clues. His eyes focused on every detail: open cupboards, knife rack, a photo from an old holiday on the fridge, food in the sink, the dishwasher, the cleanliness of the room, and the smell. He closed his eyes briefly and placed himself in the victim's head, *how would she have felt in this picture, what was life like for her living in this kitchen?*

So much can be told by the architecture of a building and the way one decorates it. Forrest was astute at understanding the person who lived in a house, as he believed it was the embodiment of the mind; he believed the home represented how we structure our minds and our desires. *Did they desire comfort and warmth? Were they busy and sought the solace of a decluttered, minimalist landscape? Were they surrounded by cute photos and nostalgic memories? Or did they surround themselves in the chromatic shine of wealth and power?* He considered everything. And as far as he had deduced, this family liked wealth, and the appearance of it. The immaculacy of the house, the chandelier, the bespoke designer furniture, the way everything just gelled... it was all so professional in appearance, like someone had been hired to design it, pulled from the pages of a magazine. Black and white in colour may mean black and white in mind.

Feeling satisfied with the results of his observations, he then scuttled back across the left wall like a crab out of water, towards Galbraith who had remained next to the body.

"Anything?" she inquired.

"There's always something, kid. How about you?"

"Quid pro quo, John?"

"I have a theory, but I need to look further. Can we be certain she died from the stab wound?"

"Look at the arterial spray on the walls. Her heart was certainly beating when she was stabbed."

"Granted, but I need to know something."

Forrest, with purple gloved hands, pulled back the victim's sleeves and examined her wrists. There were no marks and no signs she had been tied up or held. He then looked at her fingernails, cold and stiff. Each nail was in good condition, manicured recently and indubitably she hadn't defended herself with them.

"Okay Imogen, looks like she didn't see it coming. Let's have a chat with the suspect."

Galbraith shot an eyebrow up in surprise. The pair of them disrobed in the hall and bagged their paper suits for future forensic examination. Nothing was ever thrown away, even Forrest's gloves were kept for analysis. In a murder enquiry, no gaps could be left open for a canny barrister to plead an abuse of process by the police.

The two detectives entered the lounge and introduced themselves to the inconsolable husband. Forrest was thinking only one thing: He needed to see his height.

"Sir, I know it's very inconvenient at this moment but I need to ask you to leave the house for the time-being. We have a car outside that you can sit in until we are able to take you somewhere for the night. In a minute or two our forensic teams are going to be here and this place will be sealed for what could be many hours, if not days."

The husband did not raise his head.

"I understand, officer. Whatever you think is best."

"Oh, one more thing, Mr Barnes. Your clothing is completely saturated. I think it's time to remove it. I will happily go and collect something for you to change into before you leave. What clothes would you like?"

"Can I not just go and get them?" the husband replied.

"I'm afraid not. We don't want blood being spread around the house. It's best if we keep you here where you can change in peace."

A shot of anger briefly swept across the husband's visage.

"Oh, okay, if that's what you think is best. It's the last door at the end of the corridor on the first floor. Just grab me some trousers and a jumper from the wardrobe on the right."

"Certainly, sir."

Forrest turned on his heel and headed to the door. Galbraith thought about talking to the husband but had detected Forrest was up to something and wished not to disturb his flow. Instead, she took her radio out from her jacket pocket and updated the control room on their current state of affairs.

Forrest returned quickly with clothes in hand and asked the remaining officers to leave the room. The husband then undressed, awkwardly, in front of Forrest.

"Yes, unfortunately I have to stay here. I'm putting your clothes in bags sir. It's important that we separate them out in case vital evidence of the killer is on you from where you touched your wife."

"Yes, of course officer, if it helps out my-"

His crying interrupted his speech and he bowed his head once more and covered his face with his hands. His sobs were broken at intervals by his desire for oxygen.

"Can you tell me about your wife's behaviour recently? Have you noticed anything strange?"

"Well, she was a loving person. Always bubbly. She was not the type who ever really hid emotion. I don't remember her being upset or acting oddly, no."

Forrest held out a bag for each piece of clothing that the husband removed. Before long, he had the man's shoes, trousers, and his jumper all separated into individual paper bags, which he placed on to the floor in front of the husband who was now wearing a new outfit.

"Sir, just lastly, can you sign this evidential receipt for me and print your name and address on it. It shows what we've taken from you."

The husband finished scrawling on the paper. Forrest then opened the door, "Parkes!" he called out, "please take Mr Barnes out to your vehicle."

With that, the husband stood back up. He was 6.2 tall with slight shoulders. He was greying and looked older than the age he had given. He headed out of the living room, turned right and out on to the street, followed by PC Parkes, PC Legg and PC Portway. Forrest observed his every move as he got into the rear of the police car.

Forrest then picked up one of the bags containing a shoe and studied it closely. He picked it up by the centre of the laces to not disturb anything possibly on the tread. He lifted it above his head and looked underneath. He then looked inside the shoe and noted the size on the label - *13*. He then placed it with meticulous care into the evidence bag.

Galbraith simply stood there, watching.

"What can I do, John?"

"Go next door Imogen and speak with the neighbour, she's home. She might have heard something."

"She?" Galbraith replied.

"Yes, she, c'mon," he said hastily, looking towards the door and nodding.

Once Galbraith had left, Forrest radioed for PC Parkes to return to the house. The uniformed officer met him in the living room once more.

"So Brian, what did the husband say to you?"

The officer flicked open his notepad.

"He said he was out driving to collect some DIY items. He kept going on about keeping the house in order. He said that he was gone for about two hours, and when he returned, the door wasn't double-locked so he assumed his wife was home. When he walked into the kitchen, he found her. He immediately called the police and that's when we got here. There wasn't really anything else."

"Thank you, Brian" said Forrest, before shouting in the officer's face, "Galbraith!"

"Sorry?" replied the officer, jerking his head slightly to avoid spittle, some of which caught him on the cheek.

"Brian, would you please return to the husband now," said Forrest softly as he sat down on the sofa. The officer left the room, somewhat bemused.

Once Galbraith had returned from next door she hurried into the living room.

"What is it? What have you got?" she said.

"Forrest responded vaguely, "What did the neighbour say?"

Her hands instantly folded across her chest and her mouth opened slightly to accentuate her disbelief.

"Are you serious, John? You've just screamed my name through the walls and I've had to leave the lady next door for this. Sometimes... God, you're just so rude."

Forrest barely blinked.

"Duly noted," replied Forrest, indifferently, " Did she hear anything?"

Galbraith sighed. It was like telling a football fan during a world cup final to keep the noise down a bit.

"No. She awoke at around 8am and hasn't left the house since. She also didn't see anything either. No one coming or going."

Forrest stood up and walked out of the house. He paused at the door before shouting at Galbraith, "C'mon then!" He jogged down the front steps of the house and over to the vehicle occupied by the sobbing husband. PC Parkes was sat in front and the husband behind him at the rear. Forrest opened the passenger door and bent over the husband.

"Hello sir, can I ask what you do for a living?"

"Um, I manage a private security firm," replied the husband.

"Do you ever use mobile CCTV mounted cars?"

"Uh, yes, sometimes."

"And do you clamp and seize vehicles?" questioned Forrest.

"Yes, why?" he asked, inquisitively.

Dismissing the question with a wave of the hand, Forrest said, "Mr Barnes, where did you park your car?"

"It's just up there. Why, what is it?" he enquired, pointing up the road. He then looked at Forrest with incredulity. "I told the constable already that I've been out for the last two hours buying DIY goods."

"I know," the detective replied stoically. "Can I have the keys?"

124

"Yes, they're in the house, on the hallway table."

"Beside the letters?" said Forrest.

"Um, yes," said the husband.

Forrest turned and headed along the road. He already had the keys in his pocket which he had taken from inside the house. In his hand he held the husband's mobile telephone with the screen facing him. The phone was pin locked but the detective seemed not to care. Galbraith stood still, unsure whether he wanted her to join him. She felt like an overlooked child at times, sat in a corner, overshadowed by Forrest's perceptiveness and experience. He was an arbiter in the court of the character of men, and she a juror recording it all. When he looked at her, it was as though she knew the words but couldn't hear the music.

He walked along the row of sports cars and SUVs pressing the car-key button every few cars until an amber light blinked twice on a vehicle ahead of him. Scrutinising it closely, he took a walk round the entirety of the grey 4x4, checking the panelling. He touched the bonnet and then the rear tires. He then span his head around a full 360 degrees, gauging the surroundings. After which he opened the driver's door and sat inside. Forrest himself was six foot one and he struggled to fit his legs inside. He sat back and started the engine. He checked the mirrors were working by testing the electric wing-mirror controls and peered in the rear-view. He had seen enough.

Forrest climbed awkwardly out from the vehicle and locked it. He stood in the middle of the road and stared, firstly to the east, and then to the west, along the street. He was concentrating furiously, but unhappy that he had not found what he was seeking. Unconvinced, he reached for his phone and logged onto the GPS map application. His phone was old and slow and he had to wait for it to load. His large calloused fingers typed in the address and the phone displayed an aerial view of Woodlands Road where he currently stood. The street was only 250 metres long, running between two other residential streets with one small side road branching out from Woodlands Road itself, not far from Forrest.

It has to be here. He dashed off again. He headed to the small road just up ahead following the satnav of his gut instincts. Galbraith looked up the road and saw him turn off the street and disappear. She gathered herself and saw the faces of her uniform colleagues looking at her, awaiting instruction, equally bemused. As she took a pace closer to them, the sound of a car pulling over interrupted her river of thought. And she watched, as a smartly dressed black woman carrying a briefcase climbed out.

"Are you the FME?" she enquired.

"Yes, Dr Hughes," she said, extending her hand.

The pair exchanged pleasantries while donning suits before Galbraith led the Forensic Medical Examiner into the house. Crime scene or not, the body had to be pronounced dead by a medical professional. She recalled the route she and Forrest had taken and walked the doctor to the body. The doctor opened her briefcase and retrieved a stethoscope. It was a gesture of formality rather than pragmatism, and in the briefest of instances she looked up at Galbraith and confirmed the wife was dead.

The doctor rolled her left sleeve up and said the time aloud for Galbraith to record. The detective depressed her radio and updated Control with the information, providing the doctor's name and the time that life was pronounced extinct. The two suited women then withdrew to the front of the house again, passing the frozen female officer on the doorstep who smiled briefly at them as they passed.

Formalities regarding death were built on years of operating procedures, criminal investigations, legal arguments, and mistakes. The set protocol could now rarely be disregarded no matter how evident a person was dead, or how expensive the fee from the doctor. The coroner was next to be called, and once the forensic investigation was complete, the undertakers would arrive to collect the body. A post mortem would then confirm the cause of death and an inquest would be held at the Coroner's Court in Horseferry Road.

As Dr Hughes shook Galbraith's hand and strode off in the wind to her car, Galbraith caught a glimpse of Forrest bounding towards them, his coat flailing about like the black flag of a pirate ship, sailing towards them across a concrete sea. As he got closer, she saw anger had replaced bafflement. She had to intervene and began heading in his direction.

"John, stop. What is it?"

He kept on walking.

"John," she grabbed his arm, "tell me."

He stopped just metres from the car containing the husband.

"That bastard murdered his wife and I'm gonna nick him for it."

"Wait, wait, shouldn't we let Murder Squad decide?"

"Fuck 'em," he replied, grimacing.

Forrest opened the rear door of the car and the husband, none the wiser, peered up at him through swollen red eyes. The on-looking figures of Parkes, Legg and Portway listened in a state of disbelief with mouths agape.

"Oi cunt. You're under arrest for the murder of Cassandra Pinto. You do not have to say anything but it may harm your defence if you do not mention when questioned something which you later rely on in court. Anything you do say may be given in evidence."

Mr Barnes was apoplectic.

He pointed as he screamed. "This is ridiculous! You can't arrest me! I've been out all day in my car. Check the bloody CCTV you stupid man. You fucking idiots. You can see I've bought DIY products today! I've got a fucking receipt! You won't-"

Forrest slammed the car door on him, instructed the officers to take him away and turned towards Galbraith.

"Take that look off your face kid. Here, read this. Use gloves."

Forrest handed her a letter in a brown envelope. On the front it read *'Alison Cooper'*, with the full address below and a stamp in the corner. She opened the letter carefully and read the single page of writing. The letter was handwritten and signed in the name of John Barnes, dated three weeks before.

'Dear Ally,

Thank U 4 ur letter. I'm doing fine, life is relatively normal. Work is goin well and Cassie is doing fine at the mo. I hope u v well. How are ur...

Eric.'

It struck Galbraith at just how bland the letter was. It was written as though he was replying to a friend. It contained nothing of interest, just a simple message about doing well and that life was carrying on as normal.

He didn't mention his wife other than to say she was doing well. The letter went on to talk briefly about their families and that Alison should visit.

"What's the significance of this John? It's the most boring thing I've ever read."

"Precisely."

"Do I look like I spend my days reading a subscription to The Pen-Pal Times? Otherwise, what interest is there in this for me?"

"Why would he send it? It's flannel," said Forrest.

"Because he's wetter than the floor of a festival urinal, why else?"

"Where's the secret?"

Galbraith examined the letter again. The name wasn't an anagram. The address and postcode were genuine according to an internet search. The stamp was stuck on and didn't appear to hide a secret message. She studied the text some more.

"The only part that stands out is that he writes like a teenager".

"Because..." said Forrest.

"Saving time?" said Galbraith, "But that wouldn't make sense – no one posts a letter to save time."

"So he's doing what?"

Galbraith studied the letter, "The only word that is contracted uncommonly into text speak is *'very' into 'V'*. That forms the words *'U V'* when put together".

Forrest winked at her and then handed Galbraith a UV pen from his pocket. Written on the inside of the envelope it said, *'CASS IS DEAD. STAY AWAY. NO PHONES. WILL WRITE SOON.'*

*****

XVI

GRUB

Helmand Province, Afghanistan

THE British Royal Engineers were having their evening meal as the sun set in. Nothing was new to the men anymore. Routine had set in. Perfunctory smiles served leaden slop for lunch. John was irked by this, but he was irked far more by something else. The sand. John was a city boy, born in a concrete jungle, unaccustomed to tropical climates and sandy shores. Here, in the desert, the sand ruined everything. Skin crevices and cuts were paved over with it, like a tarmac truck filling holes on a battered road. It made their firearms jam and clog up. It chewed away at their lips and poured down the gaps in their body armour. In the day time, it reflected the high sun into John's eyes causing sun spots to form over his retinas. At night, despite the cold, he could still see a figment of the sun in his vision.

"How's your food buddy?" asked John.

"Fantastic!" replied Denning, sardonically, as he lifted the gruel from the tin letting it slop loosely from his spoon back into the mix. The small group of men were sat on benches in a tented off area of the base; an attempt by the brass to make it resemble in some part a dining area.

An NCO marched up to the soldier's table.

"Listen up. We need to move out ten minutes ago, so get your shit together ladies!"

"No rest for the wicked" said Blake.

The men stood up and made their way over to the sleeping quarters. Another tent, larger than the canteen, long and rectangular, with dark grey lining and metal poles holding it in place, was home to 36 soldiers. They began to pack their kits when Denning commenced one of his legendary rants. "This is fuckin' bollocks. We get fed on crap and then don't even get a chance to bloody eat it."

"I told you before old friend, don't let it get to you. Anyway, we get leave next month," replied John.

"Yeah I know. What you doing for it?" said Denning.

John continued packing but his voice took on a different tone.

"I've been saving up. I've bought this small cabin out in the country. It sits on a ridge above a stream. There isn't another house or person for miles. I'll see the kids at home and then take my wife out into the country, just us two, and relax. Just lie down with her. That's what I miss, the ability to do nothing. You?"

Denning spoke with zeal, "I miss England mate. I miss goin' down the pub, knocking back a few pints, pullin' a tart and stumbling home a fucking mess. I miss my mates, my mum, a Sunday roast. After all these years out here, you can start to miss any old thing. Last week, I even missed sitting in traffic.". He chuckled to himself. "How's your mum getting on?"

"Not great," said John throwing his rucksack over his shoulder. "I've written to her a few times but haven't heard anything. She's kind of old school like that, a real Luddite. Then I called the other day and they said that her cancer had gotten worse. I'll see how she is when we get back." He and the others headed off with their bags in tow.

Twelve men plus the NCO were packed into the rear of a transport lorry. They were heading towards the bridge that stretched out into the desert. The lorry was raucous with men shouting to be heard over the loud noise of the engine. The NCO stood up without warning and began to address the troops.

"Men! I've got some bad news from the top! Your leave is being suspended indefinitely! Intel suggests hostiles have re-gathered in our sector! And what's even fucking worse, a second rebel faction is congregating on the Iranian border and heading our way! Rather than bring more troops here, they're gonna leave us stationed until the threat is neutralised or displaced! Your loved ones will be informed."

As he finished speaking, he sat down and his face took on the same look of disappointment that those around him shared. It wasn't the NCO's fault and John and Denning were aware that he had four young children waiting for him in England.

Denning stood up and fought his way across the back of the lorry to the NCO. The lorry seemed to rock more with every step he took.

"Sir, with the most utmost respect, that's total bollocks!"

The NCO lent in to Denning and said "I know fella" before he stood up again. "Lads, it's not the first time it's happened and it won't be the last. So let's muck in and get the job done as quickly as we can."

John remained quiet all that day. He missed his family, his wife, his children, but he only worried about his mother. He worried if he'd ever see her again – he worried about who would be the first of them to die.

He pondered on his life and his work and ultimately decided that his serving the army benefitted his wife and benefitted the children. They received money every month, regular video phone calls, photos and letters. If he were to die, they'd receive a handsome sum and widow's pension. They'd grow up and move on. But his mother, she wouldn't. She got nothing for his service, just more loneliness. Out in the desert, alone in the chorus of sand swirling about him, he began to know what loneliness was. Loneliness was a crime in a time when communication had never been simpler. To John, he was closer to his family than any soldier who had served before him, yet his mind had never felt further away.

*****

XVII

POLITICS

"HURRY up John, they've been bloody badgering me ever since you arrested him. Now I suggest you just get in there and play it cool. Let me do the talking," said Inspector Walsh.

She was struggling to express herself. Her small frame and short legs could not keep up with the long strides of Forrest and this caused her words to be breathy and unconvincing.

"I'll think about it, ma'am," he replied.

He's such a shit.

There were three officers sat down at the round table in the conference room of the station. One officer, older than the rest, bald with traces of short white hair, wore a dark suit and tie, and had the weather-beaten face of a Scottish football manager nearing retirement. The second man wore a pink shirt and had a large belly that put undue stress on the buttons at his waist, and his brown hair was greasy and swept clumsily across his forehead. The third and final officer was an Asian female, younger than the men, wearing a crisp, white blouse, gold necklace and matching earrings. She had a pen and notepad at the ready.

Walsh took point and led Forrest into the room. The door was heavy and flew back of its own accord making a loud bang as it closed. Forrest had been in this room enough times to know the door would slam this way and watched to see which of the three became most startled. He and Walsh both sat down opposite the three strangers which inadvertently created an adversarial setting.

"So, you must be DC Forrest," said the fat officer blanketed in a pink shirt , an unwise choice for a man of his size, shuffling further over the desk as he spoke. "Maybe you'd like to explain why you've arrested the CEO of E3 Security Systems and why my superiors are now phoning me every ten minutes wanting an update on his detention." He grew angrier and his fists clenched, "And why, I'm having to now prepare a bloody statement to the media concerning his arrest for fucking murder!"

Forrest sat stoic as ever, with his left hand resting on his thigh and his right hand rotating an imaginary stress ball in the air. He patiently waited for the man, whom he now assumed was the detective inspector for murder squad, to finish berating him. The man continued to shout while Forrest's mind ran free. He thought about units such as SCO1 or Murder Team as it's more commonly known. He had a theory on the officers belonging to those units. In Forrest's eyes, there were two kinds of detective on SCO1. You had hard working, young, ambitious DCs who joined the police with the sole intention to become the finest investigators possible. For them, the pinnacle was investigating a murder and catching a killer. To hear the judge in your own investigation, your own case, send the suspect you found down for life. Forrest glanced briefly at the Asian female and placed her in this category.

His attention focused back on the rotund DI for a moment. He was the second type of officer synonymous with SCO1. Off-borough specialist units were fantastic places for gluttonous, lazy and cavilling officers to hide, free from the politics of figures and targets dished out to borough officers by government ministers. An old sweat detective could sit on these squads for years producing a below par standard of work with the knowledge that he could not be admonished. One false move on borough and an officer would soon find himself manning the property store or the front office for a week. But here on the specialist squad, he was untouchable.

"Well, that was all very interesting Mr? Sorry, I didn't catch your name?" quizzed Forrest.

"Listen sonny," chipped in the older man in the dark suit, "you'd better start explaining yourself before I give you a reason for never forgetting my name."

Forrest paused purposefully. He could sense Walsh was getting very hot under the collar and he savoured the smell of her discomfort. He locked eyes on the older man: an unshifting gaze.

"I went there as the first detective on scene with my colleague Imogen Galbraith, but leave her out of this, she's not cut her teeth yet. The wooden-tops had set up an officer on the crime scene already and she checked us in. We suited up in full barrier clothing and approached the body, bearing in mind the victim had not yet been pronounced dead by the medic. We took an irregular route and marked this on the crime scene log. Having inspected the body briefly, I ventured in to the back garden. It was dry outside and the sun was-"

"Hey, smartarse. I want to know why you arrested him, not what the fucking weather was like," interjected the bulging inspector.

Forrest expressed his umbrage with a quick shift of the head and a sharp stare. "This is important. I'll get to the arrest in good time. As I was saying, I assessed the scene in full. Everything will be recorded in my statement, which I was busy writing before you summoned me here."

"Constable, we can summon you whenever we bloody like, and you made us wait twenty minutes you ungrateful-" said the chief inspector in the dark suit, stopping himself from swearing.

Forrest continued, "There were no signs of a struggle. The female lay on the floor where she had been stabbed and had not been moved. The blow was a single strike from one knife. It was pushed in deep, with hate, the intention to kill. The blow landed on the shoulder, but from the angle, the perpetrator who had to be above average height could easily have been aiming for the top of her head and missed. She had no marks on her wrists or mouth to suggest she had been tied up. Her clothes were intact and there were no signs of sexual assault. The obvious motive for the murder was hate, disguised to look like a robbery."

"A robbery? Nothing was stolen."

The Asian female spoke well and there was no trace of an accent in her voice, unlike the fat inspector who was as northern as brown ale.

"As far as we know, but I am confident Mr Barnes will soon be able to state with utmost clarity and certainty that something was stolen by the intruder. I assure you of that," said Forrest.

"Okay, no struggle doesn't necessarily mean it was done by someone she knew," said the chief inspector. "Crimes of passion generally indicate multiple stab wounds, a flurry of anger."

"I agree. The window in the back door was smashed to allow the intruder entry to the property with the key left in the lock. However, firstly, the victim would have heard the glass breaking and the door opening. Secondly, the knife used came from the victim's knife rack located beside the rear door, which meant the killer apparently smashed the back door, entered the kitchen, picked up the knife, and then crept up on the victim already in the kitchen, without being seen, and stabbed her once. Unless the victim is a deaf and blind mute she would have noticed this and she would have screamed blue murder. To check this point, I sent Imogen next door on an enquiry and the neighbour who was present all day stated that she had heard nothing. And when I shouted Imogen's name from the victim's kitchen, she was able to hear me crystal clear and ran back."

Walsh saw how the three hostiles had seemingly warmed to Forrest. She had to admit, for all his bad qualities, failing to get the job done was never one of them. To have eighteen years in the job as the lowest rank and still enjoy locking criminals up was to be revered. He was a dinosaur, but that dinosaur was a tyrannosaurus.

"Okay, but he could have been hiding in there, the intruder. He could still have entered and picked up the knife and waited for her," said the chief inspector.

"I took that into consideration and went outside into the garden. The garden itself consists of a concrete patio surrounded by three feet wide, thick flower beds that encircle the patio area. It rained last night and the soil was sodden. Behind these soil flower beds is an eight foot high solid wooden fence. I went outside and saw no trace of any soil on the patio, or the steps to the door, or the kitchen floor. But when I looked at the fence, I saw clear footprints in the soil leading up to the fence which the attacker had climbed to make his escape. And before you say that all that tells us is that the intruder jumped over the soil bed when he first entered, in order to do this, you're talking about an eight foot fence, plus three feet of raised soil bed to pass to get on to the concrete patio. That's a mighty big jump and none of the shrubs had been crushed. Lastly, the footprint on the fence was large. I wear a size 11 and I compared my own shoe size with the mark left on the fence and it was much smaller. Our intruder wore at least a size 13, just like the husband."

The fat inspector looked over at his chief who seemed engrossed in Forrest's analysis, something the constable had not missed.

He continued, "The thing that bothered me most was the husband's alibi. He said that he had been out for two hours buying products to carry out DIY. This in itself worried me: the house was immaculate and had been quite ostensibly renovated in recent months, and it was an expensive professional renovation at that. The husband has a working knowledge of CCTV systems and will no doubt produce the receipt with the name of the premises he attended this morning – a premises without internal CCTV. I wanted to have a look at his car. When I got inside it, I noticed immediately that the seat hadn't been adjusted properly. I mean, the seat was pushed back, but the angle of the seat to the steering wheel was not right for a six footer and the mirrors had been set to someone considerably shorter than the gangly husband.

"That's when I realised that he must have loaned the car to someone to drive that morning. That person would be out there driving his car and all those cameras would see this. They would become his alibi, and all he needed was someone who looked like him and in the building trade."

"I'm not convinced," said the inspector leaning back and looking towards the chief. "C'mon, seriously? A guy loans his car out to someone else so that he can murder his wife? Seems a bit farfetched, but what do I know?"

"I agree," stated the chief.

The constable continued unperturbed, "To confirm this theory required the following criteria to have been followed. A shorter man to borrow the car; the shorter man's own vehicle to be out of order; the shorter man to work in the building trade, and lastly he would need to know Eric Barnes. I looked around the surrounding streets. At first, I was hoping to find a roadside repair van carrying out work on the next street over, but I couldn't see any. I had taken the husband's mobile telephone with me and kept the screen lit up. As I passed a house on Saddington Close, the wifi on Barnes's phone suddenly came on. This means he must have known one of the neighbours well enough for his phone to automatically log on to their wifi. I found the address and knocked on the door.

"A man, five foot nine tall, with greying hair and of slim build answered the door. We had a conversation: 'Do you know Eric at 71?' I asked. 'Yes', he said. Then I asked him, 'Did your vehicle have a fault this morning?' And he replied, 'Yes, it wouldn't start.' He went on to say that he was trying the engine as Eric came past and asked if everything was okay. They had a look at the engine together and the fan belt had snapped. Barnes told his neighbour that he could borrow his car so long as it was brought back in the next two hours. The neighbour told Barnes that he'd received an order on his website & needed it to travel to Chelmsford – the order stipulated that he had to collect some building supplies for a job from a specific shop. However, once the neighbour had gotten to the site, the only items listed for collection were a few bits and pieces for DIY. When he tried to contact the customer, the phone number didn't work.

"What do you think?" asked the chief of his two cohorts.

"Seems plausible, if not a little theatrical sir," said the Asian female.

"I disagree," said Forrest. "Motive, opportunity, alibi... then you have a murder."

"I'm not sure about this. If it was planned this meticulously then why would he not factor in the footprints or the noise of glass breaking," said the Northern detective inspector.

"It's either a botched robbery or a murder. Thankfully, I couldn't really give a shit. Now I've got my own crimes to investigate so I'll be off unless there's anything else you need?" said Forrest as he stood up. "Oh, I took this from the house. You'll need a UV pen to read it," shoving the letter under the nose of the DI. "You can use mine."

He waited momentarily for a response that never came and then walked out of the door leaving Walsh with the triumvirate. As he walked down the corridor he could hear Walsh's apologies becoming fainter.

Forrest winced as he headed into the CID office; the unnatural lighting pierced the back of his retina and caused him to look away and scan the floor. The chair he'd had for years squeaked and croaked as his body slumped into it. Grabbing the underside of his desk, he pulled himself in towards it. Just four hours of paperwork and he would be done.

"Pssst," whispered Martin, his supervising sergeant. Forrest looked over.

"Well done John. I've known DI McGregor for years and anyone who upsets that miserable git is a good man in my book."

Martin winked as he finished his sentence.

"Cheers Mart," he replied.

Two uniform officers were hot desking in the CID office. It had caught Forrest's attention as he surveyed the room looking for Galbraith only to find two reprobates sitting in his team's corner. Police stations were ludicrously understocked with supplies. The antiquated computers used twelve year old software, outmoded applications and had little storage space for email or documents. The force had no money to spend on upgrades and happily relied on ancient technology to get by. To the police officers who had to work this way, it was an embarrassment.

It was a fight in the morning to even find a terminal and those who arrived late would have to leave the CID office in order to find a free or working machine, inevitably, they'd be banished to work with civilian staff up the corridor, away from their colleagues, to the chagrin of their supervisors who would have to communicate with them by email for the rest of the day.

The computers themselves were castoffs, unable to even surf major websites as the browser was out of date. The keyboards had letters missing and were covered in filth. One had often wondered how much dead skin, hair, food, sweat and muck which had accumulated over the past ten years had infiltrated the cracks between the keys.

Police officers don't get work phones, or laptops, or any means to contact the public away from their desks. They don't get given cameras or GPS technology to navigate or help solve crime. The stationery cupboard was a barren drawer containing staples but no stapler, and pens but no paper. It was a shambles. The result of years of poor supervision and a non-performance related culture where doing nothing meant one was less inclined to encounter trouble or make a mistake. Forrest had never been someone to sit back and thus, his superiors always kept watch over him. He wouldn't tolerate someone lackadaisical, and he was relieved Galbraith wasn't in this category.

The two uniformed officers were sitting at their respective terminals opposite Forrest and on the machine Galbraith had tended to use. He overheard their conversation.

"Fucking hell Grubby, did you see me take that bend on Chapel St. Boom! Must have been going at least forty-five round that!" said the older of the two men.

"Bollocks, you drive like my gran mate, and she parks better than you do too," replied the younger officer.

Neither officer had typed anything over the last few minutes and they continued talking in the same vein.

"So how comes I've nicked twice as many slags as you this month, huh?" said the younger man.

"You couldn't nick yourself shaving sonny. While I'm busy driving you there, you get all the credit for the body at the end."

"Nah, you can't fucking teach it Mick. I'm a bloody natural. And anyway, I get results. You couldn't charge a mobile phone pal," said the younger man.

"A natural?" replied his colleague. "I'll tell you what you are, you're my pen. If I have to go to a call, you're doing the writing. You're like my mobile secretary. I drive, you work."

They continued talking in that overt jocular manner, expecting those around them to enjoy the camaraderie, a bit like a yob playing music aloud on their phone oblivious or without care for what others may think.

"Just because you've been in the job a couple more years than me don't mean you're any good Mick. I reckon you need to put your feet up mate and take a back office job, you're losing your touch."

"Really? When you get a little more service under your belt son and learn the ropes, then maybe I'll let you drive me somewhere and maybe I'll get my pen out. Until then, crack on. Just remember, I've got eight years' service in this job and that means I call the shots. All you have to do is bag 'em and tag 'em sonny."

"Look mate, as crap as you are, at least you're not a bird," said the younger constable.

"Yeah, ha ha, I ain't got a problem with women in the police. I mean, I'm not making the fucking tea," he laughed.

Forrest had heard enough. "Oi, Siegfried and Wilfred," he said, leaning over the top of his desk, "as much as I feel edified by your presence, I'd prefer it if you left so my colleagues due for the afternoon shift can use the terminals."

The two officers looked at one another and decided it best not to argue.

"We'll leave you fellas to it mate" said the older constable as the pair slowly waddled out of the office as the younger officer asked his cohort what 'edified' meant and who 'Siegerfand' was.

Finally she had replied to his text message.

"Downstairs near the female locker rooms. What's up?"

He swiped his phone and punched in a reply:

"Meet in the yard? I fancy a smoke. See you in 3."

The smoke poured out of his two nostrils like vapour from the cooling towers of a power station, into the sky, fading slowly, disappearing into the atmosphere but not gone. The harmful black smog crawled along his nasal hair and arched across the tip of his nose. Galbraith caught a whiff and leaned back.

"Well, what did you want to tell me so badly?" she said.

"The parcel bomb this morning. It concerns me."

She laughed loudly and then covered her mouth trying to suppress a further burst. "It concerns you? I should hope so! Everyone upstairs is bloody terrified!"

He tutted loudly. "Listen, I've seen these before and normally they're nothing to worry about. Some warning shot across the bows or a nutcase wanting notoriety. But this... I think it's part of something major on its way."

"Go on," she said assuming a serious stance.

Her shoes scraped across the wet gravelled floor as they paced slowly across the police yard.

"I called one of my pals at Terrorism and spoke to Bomb Squad. Together they confirmed my theory: the bomb was a little too sophisticated to be a lone mental case getting his information from the web and making it at home, but it's not something our active terrorist groups are known for."

"So... you're... saying?" she said.

"I don't see why he would send it, that's all."

"Perhaps, he just wants notoriety like you said. Or it was a distraction. Maybe whilst we were all out in the yard practising the fire drill, he was busy doing something, somewhere?" said Galbraith.

"I just can't put my finger on it yet is all. I'm going to make a few more calls and see what I can find out."

He flicked his cigarette still alight into a dumpster and the pair headed off back into the grey police station.

*****

XVIII

MESSAGE

THIS man continues to act with callous disregard for his colleagues, the public and the law. I am growing more concerned that his actions are detrimental to the Service and to the public. One cannot argue that the constable is a shrewd officer with a good record, but there is no doubt in my mind that he is a danger and should be relieved of front line duties.

Having finished typing their report, they uploaded the file to a central server and closed the file marked John Forrest.

*****

XIX

DECORUM

HER hair damp, clinging to her cheeks like seaweed on a rock; the once slick dark locks were now split and frayed by the wind and rain of the blustery walk home. *Where are they?* Hands met leather in a dark purse, knocking items about and listening intently for the jingle of metal upon metal.

"Lost your keys?" said the Irish voice from behind her.

Galbraith turned around and saw her handsome neighbour standing there dry as a bone, flicking the last remains of water from his umbrella which he placed against the wall. She couldn't shake off the sense of shallow embarrassment that clung to her like her wet hair.

"Yes, I think they've made a leap for freedom."

She laughed nervously. He smiled back.

"I can help you look? Why don't we retrace your steps?"

He spoke with the calm serenity of a mystic and his accent had the dulcet tone of a Sunday school teacher telling tales to young children in a soft Kerry accent.

"No, honestly, I've probably left them at work."

She fumbled nervously inside her bag once more and then wobbled awkwardly as her elevated right leg, propping up the bag, suddenly gave way.

"Look, why don't you wait at mine until your..." he said searching her eyes.

"Fiancé," she said.

"Fiancé comes home. I don't mind like, it's a welcome break from the monotony of my own ramblings," he said beaming. A wide, friendly smile encouraged a positive response..

Galbraith acquiesced: it was hard to deny his charms and his hospitality. She followed him into number 62. His flat had that modern urban chic that newcomers to London often sought and the place looked expressionless; soulless, like it had just been taken out of the wrapping. Even though the flat was aesthetically stunning, it was all too neat and perfect which ultimately detracted from any feeling of home. It was a show flat designed to woo the visitor with style rather than comfort: quickly in, quickly out. She didn't want to stay too long.

She continued her tour of the flat which had only the one bedroom and so its purpose had never been to house a family; it was for a young professional, whatever that meant. It was awash with slick chrome fixtures where the narcissist could enjoy catching their reflection at any given time. Dylan walked her to the kitchen and proffered a warm cup of tea. His flat had a different view to Galbraith's and curiosity drew her closer to the window. It overlooked a small concrete and grass play area and the wind was making the swings oscillate to and fro, as if ghost children were playing together.

"You smoke?" he said, one cigarette protruding from a pack of twenty.

"No. Thank you." she replied.

She spent two hours in the flat with Dylan. The conversation never dulled or stalled. His charm just seemed to grow. A new side to him came to the fore. At first, he had seemed rural and rugged, but the way he carried himself and his obvious desire for modernity gave him a punchy cosmopolitan edge imbued with a comforting quality only served on the Irish.

She had also not planned on drinking those two glasses of wine. It was naughty, it wasn't her. It reminded Galbraith of her week at summer camp as a child, when she had sneaked off into the boy's room down the corridor. Someone had stolen a bottle of scotch from Mr Jeffrey, the geography teacher, which led to Galbraith's first drunken experience.

"Oh gosh, it's gone eight, Dylan. I better get back over to mine, he'll be home by now."

"Time flies, huh?" he said, getting up from the sofa. "Let me show you out."

They walked nervously. He was without expectation. As they reached the door, he leaned in to kiss her cheek. A touch of formality to end an informal night. Galbraith felt the urge. An urge she had not felt in many years, dampened by the knowledge that she had the right man, and nothing else would do.

She remembered a conversation she'd had with Forrest during their many drives through the traffic laden streets of London. He argued that women, to him, were like jobs. He wouldn't quit one job before going to look for a better one, in the same way he felt you shouldn't ditch your partner until you had a better offer lined up. It was a trade. He ended his metaphor with a blunt, "And don't get me wrong, many of us work two jobs." *He could be a real git at times.*

She disagreed with him. But over the last fortnight she had become deeply aware of how boring she had become. She felt it and wondered if others had too. What a horrible thing to feel about oneself, almost the ultimate insult. We cannot change our appearance much, or our intelligence, but to be considered boring is quite irredeemable. When had she last taken a risk, upset the applecart, done something her mother would disagree with? Why should she be the one who always did the right thing, the agreeable daughter, and the meek bride?

As he opened the door, she stared into his dark eyes. Her head bent lower, her teeth sinking into, then sucking, her bottom lip. She fell into him. Her mouth now resting upon his. Breathing each other's breath. She could feel the coarseness of his stubble, the softness of his tongue. His large hand that wrapped around her cheek and then slid behind her ear and under her hair. She pushed him against the wall and ran her hands down his stomach, finally scrunching his shirt in her fingers.

They kissed for a minute, violently, passionately. Her makeup had become his and his body, like a blind woman reading braille, had become clear. Her now dry, long, white hair was ruffled about her face. She corrected herself in a mirror before scuttling out of the apartment and back to her own with quiet steps.

She wasn't proud, but felt no guilt either. She knocked on the door and was let in, which was a flat made to be a home, as the door closed behind her.

*****

XX

ABSOLUTION

THE coin span in the air, glinting in the light, blinking at him. One solitary bulb, unmasked, nestling in the corner at the rear of the smoke filled room. The coin landed in his palm without a sound, hidden by the fingers that enveloped it. He brought his clenched paw nearer to his face and released his grip. *It's tails.* He slammed the coin on to a wooden table ahead of him. The table was old and laced with circular cup marks from spilt coffee, or beer, and some other substances.

Forrest's mind unravelled before him, and then rolled back up again like a carpet, revealing all the items that were hidden beneath it, set free. His consciousness raged, burned and flared wild and uncontrolled. He scratched his face raking himself, tearing a few hairs in the process and a thin trail a blood shadowed a fingernail.

Fuck off! Just fuck off! Cunt! Fuck! Only an old photo of his sister stared back at him without reply. He rocked on the spot, on that broken sofa. The fish hooks imbedded in his temples represented those buried in his soul. The first blow shook his core, but the vodka helped him remain focused on his task and see past the pain. He was always weaker with his left fist. No matter the hours spent drilling that fist, those 27 bones into a heavy bag, his actions were not as smooth, the power was never quite achieved. He threw a flurry of punches into his own face. One punch caught himself above the left eye, splitting the worn, leathery, soft skin of his brow and a linear blood-spray splattered across his forehead. He hit quicker now. Three-four-five-six; all connecting in the temples. The final blow would hurt the most. He waited for it. Breathed in deeply a couple times. Forrest looked at the fist that would cause the damage. The right sockdolager landed cleanly on the bridge of his nose breaking it, not for the first time. His hand jarred from the blow and quivered. His neck slammed back into the comforting couch. His blood tasted rich as it dripped into his mouth. He enjoyed it.

He had succumbed to the pain now. An amplified dyspraxia overwhelmed him. His dizziness was the duality of alcohol and violence borne out of a propensity for self-harm. A sudden calm melted into Forrest. His mind stopped running away. The record that span on repeat for the last eight hours no longer revolved in his mind. The oscillations between self-loathing and general disaffection with society became blurred and he rested in the embrace of the stained sofa.

Forrest reclined and sunk into the cushion. It was his form of meditation. He could feel the pain in his face and his hands, he could feel the difficulty in breathing through his nose; he could feel. His breathing slowed to a crawl. He shut his eyes softly. He had no intention of wiping himself clean just yet.

Two years ago, Forrest began losing weight and had prolonged stomach cramps. Once he'd finally bothered to see a doctor, they discovered a tapeworm growing inside him. A simple course of antibiotics were prescribed to dispel the parasite. Forrest had a reaction that even surprised him; he waited 8 months before taking the treatment. He knew this alien was growing inside him. He could feel pain and discomfort. But for the first time in a long time, Forrest felt like something inside him was alive. Strangely, he felt less alone the world. He even named the tapeworm Tony. One day in the gym, he almost collapsed after a punch to the guts, and then went into a rage believing the tapeworm may have been harmed. It was then he realised the folly of his plight. The tapeworm died within a week of the antibiotic treatment.

The blood slowly stopped flowing from his nose. *Just another boxing injury*, he would tell them.

*****

XXI

A Priori

GALBRAITH checked her phone but there was no message from Forrest. The office door swung open, but it wasn't him either and she returned to staring at her computer screen. Even for the tardy officer, this degree of lateness was unusual.

She accepted her lack of focus and leaned back in the plastic chair at her desk and scanned the room. Martin was busy in the corner on the phone, and Lee was whining on about his marriage to another colleague a few chairs away. She saw three officers in uniform sat together. They looked happy and relaxed. She remembered her days as a patrol cop; the days of having no crimes to investigate, no stress and no pressure. She also recalled the feeling of wearing a uniform. The uniform was like a presence, more powerful than its bearer. You felt protected and clothed in cotton armour. You saw yourself as though you were another person, an inch taller, and bulletproof. You felt a part of history. One of a few thousand women who had walked the streets having sworn an oath to protect others; to give her own life to the cause. The same uniform that was a symbol of hate and oppression to so many.

A feeling of concern and doubt flushed over Galbraith. Around her, she was surrounded by the menagerie of suited men and women, giving the impression of unity when in fact, it was anything but unified. She realised how she missed Forrest. He was a comfort to her, a deflector of prying eyes and an absorber of ridicule.

Galbraith checked her work-file. She had twenty-six crimes to investigate. This was consonant with all the other detectives. Twenty-six crimes usually meant twenty-six victims to update, at least twenty-six suspects to keep track of, and countless hours of mind-numbing paperwork, statements, forms, phone calls, meetings and arse covering. This was why many crimes were commuted to lesser offences. The suspects were happy to plead and the police were happy to quickly conclude investigations.

She breathed a heavy sigh. Then a long coat appeared in her peripheral vision and a thud sounded as the owner dropped into his chair. He resembled an exhumed body, black and blue through deterioration, the incarnate of pain.

"You should see the other guy," Forrest slurred susurrantly.

Galbraith was mortified; her jaw dropped down opening a chasm of shock in her face as she winced at the sight of Forrest's mutilated face. It had grown in size like an island after a volcanic eruption from the sea. His eyes were puffy and the haematoma on both eyelids made him purblind. His nose was cut in the centre of the bridge and symmetrical rings formed a smile underneath both eyes. The right side of his lip was split and a yellow scab had formed over the red surface. Galbraith tried to avert her stare but all she could hear now was his muffled, coarse breathing over the thin murmurings from other officers in equal bewilderment.

The small team of detectives remained shackled to their desks for the next three hours running perfunctory enquiries and searching databases to uncover information. The modern building was like no other; built originally as a warehouse it lacked all the bare essentials. There wasn't a canteen or even a recreational area. Not like the old days of pool tables, gyms, onsite bars and smoking in all areas. The building simply had two microwaves and for the storage of food a few fridges, the buzz of which could be heard over the long periods of silence in the office. Downstairs, there were two vending machines with two tables beside them; but this wasn't somewhere to congregate or enjoy any mental respite. It was no wonder the sickness levels of staff within the Service were so high. The nearest shop was a ten minute walk along a motorway slip road and a lonely place to be when you're hungry.

Forrest looked at Galbraith and began gesticulating towards her, with his hands extended he acted out a driver holding a steering wheel, turning it left and right, and she nodded back in reply. The semaphore was acknowledged and the pair made their way to a CID car.

"Something is coming," he said, as they turned out of the police yard and on to the street. "That package mailed to the office, it was an omen. I think whoever sent it wanted us to make the discovery."

"I'm not sure, Forrest. Why didn't they just phone ahead, like the IRA would have done?" replied Galbraith.

"It was too obvious, kid. The bomb was sophisticated, but was made of relatively little explosive material. I reckon it was a sign rather than an actual killing device."

"John, seriously, if it weren't for you-"

"It would have killed *a* person, yes. But who? Who opens packages marked 'CID'? The office secretary. Are you telling me someone went to all that trouble to kill the mailman of a small, insignificant police team? I think not."

Forrest turned on to the high street and they stopped at a red traffic light. It was a typical drizzly London day and the rear lights of the car in front caused the officer's windscreen to glow red.

"So they sent the mail bomb to be discovered?"

"Does the pope shit in his hat? I think it's part of a larger game... Death is coming."

'Don't be so melodramatic."

His voice deepened.

"Civilisation is only three days from anarchy. The fragility of our existence formed on the daily lubrication of hypocrisy will crumble. If you remove man's ability to recharge his phone or fuel his car then prepare to bear witness to mobocracy. Four bombs in London over a decade ago and the government spends billions on protecting its citizens in order to make them feel safe. Do they even know their greatest enemy? Themselves. Terrorism is a masquerade. People have always needed to monsterize bad people: paedophiles, Muslims, foreigners, gays, anything that allows the vox populi to go without acknowledging that which, to them, is infra dig, or their own inane obsession with the worthless trappings of the fear zeitgeist."

Galbraith jumped in, "You need to start listening to yourself John. I think you need time off, or to see someone. Your bruised face, your drinking habit, I'm worried about you. Sometimes... you scare me."

"I'm the only person in this department who doesn't need his fucking head examined."

She breathed in and out deeply. It demonstrated her state of distress: her breathing was the type that sank the diaphragm and pushed out the musty air in the base of the lungs.

"When was the last time you were happy, John?" she asked, her voice ever so slightly breaking with emotion.

"I'm not happy kid, but I am awake. This life is merely a cleavage. A representation of what may be available, but unlike the cleavage of an open blouse or decollete, this cleavage of dreams is bound by lock and chain, which only the hegemonic powers are able to free. Don't be lured in by its fancy, or you'll stay trapped in its gaze."

Silence. It was a flashback to their first outing together. Forrest drove to the industrial side of the borough. Factories built in the 1930s were stacked side by side. Brick walls and barbwire fences attempted to keep the public out . Many of the buildings were shut and had been mothballed since the cost of demolishing them had proven too expensive. The police would sporadically raid these factories that had become home to dealers and users, but this was mostly a political stunt heralded by an up-and-coming police officer pushing for the next rank. Mostly, the police were happy that the drugs stayed away from the bourgeois west side of town and had become isolated here, where no one really cared.

Forrest parked the vehicle at the side of a closed factory that still had the name '*Trebor*' embossed across the side. The windows were sunk at the lintels.

"I've got a source here. You can't come in," he said to Galbraith as he exited the vehicle.

He walked off leaving Galbraith sitting in the car alone. She watched as he ducked behind the metal sheet which formed a makeshift door. He was gone for ten minutes before re-emerging from the gaping flap. He brushed the dust off his lapel before heading back to the car.

"Well? What did you ask him?"

"I didn't. I told him I need information on any new people turning up in the homeless community, especially those not involved in drugs."

"Why?" said Galbraith.

Forrest put the car back into drive.

"This bomber might need to lay low soon. I wouldn't be surprised if he came here."

They drove back to the office in no real hurry. Galbraith couldn't shake the feelings of awe she had for Forrest. That hadn't waned. She caught herself staring at him from time to time. Only when the sun peered through the visor could she see the freckles running along his nose, a sandy beach dividing two dried up waterfalls. She saw a dirt mark on his collar and it occurred to her how he was always well, yet carelessly dressed. His clothing was of a high sartorial standard, but like Forrest, it was worn and tattered from wear. Galbraith imagined an ex-girlfriend had bought him these clothes, which lasted longer than she had.

As they came to the end of the industrial estate towards the populace of London, the traffic light changed to red and the pair of detectives caught sight of a homeless man, carrying a sign, walking hurriedly towards the town in the company of a mangy dog.

"Poor thing. I hate that, using a dog to make money," Galbraith remarked, as the dog and his owner trundled past their vehicle.

"Disgusting," rumbled Forrest.

"Sorry?" Galbraith asked confused, as the final syllable inflected the question.

He didn't reply.

"What are you disgusted at John? That poor dog needs caring for. It's not right that some tramp cart him about in order to evoke pity."

"You're not right!" he barked. "You disgust me. People see a homeless man with a dog and buy fucking dog food. They care more for the welfare of that mutt, which is less intelligent than many of the animals we eat, whilst ignoring the man dying beside it. Don't anthropomorphise that dog whilst an actual person is made to feel invisible. That dog is probably his best and only friend, yet people use it to absorb their guilt when they ignore the homeless man. Well let me tell you, you are not absolved."

"You're a real arsehole, John," said Galbraith.

She considered asking him to let her out and taking the train back to the station but this wasn't a relationship, it was work, and detectives fell out all of the time. This wasn't their first outing and Galbraith wasn't going to be a silent passenger.

"Are you religious or spiritual?" she asked.

He hesitated.

"No."

"An atheist then?"

It was clear to him she wanted to engage in persiflage. He breathed out and sighed deeply.

"An atheist? No, that defines me by what I am not. I'm not a jet-skier but I don't gallivant about in a *Fuck Jet Skis* tee-shirt. But since you ask, and I sure you will, what interests me is Darwinism. What if society broke down tomorrow: who would survive? The rich, the strong, the clever, the aggressive, the quick? Let society unfold for long enough, completely unravel at its core and nature will select the winners for you. We are more overpopulated than ever before, at the exact time when life is least precious."

The buildings became larger now and the edifice of a striking glass building glared at the detectives' car as they passed it.

"You're Jewish aren't you kid?" he said.

"Yes, but how… Don't worry. Born and raised as one, but my family were never serious about it."

"Is your father Jewish?" he asked.

"He thinks he is."

"Well Jewish men can normally tell," said Forrest. Galbraith chuckled.

"I haven't spoken to my parents in three years, John."

"Why?" he said without any apparent nervousness.

"Matt, my fiancé is catholic. My parents disagree with it. Apparently, they're Jewish when it comes to posterity. Anyway, Matt and I got together in my second year of university. It wasn't such a problem then. But when he proposed to me three years ago, my parents gave me an ultimatum: him or them. I chose him."

"Is that why you haven't married him yet?" he said.

"Yes, I guess so."

Forrest's face took on the look of an inquisitor just as he had done at the rape scene and Galbraith noticed it in the tone of his voice too.

"So, were both your parents equally vehement in their condemnation of your marriage, or just your father?"

"Just Dad," she said.

"But you said it wasn't a problem prior to the engagement?"

"Yes."

"Hmm. Tell me about your father. What does he do?" asked Forrest.

"Where are you going with this, Forrest?"

"C'mon kid, play the game. What does he do?"

"He's a public notary. He works within a solicitors' office and handles property acquisitions."

"Okay, so your parents are still married. They're both Jewish. Your father works in an office. Tell me about Matthew."

Forrest seemed to have slowed the car down and he cruised in the slower lane of a dual carriageway, something he'd not done before.

"Matt is a trained accountant but now works in finance."

"And?" pushed Forrest.

Galbraith replied stutteringly, "He, um, is into sport and-"

"No, kid. Tell me about his background. Why do they disapprove?"

"Oh, he's catholic. And very catholic looking if that makes sense. His family hail from Scandinavia; he's blond, quite tall, slim and has small features. He'd never pass as Jewish, not in a million years. My father makes terrible racist jokes about him and is very offensive even at the mere mention of his name. The thing is, he was never like that in the first few years of our relationship – he was fine with Matt."

"Interesting. Your father, does he have any close female friends, work colleagues, neighbours, et cetera that resemble Matt?"

Forrest turned down the slip road under a chorus of a street lights and on to the highway into town.

"I don't quite understand, John."

"Does your father have a work colleague or friend that is catholic, blonde, young and very non-Jewish?" he said impatiently.

"Let me think... Yes, his secretary Gill. They've worked together for years now though."

"Go on."

"Um, she is Christian. She works at his office. He employed her around seven years ago. She's blonde, about twelve years his junior. Why?"

"How often does Gill visit your parents at home? Is she still in his employ?" ask Forrest.

"Um, yes, I think she still works with him, but I don't hear as much now that I'm not living with my parents. I know she used to visit regularly many years ago but I haven't seen or heard from her in some years."

"Your father is... Do you want my answer?"

He looked over at her and pulled the car over into a layby.

"What's your read, John? Do I want to know?" Forrest remained silent but maintained his stare. "I'd like to know what you think. Tell me," she spoke with reluctant acquiescence.

"Your father is splitting. Unconsciously, he has projected upon Matt his own feelings towards himself. He sees Matt as the sordid secret he has been harbouring from the past, I'm guessing, six years. When you first met Matt it wasn't an issue. But later, when he started his affair with his secretary, and when you declared your engagement, he knew then that you and Matt would be together for the long term. He also questioned his own marriage, and in doing so, discovered then that he in fact loved Gill. So Matt in your life, and around your mother and he, serves as a constant reminder that he has shamed the family, shamed his religion by loving a gentile, and it's the shame that he cannot bear. Matt reminds him of Gill, and personifies his guilt. Cutting you out allows him to cut out the knowledge of what he has done."

Galbraith felt a tear roll down her face. She knew he was right. She had visited her father in his office. She had seen how he and Gill had been close; an air of comfortableness with one another only achieved after an intimate encounter. She had spoken to her mother who regularly mentioned in an off-the-cuff remark that her father was late finishing work, had a meeting, or was out having a drink with friends. She saw it all now and the sham that the last three years of parental solitude represented. She would cry no more after today.

"Have you ever been cheated on John?" she said.

"Just once. I was quite clinical about the whole thing." He finished speaking but sensed her silent misery and continued. "I was with a woman for four months. She had her own place as I did. I knew her to be a carefree type, very laissez-faire and one unconcerned with tidiness and routine. I visited her after I'd spent a heavy week working as a UC selling guns to hoodlums in Lambeth. She invited me in and I noted just how immaculate the place was this time. I'd never known her to be so tidy. It wasn't normal. When she left the kitchen for the bathroom, I looked inside her dishwasher, and there I saw it: two wine glasses, two plates, and the pans and cutlery consistent with a home cooked meal for two. It wasn't just that. It was so neatly packed, not thrown together in any way, and thus, it was not done by her. I walked out before she returned from the bathroom and never heard from her again."

"Did you love her?" You strike me as someone who could get over a lover with just a shower," asked Galbraith.

She immediately regretted her facetiousness as Forrest momentarily seemed to turn his head away.

"Breakups hurt, kid. I'd rather take a beating than lose a loved one. What was strange for me at the time was that she was the one who told me she loved me, not the other way round, yet I remained faithful and she couldn't. Some years later I took an interest in psychoanalysis and much of this became clear to me. Freud said, '*Where they love they do not desire and where they desire they do not love*.' My job had stolen me from her that week and she couldn't face the loneliness. I doubt her love was real in the end."

"But yours was," stated Galbraith.

Forrest breathed a quiet reply... "Yes."

*****

XXII

PLEBS

ACROSS the rickety bridge lay an ever ricketier line of men, positioned in groups of three, dangling on lines controlled by rope and pulley. The bridge crept out over a canyon like the road was being proffered to the sky. One hundred and twenty feet below lay a river, stretching over the serpentine and endless sandy surface. The men hung in the white wilderness. Working as a triumvirate, Blake, John and Denning wired explosives to the abutments.

"Danny, you well down there? I'm getting pounded with sand up here," said John through his headset. "The fucking rag-heads had the right idea in covering their faces up!"

""Yeah, if it gets any worse we should call it in," replied Blake.

The pair of them were wrapping wires around the steal abutments on the old bridge. A swirl of sand enveloped their helmets and made it hard for them to breathe. Denning paused from fitting the explosive to the steel in order to wrap a cloth over his mouth and nose.

"I don't know why they persisted with this. They said a sand storm was due days ago!" exclaimed Denning.

Visibility was reduced to a wave of blurry figures in desert camouflage dangling precariously underneath the bridge. Each solider had abseiled down from above and had responsibility for his own rig. John was the lowest of the three and peered above him unable to make out any of his comrades. He looked across and saw nobody either side of him.

"All right, this is ridiculous now. Let's ascend lads, C'mon, up we go."

He got no clear response but heard a faint voice over the whistle of sand in his ears.

"I can't see anything!" shouted Blake, some metres above him.

What happened next was a phantasmagoria of horror, mystery and blood. A lump of C4 on the steel strut above the trio exploded without reason sending the men into disarray. The tawny air swirled violently as the bomb sucked and blew sand across the sky. Screaming across the plain was heard from an unknown soul. Blood flew into the face of Blake from below, from where only John and Denning hung.

"John!" cried Blake.

Blake reached out trying to find their line in the stormy air but couldn't grasp at anything.

"John!" he cried again.

Blake finally found the line but it was light and when he reined it in, the end smelt of fire and smoke.

NCO Mortlock called over their headsets: "Roll call. Barnes receiving?" (Sir, yes sir), Stewart (Sir, yes sir), Blake (Sir, yes sir), Denning receiving? Denning receiving? John receiving... Who's with Denning and John?"

"Man down sir," declared Blake.

"Right, everyone off the bridge now. It could be unsafe. Rendezvous point 3. Mitchell receiving (Sir, yes sir), abseil down to the ground with Benny, I need you to look for signs of loss of life. Wazza and Barnes, proceed with caution to John's location, confirm the situation ("received sir"). Blake, that's enough for today, debrief with me at 1600. Out."

*****

LEAVING

XXIII

ANOTHER dreary day began in the dank dudgeons of the CID office. Two detectives were discussing the ramifications of an identity parade for a robber. Somewhere else a supervisor was overlooking the figures relating to violence with injury detections against crimes reported. A gaggle of young uniform officers were huddled around an older officer whose shoulders were adorned with the reflective metal of sergeant chevrons.

Galbraith's fingers glided over the keyboard with aplomb. She was an adroit typist and could punch out a crime report with speedy precision. Forrest was sitting opposite her, thumping on his keyboard, clumsily and carelessly like a gorilla acquainting itself with a new toy; he had no problem finding the delete button. Two members of the team approached Galbraith at her desk, and she nervously tugged her suit lapel inwards albeit no cleavage was on show.

"So, are you coming to Smither's leaving drink tonight, Imogen?" said DC Lee Harper.

"Is everyone going?" she responded.

The second male piped up: "Yes, that's an order!" It was Martin Brown, her jovial detective sergeant.

"Well, I guess I am then. Where are we going?" said Galbraith.

Harper had a thick Scottish accent, almost as thick as his glasses. His skin looked pallid and appeared even more so when set against his tawny brown hair. He pushed his glasses up and seemed to squint as he spoke.

"The Kings Arms down on the Bow Road. Should be a laugh. We leave here at four."

His breath smelt of onion.

"Smither is a good lad. It's a shame you never had a chance to meet him properly Imogen. He's off to Murder Team. He deserves it," said DS Brown, who seemed to speak louder on this occasion, probably because Forrest was seated just opposite.

"Oh, John, why don't you come along too?" Brown motioned last minute.

Forrest nodded.

The pair exchanged a few more pleasantries with Galbraith before retiring to their own desks. Imogen, like a naughty schoolgirl, tipped her head up over the makeshift wall between their desks and beckoned Forrest nearer using her fingers.

She whispered, "Well, should I bother going?"

"No," he said.

"John, come with me. Please, I could do with the company."

"No, it's not my scene kid."

"Pleeease," she insisted.

He let out a long sigh and sat looking down at his desk for a few seconds.

"Okay, but just for one. My face is still pretty sore."

The pub was quiet and devoid of any customers outside of the group involved with the leaving do. A local chain of cheap pubs had opened across the street and was full to the brim with inebriated locals enjoying cut-price lager. The officers chose the quieter pub to avoid the riff-raff with whom they frequently dealt. There was nothing inherently wrong with this pub; in fact it was clean and well kept. The staff wore uniforms and a smile and it had evidently been repainted in the last year. But cheap alcohol attracts the drinker and the crowd.

The police were prepared to pay the extra thirty pence a pint for the privilege of solitude. The suits were hobnobbing around a large table surrounded by sofa chairs. Galbraith recognised many of the faces at the do. The superintendent, as well as DI Walsh and many of her cohorts from the office had come to see the departing officer leave.   Galbraith felt like a candle in a dark room. There was never a moment when a male officer wasn't hovering over her shoulder to speak to her, as though there was an invisible ticket queue in which each punter awaited his turn cordially whilst the current talker wrapped up their amusing anecdote. She had to admit it though, she was having fun. This attention hadn't been festooned upon her since her university days.

Sometime later, a short speech thanking everyone for coming was given by DC Smither, in which he made a lewd joke about his ex-wife whom he'd left behind with the rest of his 'useless colleagues' on the borough. The superintendent was also upstanding and gave a short address to the tipsy crowd recounting his fondness for the officer.

Galbraith chuckled at the puerile humour and smiled as the speeches went on. Forrest hadn't moved from the stool he'd perched on from the moment he'd entered. He listened to the speeches too, albeit with an unmistakable sense of déjà vu. The superintendent had been a sergeant when Forrest first went into CID and he remembered him for being vapid yet power-hungry and for churning out the same speech twelve years prior.

Once the hip-hip-hooray had finished, he gulped down the last fifth of his pint and stood up. The wood on the bar was old, dark and worn and had a raised, grainy texture. He rubbed his hand along its surface as he left the pub and walked towards the tube station. It was raining heavily.

"Stop!" someone shouted.

Forrest turned on his heel, looked back, and caught sight of her running towards him, meekly and humbly. The rain was in her face and her hair blew into one of her eyes so she swept it briskly aside, but the hair kept being blown again and again across her face like a zoetrope.

"Stay for one more!" she asked.

"I'm a pariah, kid. Ain't no point in it. I'd rather drink at my place".

"Well at least let me walk you home," Galbraith insisted.

He looked at her with an eyebrow askew concurring that her desire was not one of concupiscence, nor pity. But she was after something. Both of them were standing in the rain now. Her hair more dishabille and his cigarette lit in the flood like a homing beacon for the passing public. Forrest looked more tired in the rain. His face even more wrinkly as the water poured across his leathery skin. The slough of his life was written into the countenance containing such an inured mind of entropy and hopelessness. The pair headed off.

Forrest's apartment building was akin to the man who occupied it. The building's security was second to none: CCTV cameras at the access points, stairwells and corridors. There was in place a bicameral security operation: to bypass the first door one had to provide a fingerprint scan, only then would the second door be opened. Once in the second area, one had to stare into the security camera so the machine could match the face to one on the system. If the face was unrecognised, a new photo would be taken and stored for future events along with their fingerprint scan. If neither matched up, the person would be kept in the second security area until staff attended.

Despite these features, the building itself was lugubrious and dull. The walls a dirty white and the floor appeared to be sodden with an unknown dark substance. It lacked any life or vitality and where plant pots once stood were now beige atlas stones.

The pair entered the lift and Forrest pressed for the top floor. The lift was small, glassy, claustrophobic and glacial; she could smell the stale smoke on his clothes. They followed the protocol of both looking straight ahead and fidgeting nervously. Forrest knew Galbraith should have turned around at the entrance. *Why was she coming up?* Her face gave nothing away.

They entered the apartment on the 6th floor. It was one of six flats on that level and above them a large skylight danced with the rain. Galbraith was wet and Forrest took her coat and offered her a towel for her hair.

The flat itself smelt of dog and it soon became apparent why. A small West Highland White ran out from a door in the hall and jumped up at the knees of Forrest. Galbraith giggled. The little dog barely reached the top of his boots. He grunted at it and mumbled something about finding food soon.

With a glance he looked up at her and said, "Used to belong to my mum." A casual remark that allowed Galbraith to deduce that his mother had died, and that he was probably close to her.   "He's very cute," she said rubbing the small dog's head.

The male detective offered his colleague a drink and she accepted. A glass of vodka with lime, cola and two ice cubes. Forrest poured himself out just vodka. He showed her into the living room. There was no need for a tour. The flat had one bedroom, a kitchen adjoined to the living room, a small bathroom and not much storage.

Galbraith noticed the green plastic box in the corner of the room full of children's toys and a tricycle next to a hanging punch-bag in the hall as they came in. She had learned a great deal from her cohort and he seemed indifferent to whether she caught sight of these things.

Forrest sat away from her on the second sofa and they chatted calmly for five minutes. He couldn't sense any feelings from her other than that of friendship. No agenda, no uncomfortableness associated with the preamble to sex. He decided to test her and stood up, pointing out how wet his shirt had gotten. Standing opposite her, he unbuttoned the top, speaking casually all the while. He peeled the wet white shirt from his body, slowly, like a violinist drawing his bow across a stiff arm. Galbraith's intrigue coupled with Forrest's constant talking, caused her to keep her eyes on him, just as he meant it. The sight of his body was stupefacient. He had more of a muscular physique than one you would consider toned; a powerful, bulky frame but he lacked cardio and stamina. He then removed his trousers too, leaving him standing in the living room wearing only his black boxer shorts. His corpulent body was clothed in tattoos and artificial light. Galbraith made out a Trojan horse on his thigh, the skulls on his arm, and a person burning at the stake on his stomach.

"What do the tattoos represent?" she had to ask.

He saw that she was mesmorised by the sight. There was no lust, only confusion. Perhaps this visit wasn't sexual. He was glad of it, but sad that he hadn't the chance to embarrass her. He wanted her to know that she couldn't have him, but that was no longer a concern.

"Each tattoo is of a great hero. All of them died for a cause in which they believed. They deserve to be remembered... I like to remember them."

Galbraith saw the row of skulls he showed her in the car when they first met. She also recognised a face tattooed on his ribs wearing a beret.

"You know that Che Guevara was a brutal man who killed many good people, not just bad people," she said.

"I don't believe in trite concepts like good or bad, kid. I find them narrowing, myopic, and too pigeon-holed. As you know, one man's terrorist is another man's freedom fighter. And anyway, it's not necessarily his means that I'm so concerned with, it's the end he sought to achieve, and he did so with passion and the heart of a lion. He never gave up chasing his dream."

She nodded in agreement.

"So which is your favourite?"

By now Forrest had picked out a clean tee-shirt and a pair of jeans from a wash basket in the kitchen and had begun to get dressed. He had already pulled up the jeans when Galbraith asked the question.

"My favourite is the first one I got."

He put the tee-shirt on, then without speaking, he took two steps towards her and then raised the very front of the black shirt exposing his chest once more. Amidst the mass of the faces and decorated persons were words scribed across the area above his heart. He pointed to them with his hand and she read: *I will love you for the rest of my life.*

174

Forrest picked up a remote control and switched on the radio to a classical music station. He then downed his drink before pouring another glass. And another. And another. Two hours went by and despite her constant probing, Galbraith never really felt like she had discovered much more about this secret, perspicacious man.

She pulled her phone from her pocket.

"I'd better get moving, John, it's getting late."

"Don't blame time for your feelings. You want to leave, say so kid." He got up and headed towards the sink.

She laughed. "Tomorrow's a 7am start! No wonder you always look terrible."

He poured a glass of milk over the sink and returned to the sofa beside her.

"Look around you Imogen. Look at my flat. What don't you see?"

He was calm in his approach and sipped the milk whilst she thought. Her head performed a revolution one more time before she spoke.

"Well, you don't have a television but I noticed that when I first walked in."

"No. Look closer…"

She couldn't see it.

"I have removed the tyranny of time from my world, Imogen. You will not find one single clock, watch, or computer within these walls that bears the time. Time is a manmade construct once savoured for important moments, but now, it rules men. It must always be remembered as being an invention to aid, not hinder. I see it as a nonsensical edifice held up against reality to prevent us from peering through what remains, from that tiny wincing crack in the door of reality to the wonderment behind it.

People got by for millennia without it: they went to school, fought wars and worked, all without ever owning an alarm clock. It is the natural way."

"Stop, John, just stop. I can't follow you. Y'know, I've said it before but you scare me sometimes". She turned towards him with her hands in a praying position and then slapped them down on her thighs. "Is this the fucking reason you're always late-"

"I'm never late," he interjected. "I do not follow the constraints of time. I do whatever I like for as long as I please. Only when I no longer wish to pursue that activity will I cease to engage in it."

"But that doesn't account for your turning up late at work, John. Walsh is after you, you need to be careful."

"Kid, I've been living this way for three years now. I know the time. I know it without having to look for it. It's everywhere around you. People have always known it, before clocks and sundials. Take your phone out again."

He waited for her and she obliged.

"Now look at the time without showing me." He paused. "It's roughly 8.15pm."

Galbraith, still holding it in her left hand, looked down at her phone again, and the large white numbers that read 20:18. She was amazed, but didn't want to accede to his madness.

"You're three minutes out," she snapped. There was a momentary silence between the two detectives. "So how do you do it?"

It never crossed her mind that this was a trick of sorts. Forrest was a man of his word and not one for trivial ploys or showing off.

"I memorised long ago the times of sunset and sunrise, the movements of our star, the sound of birds during the Ides of March and the autumnal equinox, the noise of the vehicular traffic at peak times, the distance between passing trains across the hours, the rumble of keys as my four neighbours return home like clockwork each and every day, the eight cigarettes I've smoked since you arrived. This gives me the time; it literally empowers me with it."

"Look John, this is all a bit deep for someone who's had four glasses of wine."

He grabbed her wrist tightly. His eyes were burning with avidity and he seemed to speak into her soul.

"Time is only a linear phenomenon because we are born... we age... and we die. For us mere mortals to understand it, we need to view it as a linear, ongoing, single-strand concept. What *'time'* as we term it actually is... is decay. Time is only ever decay. And the length of our decay is relative to all those decaying and non-decaying things around us. Is it any wonder that man-made materials are often those that cannot biodegrade?"

"Well, my phone and my spate of yawning tell me it's time to leave. I've a feeling tomorrow will be a long day." Galbraith said, standing up.

"Quite right. You have to leave anyway, I've a visitor due any moment."

Her interest rallied.

"A visitor?"

"Yes, I haven't had sex in a few days, and I stopped masturbating over two years ago. I find I get distracted if I don't have sex regularly and I need my most vital component, my concentration, so I've arranged something."

"Oh," she replied.

"See ya tomorrow, kid."

Her walk home may as well have been a day dream. Her mind raced continuously, trying to process what had just happened. *Was this for real?* She thought about how this man lives a life without time. How he arranges sex like a commodity, like purchasing fresh bread. She contemplated his thoughts on time and decay, and whether this was an accurate reflection. But her most common thought, and the one she battled most, was whether Forrest was mentally stable. *Could he continue his job in this vein? Was he safe out on the streets whilst harbouring a nihilistic temperance towards humanity? Should I tell Inspector Walsh?*

*****

XXIV

COCOON

A message board comprised of red LED words scrolling along a black, rectangular screen pulled the eyes of those in the lobby towards it. The quiet, bored people in the waiting room sat dutifully, ticket in hand, awaiting their turn. An even more bored row of faces mirrored back at them from behind the counter. The faces of people so alienated from pleasure or purpose that they had died inside a long time ago. Passionless like the end of a long marriage, and as tired and worn as the items left unsold at a boot sale.

The lobby was cocooned in glass revealing the drabness of the London sky, the beige of the street outside, and two employees in office-wear smoking by the exit; neither talking to each other but instead glaring at their mobile phones in their hands. They were the same age, worked in the same building, but completely disinterested in one another.

A young girl in the lobby stared at a man in a wheelchair; the stripling gazed bemusedly before tugging on her mother's skirt and asking why the man couldn't use his legs instead? The man in the wheelchair pretended not to hear. The waiting room was densely populated with a menagerie of accents and fashions, knitting the room with a multi-cultured narrative.

The message board flashed and beeped twice as its red dots formed the name Trevor Jackson. A second man accompanying Trevor Jackson rose up and pushed his chair towards counter number 8, towards one of the bored faces.

"Welcome to Newham Council, how can I help you today?"

It was a rehearsed statement rather than a question. The lady serving them was Afro-Caribbean but had an East London accent that was thick and palpable.

"Hello, we're here for our housing appointment. I've been on the waiting list for two years now and still haven't been given a place. I was told to come in to discuss the situation?" said the man in the wheelchair.

His brother, tall and athletic, an almost complete contrast, was stood beside him.

"Let me have a look at your file," said the council worker.

Trevor gave his details while the sullen woman punched them into the computer in front of him. The man's brother finally took a seat beside him. Every now and then a shrill beep could be heard coming from the message board hovering above them like a barking demagogue.

"Okay Mr Jackson, I've seen that you were offered a place last July in Forest Gate and you rejected the property, is that right?"

He seemed quite upset by the council worker's remark.

"Yes, but it wasn't suitable for me. I need a ground floor apartment and that was on the eighth floor of a housing block with just one lift. It's not safe for me."

"I understand but you've been assessed as being suitable for any property on any floor Mr Jackson. Therefore, we can't prioritise you for a ground floor flat," said the woman in her broad Cockney accent.

The brother interjected, "Sorry, prioritise? For whom do you prioritise ground floor flats?"

"Well, families with children, the elderly, anyone who meets our criteria for one."

"That's ridiculous!" said the brother. "Trevor has worked his entire life. He only lost his ability to walk through some botched hospital operation. And now, now you can't give him a flat because someone comes above him who, I'm guessing, has never worked a day in their life?" His anger grew as he spoke.

"You have to calm down sir or this conversation is over." The woman was stern and repeated this numerous times almost goading Jackson to interrupt her. "Listen, I don't make the rules. You get assessed by the Assessment Team. I can rebook you in for another assessment but I already know they won't put you ahead in the list. Only disabled people in need of care assistance get that."

"You are an ethical vacuum, you know that. Basically my brother isn't quite sick enough, but when he is, or if he has children, you'll happily oblige him with the flat he currently needs," said the angry brother.

"Well we offered Mr Jackson the flat in Forest Gate."

No sir this time. The woman behind the desk became somewhat defensive. This type of reaction wasn't uncommon from those seeking housing.

"John, please don't make a scene," said the man in the wheelchair. He then turned to the woman. "Look, can you book me in for a re-assessment or just see if there's anything that is on a higher floor but where the building has more than one lift. I don't want to end up a prisoner in my own home when the lift inevitably breaks down. My brother works abroad and my mother isn't well," he said with compassion and a wobble in his voice. He was desperate.

"Sorry, but when you rejected that last property you were placed at the back of the list again. It'll probably be at least another two years or so before anything comes up. We're pushed for houses at the moment. The right to buy coupled with London becoming more affluent means we don't have anywhere near enough places for people in need. I'm sorry but it's only going to get worse. I suggest you just take the next thing you get offered."

His face curled up and darkened like a sheet of paper exposed to a flame, his moral compass being eroded in the same vein. He looked behind him at the multi-cultured room, at the children running around freely amongst foreign garbs and darker pigmented people.

"I want to speak to whoever assessed my brother. Who was it?" demanded the angry brother.

"John, please don't make a scene," Trevor said, patting his arm.

"Who was it?" John repeated.

"Well you would have received that name on the letter from the Assessment Panel. The head of that department is Mary Combs but you'd need an appointment to meet with her and I already know what she'll-"

"This is a fucking disgrace! I fight for this country. I've nearly died for this country. Look at this fucking debacle that is our council. This artifice! You hand out freebies to any economic migrant like they were sweets at a school fare because some Lithuanian got pregnant whilst her boyfriend claimed benefits here or to some paki who married a shopkeeper with a UK passport!"

He was pointing at the woman now and raising his voice for all to hear.

"If you don't leave now, I'll call the police, I'm warning you," said the woman who was no longer bored, but was now scared, vulnerable and giving the pair her complete attention.

"Call the police! Tell them we've been burgled and the culprits are all these cunts sat here, waiting to steal the Crown Jewels from under our feet. They've snuck in unnoticed, trespassing on sovereign land, and have usurped the government. In South Africa it was called Apartheid, but over here, it's called multi-fucking-culturalism."

He stood up swiftly, turned around and looked at the crowd in the lobby.

"You all make me sick!"

John spat on the floor in disgust. The room fell silent and two of the children running freely now bolted over to their mother. He then calmly wheeled his disabled brother through the glass windowed lobby. On their way out, Trevor turned in his chair and whispered "sorry" to the woman behind the desk.

*****

XXV

FUTILITY

TWO police officers in uniform entered the CID office carrying paperwork and exhibits; they were clearly apprehensive. Detectives were finicky judgers of the uniform's work; fastidious pedants, hard to please, and keen to pick apart the uniform's primary investigation. The shortcomings of their initial investigation would always come out through the Detective Sergeant's scrutiny.

The officers had brought in clothing in paper bags they must have seized from the suspect. The bags were heavy and cumbersome, and one of the officers dropped one in the middle of the room. The other officer was carrying a stack of paperwork. The pair approached DS Brown at his desk. They lingered there, a little afraid to approach. The DS was aware of their presence and made them wait on purpose.

"Serge, can I tell you about an assault prisoner?" the younger male asked.

DS Brown remained peering at his computer for a few more seconds before swivelling slowly round to them.

"What is it, fellas?" said the DS.

Both of the officers stood there, feeling awkward, like a new boyfriend at a wedding, trying to please but just wanting to leave. The uniform made them stand out, like they were wearing fancy dress at an office party.

"Cell 19 Serge. We got a call to a flat by one of the neighbours who heard screaming. Apparently, this is a nightly occurrence but tonight was worse than usual. We made entry and found the victim black and blue. She's in a wheelchair and is quite frail. She was bleeding from a head wound. When we checked her over, seems she's been suffering from prolonged abuse. She had bruising all over her body; some of it was days or weeks old. The suspect was at the location."

The DS turned back to his computer, unfazed by the officer's remarks.

"Who is the suspect?" asked Brown.

"It was her sister, Serge. She's in custody."

The DS didn't look at them as he spoke.

"Yes, we're aware of it. I've already got two of my DCs on their way to the scene."

Galbraith felt a phantom itch on her neck as the pair climbed the stairs up to the first floor. The block of flats smelt of urine and damp. The stairs were painted a jaded green, worn and bruised from wear. Forrest followed up behind her. He was a slow mover, but his stride was long and strong, so he climbed the steps just as quickly.

Galbraith sensed he was different tonight. Two hours ago, Forrest was his usual enigmatic self, but right now, he just seemed dull, almost lifeless; far quieter than normal. She grew concerned. As they bounded along the corridor, aware of what was before them, she had to ask.

"Is everything all right? You've been acting differently since we left the nick."

He looked at the floor.

"I hate these ones," he said softly.

"What ones?"

He fidgeted with his coat before stroking his cheek twice.

"I just don't like these crimes. I mean, I can walk into a hanging no problem, I can pick the pieces of flesh out of an underground train, or roll around in human excrement without furrowing my brow, but this type of crime... it keeps me up at night: it keeps the invisible demons circling me like a kettle of vultures."

She didn't understand. Perhaps she never would. In terms of heinousness, this crime was in the median. There was no death, no body mortification, no long term psychological harm, and no goriness.

They ducked underneath the blue and white cordon tape and entered the scene. There was no need for full barrier clothing and the two detectives strolled in quite nonchalant. The flat was messier than a nightclub toilet at closing time. There were clothes strewn about, piles of dirty cups and plates in all rooms, and Galbraith was sure she'd seen a rat running behind the sofa.

The two detectives trawled the crime scene looking for a history of violence. 'We'll need to seize this,' said Galbraith, pointing at a belt. At first, it appeared burgundy in colour, but upon inspection, she realised it was awash with dried blood. Forrest had found a blood soaked top lying in a corner amidst a pile of clothes. He left it where he was.

The two officers had finished looking around as the Scenes Of Crime Officer arrived.

"Hi John, how's things? Still coming second in the boxing I see?"

"We can fight if you like. I promise I'll come first," said Forrest.

The SOCO laughed, "No, it's okay big man. Anyway, as my girlfriend tells me, sometimes it's best to come second."

The SOCO was led around the small flat by the two detectives. They pointed out to him the items that needed seizing. A forensic specialist was best suited to seize such evidence: they knew how best to protect the objects from forensic erosion, to prevent the destruction of fingerprints and DNA. It was a science. Dependent on the object, it required a different bag. Clothing into paper, damp items into breathable bags, hazardous items into plastic containers, sharp objects into tubes, and lastly, electronic devices into metallic bags.

The SOCO photographed the entire scene, marking each object he seized with a number card. He then photographed each individual object in situ, before sealing it in the correct bag. For the most serious crimes, measurements were taken of the entire venue. Once the case was in court, the scene could be computer mapped so the jury had a full visual replication of the crime scene to look at, as though they were in it, immersed in it, inculcated by everything but the relative pain felt on the night in question.

The victim had been taken to hospital and that's where the detectives would head next. Forrest shook the SOCO's hand and said goodbye. The two veterans had been to many crime scenes together, shared many deaths, many rapes, and were equally cut open by their visions. And yet somehow, these two men barely knew each other. They'd never shared a drink, or spoken of personal matters. It was just another job to them, and that was all it ever would be.

Galbraith and Forrest drove to the hospital. As he drove and focused on the traffic, she wanted to know more about her colleague. She was intrigued by him. In front of the SOCO, he seemed perkier, but it was clearly a front., and something bothered him that now bothered her.

"What is it that you dislike so much about this crime, John?" she asked.

Breathing heavily, he responded, "Some things, Imogen, don't need an explanation. And some things don't have one."

The victim was in a curtained off hospital bay amongst others in a similar plight. A solitary doctor was doing their rounds, overworked, young and lacking sleep. As the two detectives arrived, a nurse came out from behind the curtain of Bed 4. The two detectives entered slowly. The victim had only a young male officer for company. Surprisingly to Galbraith, it was Forrest who took the lead.

He sidled up beside the woman. She was lying prone in the bed. Her eyes were heavy and numb. The lids were closed from severe bruising that caused them to puff up like black eggs, cracked and gloopy. But despite her obvious wounds, she seemed settled, at peace.

"Margaret, can you hear me okay? My name is John."

The woman's head rolled over slowly, to the side of her pillow, as she strained a small, but beautiful smile.

"Hello dearest, call me Maggie," she whispered.

"Maggie, I don't want to cause you anymore hurt, and it saddens me to bother you in this state. I don't expect you to be able to give me a statement at this moment, but we need to access your medical records. Would you be able to sign a document to enable this; it's very important."

The woman was still for some time.

"My sister," she whispered. Forrest leaned closer. "She isn't perfect, but she's all I have left. I will sign your document but I don't want her to be punished. She just needs help."

"Maggie, we are here to help you." He took her hand in a gentle grasp. "And by helping your relationship with your sister, we can do that best. I promise you, from the bottom of my soul, that I will help you," said Forrest.

"I hope you will, John."

Forrest stood up slowly and nodded towards the young male officer who sat bemused by the spectacle. The three police officers left Bay 4 and had a quiet discussion down the corridor.

"Dennis, I'm not here to teach you to suck eggs, but here's what you're going to do. I need you to write down anything evidential she says whilst she's in your company. My colleague Imogen has brought you some evidential bags. You're going to seize Margaret's clothing in there and deposit it at the station when you're relieved."

"I understand," said the young officer, nodding enthusiastically.

"Hang on, I'm not finished. Here's a camera. Take photographs of her injuries when they next dress the wounds. We need all of them photographed to a good quality. You can start with her face as she is now. We'll take care of getting her medical evidence sorted, understood?" said Forrest.

"Yes, of course, no problem."

Dennis rushed back into Bay 4 with evidential bags at the ready. Forrest bounded over to the on-call doctor and seemed to interrupt him at his work. Following a brief confabulation, the doctor called over another colleague who printed out the medical notes. Forrest read them in the doctor's presence, not to judge the doctor's work, but to assist in interpreting the medical jargon that was scribbled on the pages like a litter of tiny black spiders.

DS Brown was still at his desk when the two detectives returned to the office. Forrest didn't dislike Brown, but their relationship had always been strained. Brown struggled to manage the sleuth. At first, it was almost unbearable, but as a good supervisor, he realised that Forrest's strengths didn't lie in his punctuality or coarse demeanour; it rested on his ability to solve crimes, his penchant for locking up bad people, and his guile. The DS, learned too, not to ask questions about the means, but to focus on the end.

Forrest didn't hate authority, he sometimes welcomed it; but what he did hate was misplaced power and people's search for it. Forrest also realised that people detested him quite the same. It wasn't hatred though. One can detest a person and still say 'hello' to them in the corridor, but when one hates you, such a passing moment in a building becomes an impasse, and the 'hello' mutates into an expletive under the breath.

And when it comes to accepting, Brown and Forrest knew that they would never be friends. They weren't the kind to have drinks after work or discuss personal affairs, but in this sphere, one could thus remain purely professional, just how Forrest liked it. To the Detective Constable, DS Brown was as intellectually engaging as a Scotsman overly obsessed with the smell of his own farts. He had a moral incontinence and lacked integrity, but irrespective of that, he knew his shit and that's what mattered.

Forrest and Galbraith pulled up a chair beside Brown.

"What did you find at the scene guys?" said the DS.

"SOCO has seized a blood stained belt and some clothing. We've got photos of the entire place. Seems like a neglect case as well as the assault. Is our suspect ready for interview?" said Forrest.

"Yes, but she needs an appropriate adult and a solicitor. I've already got them running for 8pm," said Brown. "Did you manage to take a statement?"

"It wasn't possible, Martin," said Galbraith. "We've got photos of the victim's injuries, her clothing and her medical notes. It should be enough for a GBH charge, but she isn't fit to make a statement. She most likely requires a video statement to be taken to cover the abuse."

"Good work," said Brown.

"Martin, we'll need to find her a new carer. Her sister clearly can't continue in this capacity," said Forrest.

"Well, I'm afraid that might not be possible," said Brown. "I had Stones get in contact with the Disability Home Team and they've stated that they had her accessed last year and she didn't qualify for a care package; it seems the sister was fulfilling this role voluntarily. We can arrange for an assessment but nothing's gonna happen overnight."

"That's what I feared," said Forrest, retreating into himself.

The interview began like any other. The two detectives on one side of the table, and the suspect on the other, accompanied by their solicitor, and an appropriate adult to oversee the fairness of the police and assist the suspect's understanding of the process. The room was lit up by intense tube lighting. A machine hung on the wall showing times and recording the whole affair. All the chairs were bolted to the floor to prevent a melee, and panic-strips ran along all the walls so an officer in peril could call for help. Forrest put the allegation to her immediately.

"You're here because of the gross neglect of your sister, Margaret. You're also being investigated for an offence of grievous bodily harm. These are very serious allegations Angela and you could be facing a long time in prison for this. Please tell me what's been happening?"

"No comment," replied the suspect.

"Angela, I understand your right to say nothing to me, but hear what I'm asking you. I'm accusing you of beating your sister with a belt and various other implements. I'm accusing you of neglecting a woman in a wheelchair unable to care for herself. Aren't you going to defend yourself?" said Forrest.

"No comment."

"Angela, if it wasn't you, then it was someone else. I want to find the disgusting person responsible for this sickening crime. I need you to help me, and for you to help Margaret. Now tell me what happened!" he said.

"Officer," said the solicitor, a white woman in a black suit, wearing fashionable spectacles and with her hair loose about her shoulders. "My client has already replied to your question and has exercised her right to give no comment. If you persist in questioning her along these lines I'll argue you're being oppressive and file for a breach of process."

"Thank you for that," said Forrest, without looking at the lawyer. "Angela, I find it quite despicable that you won't even defend yourself against these claims. Look at these photos." He placed the photographs of Margaret's face on the table in front of her. Her eyes, black and bulging. "Did you beat this defenceless woman so badly she may lose the sight in one of her eyes?"

"Oh yeah! She's the victim is she? That fucking bitch deserved it!" shouted the suspect. "All my time is spent caring for her and I get nothing for it. You don't see what she's like! Always moaning, always calling me, shouting, throwing her food away. She's not the only one with problems. I've got problems too! No one looks after me."

"I would like a private consultation with my client if you please, officers," said the solicitor.

Forrest stopped the interview.

When the interview recommenced, Angela Bowen continued to give no comment to the questions the two detectives put to her, and so the interview was terminated some forty-eight minutes later. The detectives showed her their mass of evidence: the blood stained clothing, the belt, the photographs of the scene, the reports from the neighbours, and the medical evidence of Margaret's injuries, but the suspect did not comment once.

Following the interview, the suspect was led back to her cell to await her fate. A mental health team had had reason to assess her in the past. According to her file, Angela Bowen had a personality disorder, ADHD and a predilection for violence. She'd been remitted to mental health facilities on a number of occasions but hadn't had an intervention for the last three years. The mental health team accessed her in custody and reported that she needed to be sectioned under the Mental Health Act.

Whilst this took place, Forrest spent the next three hours writing up the reports for the Crown Prosecution Service. He and Brown sent the file up to the CPS that evening who authorised that Bowen be charged with neglect of a vulnerable person and GBH. It was Galbraith who charged Bowen before she was transferred to a mental health hospital and bailed to court.

"Going home Forrest or time for a drink?" asked Galbraith.

"I dunno, kid. Not tonight," he said.

She didn't feel comfortable with his going home alone this evening.

"C'mon John, the drinks are on me. Just say yes to one."

He nodded solemnly.

The detectives found a quiet pub on an indiscreet corner shadowed by the City of London and the large, glassy, phallic plinths that cast a shimmer on the night sky. Forrest had put his suit in his locker and changed into a grey tee-shirt and black jeans, which coupled with his long black duster coat, made him look like a Hell's Angel without a motorbike. Galbraith remained in her dark green suit; it was a few years old now, but to her, irreplaceable.

The pub was tinged with amber, like a sepia filter had been placed over a photo of the room. The pub was quiet during the week but the scattering of glasses and a cluster of seats facing a projector screen that hadn't been reset indicated to Forrest that the pub was busier not long ago, most likely broadcasting a football match. He felt more at home in a quiet pub.

The pair settled down into a nook beside a disused fireplace. The seats in the pub were mismatched, old and worn, with a choice between red cushions sewn on to tiny stools or large brown leather padded throne-like chairs. Forrest and Galbraith chose the stools.

"I know you want to ask me why I've been different today, so go-ahead, ask."

"Okay, what's the story?" said Galbraith.

"I regularly ask myself why I joined the police. Why would I sacrifice an easier life to do what we do? On those days, when you uncover a baby in a washing machine and a drugged up parent asleep with a needle sticking out of their arm none the wiser, you have to sit and contemplate just what you're doing with your life. Should anyone be exposed to such things?

"But over time, I built up an armour. My casing protected me from being affected by these sights and images. To me, it was just a spectacle of a reality that existed in the shadows but wasn't real. It's why some cops become devoid of humour or compassion – like robots walking the earth. The choice is become robotic, an automaton, or feel and see what is truly there and destroy the self. But over time Imogen, this armour has been eroded. My armour is now a husk, and inside the shell, there is nothing.

"I can understand a death, kid. I get that we die and death doesn't scare me. However, mental illness does. It's the death of the self but the body ceases to die with it. Margaret is suffering along with her sister Angela. They suffer differently. You can no more blame Angela for her crimes than you can a bear for attacking a person: they don't have the capacity to make that choice. There are no winners in this case, just losers.

"As sad as it is, Angela will lose her liberty, and Margaret will lose her best friend, her carer, and her sister. And that's what saddens me."

After their beer together, the two detectives went their separate ways at the pub door. Galbraith headed home on the tube as Forrest made his way to the boxing gym. It was late, but the place was a refuge for the insomniacs of society.

He saw an old face in the room, one with whom he'd boxed many times. The pair exchanged a friendly greeting, both gloved up ready to throw. A young man sat at the entrance and he alone was the only other figure in the building.

"Frank, I'd like to work on my defence tonight, fancy coming at me for a minute? I'll only pop you back if you drop your guard. Sound good?" said Forrest.

His opponent took up position in front of the bulky, tattooed edifice ahead of him.

"You sure you don't want to wear a head-guard John?" said the boxer, gum-shield in his glove.

"No, I won't have one in the real world pal, so I won't be wearing one here."

Both men popped their gum-shields in and began bouncing on their feet. Frank was shorter than Forrest but in better shape. His body was lean and carried hardly any body fat. His shoulders had been rounded by relentless training and his punches were quick and deadly.

Forrest held his heavy arms up shielding his face and chest. Frank danced about him throwing a few jabs which the bigger man simply pawed away without difficulty. As the smaller boxer warmed up, he began to throw combinations. The odd punch crept through Forrest's guard, jarring Forrest's neck back, flipping his chin round, and a quick left plunged into the ribs of the detective.

Forrest breathed out each time he got struck. It was quite a breathy affair, as Frank exhaled each time he threw a punch. Forty seconds had passed when it seemed to Frank that Forrest's guard had come loose. The quick fighter threw a melange of light blows to the face of Forrest, without much resistance from his opponent. His punches grew in ferocity as he rained down blows into Forrest's gut. The shots were untrammelled and Frank suddenly stopped.

"What's up?" he muttered. "You ain't blocking nothing."

"That's because you punch like my daughter. Now put your handbag down lady and hit me with whatever you've got!" said Forrest through his gum-shield.

Frank exploded upon the detective. Each punch seemed to bypass the glassy guard and strike a different tattooed figure on the physique of Forrest. The breathy retort from him now became a grunt as the punches landed on his bones. Frank was unceasing and his flurry of blows had an almost perfect strike rate. It was then, after another thirty punches had landed cleanly into the face and body of the wreckage before him that Frank realised his friend didn't want to work on his defence. He wanted to be punished. And he stopped.

Forrest slept terribly that evening and knew in the morning he would feel even worse.

*****

XXVI

DISTENSION

A digital yodel sprung from the alarm. It forced her hand to creep towards it. She blindingly searched for the off button like a new born searching the air for substance. Looking down at her phone, she read an awaiting reminder displayed on the screen: *'Day of Mindfulness'*.

Some years ago, to circumvent the onslaught of depression and compassion fatigue, Imogen sought the help of a psychologist, much to the secret of her employer. An officer having counselling invokes the bitterest, cavil response and can reduce an officer's chances of promotion for fear that the unit will be taking on a mental case. She learned through this period the joy of mind extraction and to recognise the conscious from the unconscious: recognising one's automatic settings helps to prevent one becoming an automaton.

Since this time, she set monthly reminders to indulge in a day of pure mindfulness. Typically, a reminder on her phone would go off to alert her to the event. She would see the reminder and from that point on she couldn't indulge in anything that would distract her from the present moment. Conversations would be reduced to a minimum, her telephone would be turned off, and she would spend most of her time carrying out tasks such as cleaning, washing, shopping or going for a long walk, or in her words – *'creating mastery'*.

Galbraith remained supine and breathed in deeply before exhaling long and slowly. She rose up at minimal speed like a drawbridge and turned off and out of the warmness of her bed. Matt was rousing beside her and mumbled something incoherent.

"Good morning, darling," she said.

He looked over at her with one eye slightly open and said, "I would get up too but I'm trapped under a heavy duvet." Galbraith smiled.

She brushed her teeth twice as slowly as normal, before taking three times longer in the shower. This was followed by fifteen minutes of cradling and sipping a cup of tea, all the while wearing a half smile. She then did the laundry and took her time ironing and folding her work clothes. Her mind was kept clear throughout. She pictured herself as a train on a journey, and no matter how many things passed-by, she continued on that journey and didn't stop to contemplate any of the hitchhiking thoughts along the way.

Over an hour had passed before she returned to her dozing boyfriend who was still only an adumbrated heap under the covers. He had the radio tuned in to BBC Radio 4. A newscaster was speaking in a morose tone. Something serious had happened.

"Have you heard?" he grunted.

"Heard what, Matt?"

"There's been a terrorist attack. I thought you would have been called by work already. It happened just after you woke up."

Her face became a clenched fist of anger, "Fucking hell! It's my mindfulness day. I turned my phone off!"

Galbraith reached over for the TV remote and put on one of the 24 hour news coverage stations. A male reporter in a suit and tie was overzealously shouting to the camera over the heavy background noise at the scene. The words *bomb* and *terrorist* repeatedly ran across the text feed scrolling at the bottom of the screen.

"Over the last hour, fire crews have struggled to battle the inferno engulfing the Newham Council building. The heat here is almost unbearable. I don't know if you can see behind me, but the building has been completely decimated. The police, the police," he said touching his left ear, "have cordoned off an area spanning eight-hundred metres bringing this whole place to a standstill. We can confirm it was a bomb which the police have said, they believe, was planted in the car park. What has come to light is that a fire started inside the building drawing the employees outside to the car park where they were expected to rendezvous until it was safe to re-enter. It is thought that the bomber caused the fire and planted a bomb in the car park in order to kill as many employees as possible. The fire itself damaging the building..."

Galbraith observed the broadcast with shock and disgust. So many questions ran through her mind. *Who would bother to attack a council building? A soft target like this is not the usual work of Middle-Eastern terrorism. Perhaps the IRA had resurfaced?*

She saw that there were four voicemails on her phone and a number of text messages from co-workers discussing the day's events. There was nothing from Forrest. As she sat there, Matt seemed to lean towards the television more closely.

"Christ, what a shame. How many do you think have died? I can't believe it's still on fire."

"I know, terrible," she said, making sure her reply wasn't too perfunctory.

Galbraith held the phone against her ear but it rang without answer. Forrest's voicemail had an unexpected message: 'Sorry, this mailbox is full. Please send a text or try again later', stated the automated voice on his phone. *He's probably collapsed in a ditch somewhere*, she thought.

The news coverage kept on recycling old clips from the scene and playing a montage consisting of the fire in the building, the ambulance crews racing to the hospital, police officers lining the streets with cordon tape, dead bodies covered in white sheets, and an overhead pan from a helicopter to capture the entirety of the horror. The camera showing the fire seemed to be at a distance behind one of the police cordons and it was zoomed in on the Newham Council sign above the entrance which was melting like candle wax due to the intense heat. As the camera appeared to zoom ever closer, a figure was seen emerging from the building.

"What was that?" Galbraith said jumping up.

"What?" replied Matt.

"Give me the remote, quick, quick", she barked.

She rewound the television feed to the shot of the melting council sign and the man emerging. She watched it a second time. She saw someone walking out of the building with his head down and a long coat swinging about his knees. She could see his short messy hair, unshaven face and dark eyes as they caught the camera almost square on before he looked away. It was definitely him. It was definitely Forrest.

"I have to go."

"Go where?" said Matt.

"Later. I'll be back as soon as poss."

She grabbed her belongings and rushed out through the door. Her fiancé resumed his slumber.

Galbraith drove to his apartment. It was a hunch, but one which she could rely upon in these circumstances. It was unlikely he had gone back into the office. The level of pandemonium would have dissuaded Forrest from going in. He would much rather work on this alone from the safety of his home and with the comfort of his alcohol cabinet.

She took from her inside pocket her fire key and allowed herself entry into his building bypassing the fingerprint system at the first door. For the second, she needed only to let the machine scan her face, as it had remembered her from previously. She took the stairs to his floor and placed her ear against his front door listening for sounds within. The platitudinous sounds of clanging and susurrant voices in the distance were carried by the wind to be picked up by her ears. She wasn't sure if they were coming from inside Forrest's flat or elsewhere. She pressed against the door harder, her ear conflated with the wood, cold to the touch, but there was nothing. She held her nerve and closed her eyes, her breathing controlled and almost silent. She remained still, focused and pressed against the door.

"Can I help you, kid?"

Galbraith flinched and jolted so hard she banged her head against the door.

"My God, John, you scared me."

"What are you doing creeping around outside my flat?" he asked, taking his keys from his pocket and folding his arms.

"And why were you seen skulking out of the Newham Council building whilst it was going up in smoke?"

"Come inside. I'll tell you."

He motioned with a tilted head towards the open door.

Galbraith could smell the fire on his body. His face was blackened and sooty. In the closed confines of his doorway, she suddenly saw how tall and powerful a man Forrest was when compared to her. He overwhelmed her in every way. She felt trapped and isolated. It was the first time in their relationship that she feared him. She questioned whether going inside his flat was the worst possible thing that she could do. But her own intrigue made her acquiesce, and she walked inside.

Stale smoke lingered in the flat and its smell had permeated the furnishings. The ceiling was stained in an area above the sofa where a Forrest-shaped groove had formed through use. He had clearly spent many an hour sat there smoking, drinking and doing God knows what else.

"Drink?" he said, opening a fresh bottle of Russian vodka.

"You can whet my appetite. What do you have?" she asked.

"Scotch or this?" he said banally.

"Just a water... thanks."

"Hey, we're not technically on duty. It's all right," he said as he poured 70ml of the vodka into an empty glass. Galbraith knew this fact rarely made a difference.

With a lit cigarette dangling from his mouth, Forrest searched the inside of his leather jacket. Galbraith sat down on the sofa away from the groove and made an attempt not to touch anything in the process. In the daylight she could now see the place clearly; the flat hadn't been cleaned in an eternity. There wasn't a single hint of femininity in the flat and Galbraith surmised that Forrest must have only ever lived here whilst single, or at least banished any trace of a female tenant. The furniture was bland and ill-fitting, without colour-coordination or love. The walls were peeling and the carpeted floor looked jaded. She kept her hands resting on her lap and suddenly scratched an invisible itch behind her neck. The place was worth far less than he could afford; it was like a penal colony in which he was the sole prisoner.

"So I pulled this from the fire. Take a look."

Forrest threw down a rolled up jumper. Inside it was a plastic bag which contained a computer hard-drive that had clearly been ripped from its housing.

"I should be able to resurrect this with the tech boys at the station," he said.

"Oh, just plug it into your laptop or PC," she replied promptly.

"I don't have one."

"John, it's the bloody 21st century, how do you not own a computer?"

"I just don't. I find them an abominable distraction."

At that point Galbraith's arm swung and knocked her glass onto the floor causing it to shatter. She rushed down to the ground on hand and knee to collect the broken pieces. Forrest didn't move to assist.

"Don't worry about that. We need to view this footage. I think Alan's team is on at work, perhaps he can play it for us," he said.

Galbraith was still on the floor trying to collect the pieces of glass.

"Oh for God sake, look, I don't live that far away, let's just watch it at my place."

Finishing his drink off, Forrest enjoyed the view of Galbraith bent double before him. *No harm in looking*, he mused.

The drive across town was surreal and effervescent as they floated across a sea of worry and hateful derision. The lights of the emergency services shone them a blue lit path like a ship, out at sea, swaying to a lighthouse's beam. The Moloch of terrorism was hungry for sacrifice; not of those already killed, but the fearful souls of those living. The line of acceptable combat crossed the terrorist, the terrorist didn't cross the line. As he drove through burning London, Forrest could feel the palpable latency, the seed form of further death, ready to flower into chaos.

The pair spoke seldom as an operatic aria flowing phlegmatically out of the car stereo soothed the silent ride. Both officers were deep in thought; impelled by their love for detective work, the anodyne of being surrounded by those in distress distracts one greatly from their own shortcomings.

They passed the city's agrarian landscape where people are sheep and pavements are beaten paths of grass. Those stupefacient faces of sorrow uninured to the pain of loss, to solitude, unlike the two detectives, cataracts removed, thresher beaten and worn.

The pair had arrived at Galbraith's flat. It was more humble than Forrest's and even the street outside had a lovely smell of freshly cut grass in the air. He parked outside and she led him to her apartment on the 5th floor. The building was lighter, more welcoming and a passing neighbour said 'Hello'. She lived in an affluent suburb with fine schools and more green spaces, something that was a priority when one had to consider children.

Forrest hadn't been to a colleague's flat since Georgina had left. He stepped inside slowly, like a child's first dip into the sea. A soft breeze met his ever-growing facial hair and his coat billowed like a small sail. Galbraith called out for her fiancé, and he met them in the corridor. It was an awkward moment: the three of them, huddled tightly in the small corridor of the flat, with Galbraith in the middle. Matt reached out a hand to greet the big man, who in turn proffered his clumsy paw. They shook hands: in medieval times this showed one was without sword and not a threat, but with modern man's paranoia does the sword of Damocles always hang above one's head.

"I've heard so much about you, Mr Forrest," said Matt.

Forrest laughed louder than Galbraith could ever have imagined, a laugh so deep that it made Forrest struggle for breath.

"I haven't been called Mr Forrest since my army days, ha-ha, you've a great girl here, kid." He said, patting Matt on the arm.

Galbraith blushed with embarrassment.

"Listen, you've caught me at a bad time. I'm rushing out to meet the chaps down at the club. Sweetie, I'll give you a buzz later on. Ta-ta!" he said pulling on a jacket and heading out of the door.

Forrest pretended to salute as the door swung closed and then turned towards Galbraith and pondered the scene.

"What?" said Galbraith.

"Nothing."

"No, c'mon, you've always got something to say. What is it? Spit it out Sigmund."

"He seems nice."

He coughed.. She wasn't sure if this was meant to mock or if it was down to the fact that he was a heavy smoker.

Galbraith loaded the footage into her computer; a sleek modern tablet with a light projector, touch screen and holograph keyboard – it was state of the art. He watched her as she booted up the CCTV, marvelled as her fingers danced across the projected keyboard. He saw how freely her hands danced across the keys like a grade 8 pianist. It reminded him of age, of his decay. He recognised how he was becoming obsolete like a product still being churned out, but no longer desired by today's consumer. A human victim of planned obsolescence: the designing of products that are specifically manufactured to break and require replacing. From the lightbulb to the latest infospecs: man is now a product with a limited lifespan whose value has been realised and surpassed; its replacement produced on a mass scale.

Something inside Forrest seemed to snap. The Luddite spoke out of turn: "Why do you surround yourself with such technologies? Is this your doing?" he jabbed.

"Huh?" she said, turning her head askew.

"Look around this flat! There's nothing human here."

"John, I don't need one of your didactic lectures right now."

"It is the organised creation of dissatisfaction, and the invention of a nasty tradition. Kid, when one looks through the windows of consumer paradise and feels that emptiness inside them, and inside their wallet, the void creates need and unhappiness. An elevated ideological struggle to consume: a riot. I watch consumers at shopping malls behaving like zombies in 'Dawn of the Dead' aimlessly wandering around trapped in a dumb hypnosis; a story of delirium."

"Whoa, whoa. Stop. Just stop. Just because your place doesn't even have a microwave don't start coming over here telling me that because I like to decorate once in a decade, I've somehow committed moral turpitude. If you wish to discover who is trapped in a void of unhappiness you need only look in that analogue mirror over there!"

His anger subsided. He seemed almost delighted at his cohort's ability to defend herself.

"I'm prone to the odd ephemeral outburst. I apologise." He meant it. Even he was surprised by his reaction.

Galbraith finally accessed the hard-drive and managed to locate the footage it had recorded. She played it on her computer screen and the pair watched in silence. It was surprisingly clear and vivid with detail. Most of the building had coverage and Galbraith noted a swipe system was in use to access different areas of the building.

"We need to get that swipe data," she remarked, pointing at the screen.

They continued watching until the cameras showed smoke billowing across a corridor. Galbraith was able to locate the camera that covered the door to a cleaner's cupboard. The incendiary device appeared to be hidden inside the cupboard as smoke could be seen initially swooping out from underneath the door.

"Why would anyone set alight to a cleaner's cupboard?" she asked.

The footage was wound back and a cleaner, wearing a blue boiler-suit and cap carrying a bucket without a mop, was seen walking along the corridor. They both noted that the cleaner could be the instigator of the fire, and that the bucket could be holding the incendiary material.

Eventually the entirety of the footage was seen and Galbraith was able to plot the different times, cameras and footage on to one linear timeline like an edited movie. The pair watched her creation. The cleaner entered the building via the basement carrying the bucket. He took the stairs up to the third floor of the four storey building. He accessed the cleaner's cupboard which was locked using a card key. He spent fifty-four seconds inside the cupboard before exiting and closing the door behind him. Thick black smoke is seen only two minutes later billowing out from underneath the door. The fire alarm system activates and the building empties quickly of people.

The cleaner, a tall yet slim man, exits via the basement and on to the street. As the smoke engulfs the building, hundreds of people can be seen gathered at the far end of the car park. It is at this point, only when everyone has congregated at the designated fire assembly point that the bomb detonates. A bomb hidden in a wheelie bin. Twenty-two lives were ended that day, but many more destroyed. Many of them left their loved ones for the last time that morning, saying a casual goodbye, leaving on a dull note, and fading out without a song.

The landscape of the car park turned into a late Monet painting, red and blurred; or was it a Picasso? - a phantasmagoria of shapes shifted and displaced. The former mass of people now a uniform mess, conflated into a story of horror, into a memory of loss. This human tautology of death had a meaning to someone yet to be discovered. Galbraith vomited on to her shirt; a whimpering vomit that spluttered slowly out of her mouth and clung on to the tip of her heart-shaped face, trickling down.

Forrest rose and poured a glass of water for Galbraith who was busy patting her shirt with a tissue. She didn't want to lose face. The footage continued on in the background. Some of the bodies in the car park were still mostly intact, with perhaps an arm missing, a foot destroyed, or a corpse sat up headless against a wall. These twenty-two cadavers had names, lovers and lives.

"Don't mind me. Let's scrum down, what is your thinking Forrest?" she began.

"I don't wish to assume. We only have assumption here."

He was blunter than usual, and it surprised her. He was usually like an investigative artist who painted without drawing an initial sketch.

"Okay, let's just do haves and have-nots."

"If you insist," he replied.

"We have a brief description of our man, tall, slim, light skinned, wearing a cleaner's uniform. An image to circulate to the media. We have the time, location and some witnesses. We have forensics from the bomb site. We should have a list of all employees present, injured, dead and those absent. And the swipe data from his key-card could be a good place to start."

Forrest nodded.

She continued, "We don't have motive. It is a soft target, a council building, and that seems a far cry from current domestic terrorism. No one has claimed responsibility-"

"Kid, you need to learn to pick your battles. Let's just copy the footage and hand it over to Terrorist Command."

"What happened to 'a true warrior seeks a good fight'?" she said, looking down at his arm.

"I already have one."

"Do you think this guy will strike again?" she asked.

"He who rides a tiger is afraid to dismount."

"Meaning?"

"If you partake in a dangerous venture, it's best to see it through."

*****

XXVII

DEIPNOSOPHIST

THE next day at the office was like any other. Galbraith saw the same usual faces that littered the same room of usual content. Even Forrest turned up when his shift began and the cohort of suits buzzed and tapped away. A detective in the corner was plotting a spider-web, marking out names of companies to investigate a complex fraud. On the near side of the office a young female officer with pretty blonde hair was having a rankling phone call with a disagreeable witness.

DS Martin Brown was with his gaggle of detectives grouped conveniently near to the latest young female colleague to join the office. Looks of agreement were exchanged between the concupiscent men who egged one another on to approach her.

A shadowy DI Walsh, silhouetted by an overhead light, stared out across the room. But this wasn't what was bothering Galbraith. The officer's mind was fixated on the night before. She had a strange intuitive welt in her stomach. There were too many questions to be asked, too many holes left open. After they viewed the footage, Forrest said he would forward it on to Terrorist Command and that it was best to leave it to them.

Galbraith had a friend in Terrorism. She just needed to confirm it. She sent an email asking DC Maddison if she had gotten the CCTV tape through, and what updates they had. Maddison sent her reply:

'Hey Immy!

Hows u?! Long time no see. Everything well with hubby?

We're just going over the motions now for this job. Pulling all the CCTV locally, forensics are getting to work on the site, lalala. Hey, your colleague John Forrest came and dropped the footage off himself yesterday. He said we would probably find his prints around as he spent time looking about before the fire got too bad. Brave guy or what! Did come across as a bit thick tho?!?! Oh well stay in touch. Must grab a coffee soon!

Mads'

Galbraith looked over at Forrest who was fresh and sprightly. *Was he smiling? No, just a smirk.* She dwelled on Maddison's email as thoughts raced like bubbles towards the surface of the sea. *The email confirmed he had forwarded on the CCTV footage, as promised, and he'd actually hand delivered it to the officers. He was honest about being at the scene and it's no surprise they thought him somewhat stupid as he can sometimes appear more brutish than cerebral.* Galbraith's phone beeped loudly. She looked down and saw who it was from before heading out of the office to respond.

"Imogen, you haven't been in touch lately and I've had no messages from you. How is our friend Forrest doing? Any incidents of note?" she asked sitting at her desk.

"Ma'am, in fact, I've been meaning to speak with you. John has been great lately. I've visited him at his home and he has been sharing information with me about his cases. I honestly have no worries about him whatsoever," replied Galbraith.

The inspector leaned forwards. "I don't understand you, Imogen. John Forrest is not a very likeable character."

"But ma'am, he isn't meant to be."

She walked round her desk and sat on the edge, her legs almost touching those of Galbraith who sat below her, looking up. Walsh leaned over her, "You would tell me if there were any problems, wouldn't you Imogen? I'm only asking you to help me, so that I can help him, you do understand?" said the inspector.

"Of course, I understand fully Governor," said the detective.

Forrest returned from one of his many jaunts out to the smoking yard in the same long black coat now antonymous with his demeanour. He appeared to have an extra spring in his step. Galbraith was immersed in one of her many crimes and was struggling to reduce the mass of paperwork strewn across the desk that had become hers for the day.

"Kid, there are drinks tonight for a friend of mine in the Robbery Squad. Fancy coming?"

He smelt of stale cigarettes.

"Um, yes, who's going?" Galbraith said.

"Quite a few people from here. Come, it'll take your mind off what's happening."

"Yeah, sure John, let's do it."

"I'll send you over the details," said Forrest.

He walked off and whistled the tune to Swing Low Sweet Chariot quietly under his breath.

Galbraith had stayed at work to finish dealing with a prisoner. A young man arrested for stabbing another even younger man in the face with a broken glass during a nightclub brawl. One moment of madness would inevitably cost this suspect his freedom for a few years, and the victim his eyesight in one eye.

Having charged the suspect, Galbraith filed the paperwork in the now quiet office and headed to the bathroom to check her appearance before embarking on an evening of drink. The mirror in the bathroom was dirty, with the addendum of poor lighting, she peered at herself through a lugubrious aperture. She slowly painted her lips a subtle pink, coating them from the centre outwards, rubbing her lips together and smoothing the gloss out. Finally, she sucked her index finger making a popping sound and wiped it clean with a tissue.

Upon entry to the bar, she was met with raucous laughter like a homing beacon drawing her near. She decided to buy a drink before the inevitable awkward approach. Her hands clasping the wet rum and coke, she powered into the group. Her moment was ill-timed and came at the end of a Forrest anecdote.

"So I said, 'anyone who doesn't know what insomnia is should stay up all night thinking about it'!"

The group laughed loudly. He seemed to be utterly captivating the fraternity of overweight, tight-shirted men. Each one of them lapped up his words like dogs eating a bag of chips. He saw Galbraith standing within the circle of men but didn't alter his position as he continued to throw them bones they were happy to chase.

The mood carried on in the same vein for the next two hours. Forrest at the heart of every new discussion, seemingly knowledgeable on all matters yet light and witty, like the cream atop a dense biscuit complementing everyone as they joined him. The group consisted of a mixture of police officers and armed forces. At one point, a slender man went and stood beside the pub's jukebox. He called towards the group.

"Oi fellas! What music shall we put on?" he said.

"How about The Beatles," Forrest said.

Another of the group interjected, "Let's not bother with music. Silence is golden."

"Ah, but The Beatles are platinum," Forrest fired back.

And with that, the slender man placed a coin into the machine and John Lennon's voice crackled through the pub.

The group danced to the verbal cues of Forrest. Vodka in hand, he was like a snake charmer blowing his pungi wowing anyone that wished to watch the show. Galbraith was relatively ignored, her sexuality nullified by the alpha male; her musings met by laconic replies from the group. The protoman continued to regale them with stories from his past and funny incidents: "A man creates an object from ivory worth more than himself." Galbraith noticed that no matter how much Forrest spoke, or how much he revealed of his stories, one never actually learnt anything about him. He remained a closed book whose pages had been conflated from years of being unopened. But there was one thing more evident tonight than ever before to Galbraith: *He is happy. This is what Forrest looks like when he is happy.*

He raised his glass bibulously and glanced across the group of men, "Dulce et decorum est pro patria mori."

The group of men nodded solemnly and raised their glasses in tow. She copied them coyly and without understanding.

Galbraith left the pub solitarily, looking back at the inebriated stranger she had come to find and yet never to discover. Her route home was accompanied by a hip-hop soundtrack coming from her earphones.

She turned the key to her apartment and saw that Matt had gone to sleep. Sneaking about her flat quietly, she readied for bed and pulled the covers upon her naked torso. Stillness provided the means to compartmentalise the day's events.

Something played on her mind. She thought over the email sent from DC Maddison. *Why did he hand deliver the item? Perhaps this lets him see who the investigating officer is. He told them his fingerprints would be at the scene: is this a double bluff? Did he purposefully place himself at the scene knowing he'd been caught on the news footage? And he came across as stupid to Maddie, and despite his brutishness, and other flaws, he's never been considered stupid. Is he pulling the wool over their eyes?*

As her eyes slowly began to close one last thought came to her: *Dulce et decorum est pro patria mori*. She took her phone from beside the bed and opened the translation application. Typing in the words one by one, the application revealed the meaning: *It is sweet and right to die for your country. Was that why he was happy?* She thought, as she drifted off.

*****

XXVIII

H3RRING5

HE wasn't sure if one of his teeth was loose, as he sat there, in his old chair, licking it repeatedly, making enquiries with his tongue trying to discover evidence; but what he did know for sure was his unbelievable boredom at the briefing being wittered out by the detective chief inspector. His mind began going off track: he was pontificating his plans for the week ahead, whether he should take more ibuprofen for his hangover, and the name of the prostitute he had fucked the night before.

Galbraith, conversely, sat there listening intently to the words uttered by the DCI and scribbling away on her notepad. She was interested in the operation and her task. She felt part of the bigger picture, just as she'd imagined it those years ago; a true detective. She looked over at Forrest to gauge his response. He barely looked alive. His face was grey and sallow, and he resembled an old cushion, full of dust, wedged into a corner of a room between other newer furnishings. Galbraith observed him. She saw that he was walking around with open wounds that had yet to turn to scars. She finally saw how vulnerable and scared he was, and how dangerous that could make him.

"I would like to thank you all for being here so early, granted none of you had a choice, but it's the thought that counts," said the DCI. A few of the crowd chuckled at his banal joke. He continued, "Terrorism are inundated at the moment with this Newham Council attack. They're personally visiting each of the victims' families and taking statements from them. We need to know everything about those who were killed in case there was a specific target..."

Forrest finally pulled the lid off of his pen. He wrote down *specific target* on his pad and leaned back in his chair tossing the pen contemptuously down onto the desk once more.

"... We were conducting facial recognition on the images captured. Unfortunately, I've since discovered that the footage is too grainy to establish an identification of the suspect."

Forrest wrote down another note on his pad. *Image to media.*

"At the moment, we're cross-checking all persons on PNC with knowledge of bombs and bomb making, including those in the army, the police, or any known terrorists that have links to Newham Council. We're especially interested in those retired army personnel, since the bomb used is similar to the IEDs used in Iraq by the militants..."

Forrest then wrote down *retired army police terrorists* on his pad.

"At this time, we have no DNA or fingerprints linked to the suspect. But once we do, we'll be sure to keep you all informed..."

The briefing lasted around thirty minutes. A few officers in the room asked questions of the DCI, who gave laconic responses. Forrest had questions boiling in the pot of his mind but not ones the DCI could serve up. At the end, the DCI asked the sergeants to assist Terrorist Command by delegating tasks around, in essence, visiting the families and taking statements – something Forrest considered a waste of time. *If you wanted to make the victim's feel better about what had happened, then catch the person who did it*, he thought.

"What did you make of that then?" asked Galbraith.

"I'm going for a coffee and a cigarette," he replied.

"That good, huh?"

He stood up but stopped himself in the middle of walking away.

"Hey kid, that CCTV footage, did you get it burnt on to a computer?"

"Yes."

"Can you get it sent over to your phone so we can watch it on the move?" asked Forrest.

"Yes, I can do one better and download it to my tablet."

"Good," he said, as he walked out of the office, cigarette packet at the ready.

He returned seven minutes later and picked up his coat, and with a simple nod, she ascended from her chair and the pair made their way to the car.

"Where are we going?" she asked.

"Back to the council building; it seems our dear DCI and his goons may have missed something."

The car rolled slowly to a stop next to the outer cordon. The whole pavement was still shut off on the side where the building stood. The traffic moved slowly past as the drivers tried to catch a glance of the wreckage. It was common for a small accident on one side of the motorway to cause a much larger one on the other side, all thanks to the nosiness of the public.

The two detectives ducked under the cordon and held their badges up to the uniform officer on scene who was clutching a cordon log to mark those arriving. Galbraith had her tablet in hand at the request of Forrest.

"Is it safe to enter now?" she asked.

The uniform officer on the scene nodded and asked them for their details.

The council sign above the door had now melted into the wall, a long streak of burnt plastic rolled down the side of where the door once was, as though the wall was crying red tears, like the smudged make-up of a bedraggled wife. The two detectives stepped in slowly. The fire had damaged much of the building. They both looked upon it with awe. It was dusty and black, and smelt toxic and smoky. The stairs were not safe to climb and the floor was covered in rubble and detritus from the ceiling which had partially collapsed. The room's original ceiling now lay on the floor in pieces, creating a long chasm above them and into the dark some five floors up. A small crack of light filtered into the middle of the room from a burnt out window.

Galbraith, whose lungs were used to fresh air and the countryside, found it difficult to breathe. However, Forrest, whose lungs were already blackened, felt strangely at home.

"Okay kid, let's get that footage up now."

Galbraith turned on the tablet and booted up the CCTV from the Council's internal cameras from the day of the bombing. "What are we looking for Forrest?"

"I always visit the scene of any major incident. It gives you a good picture of what actually happened. You're quite literally inside history Imogen, don't ever forget that. But more importantly, the DCI said they didn't have any DNA or fingerprints of our boy yet. I'm guessing none of them have bothered to do a forensic scene trawl using the footage."

"How do you mean?" she asked.

"It's simple. We can play the footage on the tablet and see where exactly the bomber touched when navigating the building. If he touches a certain wall, or door, or area where DNA or fingerprints could survive the fire, then we can still take a sample from that contact point."

"That's great thinking!" she said jubilantly.

"Don't get over excited kid. It's a shot in the dark, quite literally," he said, looking around the black room. He switched on his torch and shone it about the scene.

"Okay, so I'm just going to forward the clip to where the bomber enters the building," said Galbraith.

The pair hovered over the device, their faces lit in blue. The footage played out and the bomber was seen, clad in a navy outfit, bucket in hand, entering the basement. They watched closely as the bomber walked through the corridor and out onto the staircase.

"There, he touched the door of the basement to enter the stairwell," she said.

"Nope, that door is wooden. It wouldn't be any good," replied Forrest.

They continued to watch the screen, as the bomber was seen to climb the stairs up to the fourth floor. He entered the cleaner's cupboard as previously and then the fire was started.

"Do you think we can get to that cleaner's cupboard?" she asked.

"I'm not sure it's worth it. It's where the fire started so the chances of excavating any forensics from there are extremely slim. We need some luck here I'm afraid."

They watched the footage some more. The bomber left the cupboard and descended the stairwell once more. The bomber flew down the stairs more quickly than he had travelled previously, probably nervous of the sprinkler system coming on. As he rushed down the stairs, the fire alarm activated. He managed to reach the first floor before a pair of smartly dressed women entered the stairwell, likely deterred from using the lift by the sounding of the alarm.

"There it is!" said Galbraith, her hand pointing to the screen. "Look! As these two women enter the stairwell on the ground floor, he moves over to the right, wobbles slightly and grabs the handrail for balance. You can see his entire hand wrap around it. That's perfect."

"Let's get forensics down here. Good spot kid. You can let the DCI know."

The office was on the second floor of the miserable police building. Like the detectives' office and the custody suite, his office had no windows either. It was bland and soulless. There were no plants in the corner, no fancy décor nor any stylish ornaments. An air-conditioning vent in the ceiling produced a constant, low, dull buzzing. The room could have belonged to a night watchman at a carpark, but instead it belonged to a DCI in the Metropolitan Police.

"Excellent work you two. I wanted to personally thank you both for your help with the forensic find. Right now we're running the DNA to the lab and checking it against the database. If the bomber is known to us, we'll have our match in the next hour."

"Thank you sir, but it was John who did the work," said Galbraith.

"Can I ask something boss," said Forrest, "what if you don't get a match. What's the next move?"

"If the DNA hit is strong enough to identify familial links, then we can run it against anyone who is close to our bomber. This could be a direct sibling or a parent. And if that isn't fruitful, we'll start asking people to volunteer their DNA to us so that we may find our man."

"Thanks for your time boss," said Forrest rising up from his chair.

"Oh, one more thing, tell the office that I'll be holding another briefing in two hours' time."

The pair left the office in silence. Galbraith knew when Forrest was being genuine, and this wasn't one of those instances.

"Do you have doubts about their strategy?" she asked.

"Yes. If the DNA comes back as a hit or familial hit, it could be a great result, but I'm not confident. If the bomber really cared, he would have taken more precaution, y'know, worn gloves or hidden his face better. I'm not confident we'll get a match, but perhaps he just didn't factor there'd be any DNA or CCTV remaining. Whatever happens, conducting voluntary tests is a great idea when you have a protracted murder enquiry, but this is a bomber most likely looking to kill again in the near future. We can't pussyfoot around testing people. That could take years and I don't think our resources should be used that way... and guess who the resources are likely to be?" he said, looking at her disappointingly.

The second briefing of the day was different to the first. The ambience of the room had changed. People were slumped in chairs, their faces drawn, a smell of sweat wafted about the air, men's ties were pulled loose and buttons on shirt collars were undone. They were tired from the long day. It seemed Forrest was the only person who had consistency in his approach to the task at hand – he'd been tired of it since the moment the day had begun.

"Thank you everyone for all your work. Yes, the bomber is still at large. I have some unfortunate news too. You may have heard that we found the bomber's DNA on site this morning. However, forensic testing has shown that the bomber is not known to police, and the strength of the DNA, even when our specialists have tried to restore it as best as possible, is not complete enough to be used to match against any familial links he may have in the system. We have no further leads in this respect."

Forrest listened impassively.

"On the other hand, our Intelligence Team has been looking into all those serving and retired personnel with links to both Newham Council and a background in explosives. A list has been drawn up comprising of fourteen names. We've been able to eliminate ten of these names already. Some are people who were serving abroad during the time of the bombing and could not possibly have been involved and others have already been interviewed. I've got three persons for you to visit this afternoon and knuckle into as to their whereabouts on the day. Don't be afraid to throw a few fucks in when needed, okay team," said the DCI.

He asked for volunteers to chase the three names and obviously, Forrest raised his hand along with a few other officers in the room.

The DCI overlooked him and gave the three dockets out to different pairs. Albeit Forrest didn't appear at all dejected by this, Galbraith continued to observe him at a distance. He had a true poker-face and his feelings were completely undecipherable to even those who knew him.

As the room cleared out and people returned to their stations, Galbraith made her way over to Forrest. He was sitting back in his chair, pensive and still.

"What is it, John?" she asked.

"Probably nothing," he murmured.

"Something isn't right is it? The Chief said fourteen names needed to be investigated, and they'd eliminated ten already. He then said that three further names needed eliminating. That leaves one name unaccounted for, right?"

"I know," he said softly, "the last name on that list is John Forrest."

Forrest was smoking outside as the sun fell behind an electricity pylon. He heard the tapping of shoes coyly closing up on him.

"Why would they have your name, John?" she asked.

"Do you know that ninety-seven percent of thoughts in a day are repeated. Over and over, like a bad film on loop, like a nagging aunt, constantly, repeatedly, berating you."

"Don't equivocate, why you?" she asked again.

"I would like to say it's because I represent the bad time in a person's life. I am that darkness which they seek so they may see the light in themselves. I would like to say that it's because they're wrong, or their facts are flawed, or they are prevaricating, but I can't. I'm as guilty as any other name on their list."

She was still unsure of how to take his remarks.

"What are you saying?"

"I'm saying the shoe fits me kid, It's just I walk to a different beat." He threw his cigarette to the ground and walked off, turning around as he pulled the door open to exit the police station, "but they're looking at the wrong shoes."

"What are you going to do?" she shouted.

"I don't know, it's a choice between whiskey or vodka. Yes, vodka it is," he said joyfully, as he walked out of work.

*****

XXIX

SUNDOWN

THE following morning both officers were contacted by the Special Aid Department requesting that they attend despite being on their rest days. Like the armed forces, the police are technically always on call, and both accepted the summons to appear.

Galbraith felt invigorated from her routine a.m. fruit smoothie and long shower. She apologised to Matt for the inconvenience caused by her call to work and he was left to cancel their afternoon plans. Matt who was wearing only his beard sighed as she headed out saying a brief goodbye.

On the journey to work, the tired faces on the underground train seemed ever more hackneyed. The *bump bump* of the train through the tunnel chattered a plaintive melody to match the myriad of amorphous countenances terraced across the carriage. What had she done to be led to such perdition?

She closed her eyes and sought beatification through the breath, touching the tendrils of her heart with calming green and silent mental address until she reached work, '*a breathing space*', she called it.

In the office, the DS laid out the day's plans. Those seconded to work for the day were placed on stand-by. If the bomber should strike again, they would be expected to act swiftly. Other than that, the four officers on aid were allowed free reign to do as they pleased in the meantime. Forrest had been in this position before. He signed to Galbraith that the pair should grab coffee and without her saying yes, she stood up with her bag.

227

"How are you and *lover boy* getting along?" asked Forrest.

"Jealous are we?" said Galbraith. "Why, we're fine."

"Really?" he said. "When you first came up here you'd be on that iBerry of yours all the time, but now you barely glance at it."

"Don't worry about me Mister Analysis. Here's one for you. Have you ever read about Kafka and his relationship with Felice Bauer?"

Forrest placed the radio on the coffee shop table. He pulled out a cigarette from the box, tapped the end twice and stuck it in his mouth. It muffled his next words but they were clear to Galbraith.

"I've read Franz Kafka but no, tell me more."

He lit the cigarette.

"Kafka and Bauer had a somewhat distant relationship, to say the least. He lived in Prague, she Berlin. He would write to her, almost daily, asking her where she was, what she was doing, who she was with. It was an intense relationship constructed almost entirely by letter, way before phones and email and Facebook. Kafka was an irritable, controlling man who proposed to her twice, and called it off on each occasion. For Kafka, being apart from her was almost unbearable. If she failed to respond to him quickly he would lose his temper and become outraged. They met only ten times in five years! Can you imagine that? Of course, they never did get married. So why did he bother? The person Kafka wanted most in this world, the one he most desired and thought about, was the one person whom he kept at bay. The only thing worse than not having Felice present, was actually having her present. With Matt and me, I guess I'm becoming more oblivious to his needs and more of a Bauer to his Kafka. He's forever working and I'm learning to leave him to it; to stop peppering him with messages and questions." She smiled at Forrest. "In short, I'm keeping my distance. Absence is supposed to make the heart grow fonder or so they say."

"Hmmm, okay," replied Forrest, stoic as ever.

"What?"

"Nothing."

"John, what?"

"No. The last time I spoke we fell out. I'm done with my pejoration of your affairs."

"Don't make me ask again, Forrest," she said bluntly.

"Then why have you fallen for me?"

Galbraith's mouth hung there. Her red lips exposed in the light. Forrest wasn't looking at her but he mirrored her reaction. Both sat still, unmoving. The blood in Galbraith's chest ran warmer, distended in the vessels, pumping wildly. Forrest fiddled nervously with some loose change in his pocket. It seemed amplified compared to the quietness that encroached upon them. He wondered if he should help her, help explain it all to the younger of the two. She had never appeared so vulnerable to him as she did right now.

"Look kid, it ain't real anyway. What you're feeling, you're lovesick that's all."

"Huh?" she shook her head. Her eyebrows fell askew.

"You long for intense closeness which *lover boy* doesn't give you. You're like a child begging for her mother's embrace. This is amplified when we're most upset or lonely or stressed. Listen kid, infatuation is the fun bit at the start. Real love is the dull bit at the end. Reality is the guy waiting for you at home and who has been there for the past eight years; I'm just a fantasy clad in bruises."

Was he mocking me? "Well you're sadly mistaken. I admire you... for work reasons. Trust me, there is no attraction."

"Okay," he said sardonically.

If Forrest was trying to be annoying, he had succeeded.

"This is banal. Let me know when I'm really in love with you then won't you, John."

Forrest swigged down the black coffee and flicked his cigarette into the road. But it was Galbraith who spoke next.

"I've got a more interesting question for you. What's your take on the privatisation of the police force?" she inquired.

"Are you asking whether introducing capital gain into policing is a good idea? Then I must insist it is the most ridiculous of all ideas conjured up by the bourgeois buggers in government."

"I can see benefits, Forrest. Competition is healthy for any industry. If the police have an active competitor then it must raise its own game or fear being replaced. It'll shine a light on how inadequate our resources are. Imagine if Google decided to go into law enforcement? For a fee, they could investigate fraud for your business, or the theft of your vehicle. Can you imagine how successful they could be with their vast technology and resources? It would be amazing," said Galbraith.

Forrest was blunt. "It would be a tragic misstep in the evolution of policing. You are right, kid, they would investigate it brilliantly. The police are drastically undervalued and under resourced. We're a malnourished, antiquated whale that was beached years ago and is stuck on the sand smeared with racist overtones and widespread condemnation. Even our fucking email system is 14 years old. The Police National Computer system was invented in the 80s, can you believe." He lit another cigarette before continuing. "From where do you think Google will recruit their staff? The police will become the dumping ground for the waste of law enforcement. Those officers with any nous will be lured by the bigwigs to the detriment of the poor who can't afford a private police force. It's the same for schools and health kid, and I don't want any part of it."

"I think competition is healthy. And if you can pay for it, then why not make it available?"

"Because money creates corruption. Back in the day kid, I'd have stuffed a few doses of Ayahuasca down some shit's neck and waited for the effects to kick in. When he's nodding away like a shaman's stick I'd get whatever answers I needed. But that doesn't make it right. Throwing money at cops to make them work doesn't make it right either."

She replied, "Power, not necessarily money, creates corruption. Anyway, I expect with the incumbent technological advances and ever increasing surveillance I imagine crime will naturally diminish."

"In a total surveillance society, there will be no crime, you're right, but there will be no defences to a corrupt state either. No fear. Nowhere to hide. No secrets. No self," he said. "I like danger. And anyway, if there wasn't any crime, I'd have to go back to being a civilian. And I say fuck that."

The pair sat at the quiet, urban café both eating breakfast and enjoying their food. They were comfortable now, a partnership that spent more time with each other than with any significant other. They sat in the comfort of silence and feasted on beige.

Galbraith checked her phone quickly and saw, once more, the litany of sadness and news reports on her social media feed expounding hatred for the bombing. She'd had enough and put her phone away into her jacket pocket.

As each item passed their lips and tumbled around their teeth, the world went on by in front of them. The faces of the people etched the torment felt inside. The bomb in the council building had stoked much debate about why terrorists were now going after soft targets. A palpable fear hung in the air like humid heat at the end of a cloudy summer day.

A group of school children in yellow blazers walked on by against the wind. They were the first people Galbraith had seen that were unchanged by recent events. They acted naturally, playfully innocent, unbridled by the meaningless of death.

"John, tell me about your time in the army?"

"The Royal Marines. I was a marine."

She winced.

"Sorry."

He breathed out heavily as though bored of the topic.

"I served for six years, fought in two campaigns, got a pat on the back from the big man and handed in my notice when I realised I could work for the police for more money without getting my legs blown off."

"As simple as that, huh? Do you miss it? Did you enjoy it? Why did you join?" said Galbraith quickly.

"Slow down, kid. I joined because I was young and stupid and, well, guys like me didn't have anyone smart enough to tell them any better. I hated it and I don't miss it. But I don't regret a single kill I made."

The remark seemed malapropos. Galbraith wondered whether to push it.

"isn't all killing wrong? Who's to decide?"

"I wouldn't say that. Euthanasia is justifiable for a start. Just ask my father." He took a bite from his food before continuing. "Kid, if you were Superman, would you wanna go around and save people, or would you let nature decide and play Clark Kent?"

He was masticating as he spoke.

"Umm… I guess I'd like to think what I already do is more Superman than Clark Kent, so I know I'd try to save people. Isn't that obvious?" she said.

"You know what I'd do?" he said sharply. "I'd kill every fucking person going. Not just rapists, murderers and molesters. No. I'd kill 99.9% of the population. People are a plague on this planet. We will ultimately destroy it and ourselves. I don't think life is sacred, I think it is pointless. I believe the moral compass of mankind shifted a long time ago; tilted away from group empathy and became transfixed on individualism. Blame modern desert religions focused on the individual's relationship with 'God', the forgiveness of sins, blind faith; blame materialism, and the removal of pagan beliefs and community living, and blame yourself. If I had the power, I would keep only the brightest and best and wipe out the anathema that is man.

"Ultimately, there is no meaning to life. You may argue it is to be happy, but then wouldn't the meaning simply involve taking as many happiness producing drugs as possible regardless of whether you die. Happiness boils down only to whether our brains produce a chemical that makes us feel happy. Spreading happiness falls into the same trap. Some say it is to live a meaningful life, but meaningful to whom? The meaning in your world is of no significance to others. Others argue it is to obtain knowledge but in what respect does this affect anything outside our world or from handing over complete power to a super-computer far more intelligent than us? If the entire world was destroyed tomorrow, and with it all known life in the universe, what difference would that make to existence? A planet of rocks continues to be a planet of rocks, meaningless, unfulfilled, unhappy, it just is. Life just is.

"Forrest, you're not serious, are you?" said Galbraith.

"I am serious! Look in the faces of these people. Look at them!"

Galbraith turned towards the street; crowds walking past were unsmiling and indifferent. Some people had their phones out, staring at them, others stared at the floor, and some had headphones in; all of them lived inside their own little worlds.

He continued, "None of them care about anything further than the end of their noses. Empathy is dead. Try and get them to raise money for a sick kid, sure, you'll get the figure you need. But try and raise taxes to pay for schools and hospitals, or take money from those with it, and everyone is a fucking miser. The selfish will do everything in their power to retain the ability to drive their white 4x4, diesel guzzling, off-road cars in bloody London but complain about helping out others for the greater good. People disgust me."

At that moment, Forrest's phone rang so he got up and walked off to take the call. He seemed to be gone a while.

Galbraith sat back in her chair feeling like a hairdryer had just been blown into her face. She reclined in a state of lethargy and the food had distended her belly. The radio crackled and the controller, usually calm in her manner, expressed in a grief ridden tone that another bomb had exploded.

*****

XXX

BISMILLAH

THE pair raced across town with the blues and twos sounding and Hollywood tyres screeching at each roundabout. Forrest was his usual enigmatic self as he drove, silent, peaceful and floating. Galbraith had to remind herself to stop squeezing her car seat so hard and to relax her fingers. Forrest looked over towards her, sensing her fear, and spoke softly.

"What do you call a black policeman?" he asked.

"I don't know?"

"Officer, you racist bitch."

His laughter merged into the sound of the siren above them.

A plume of black smoke swept across the bright sky scribbling dusk on daylight. It was a homing beacon pulling the emergency services towards it - a cop magnet. The bomb had blown a large hole in the mosque's opulent dome morphing it into a giant candle stick. The flames grew and peaked out from the tip..

The bomb had annihilated everything within a forty metre radius, living or otherwise. The mosque walls had folded down and debris had been sent flailing for miles. Anyone just outside that radius could have still suffered heinous injury from the detritus of falling brick and shattered glass.

Forrest pulled into the emergency vehicle zone but quickly drove back out. Galbraith sent him a look and he explained that they wouldn't be able to get the car out for the next ten hours if he didn't move it now. He parked two streets away and the pair walked back.

As they approached the cordoned area of the bomb blast, the extent of the massacre dawned on them both. The high street was awash with uniformed personnel conducting life support for the injured. Ambulances seemed to leave as quickly as they had come. People rushed about cradling the injured and carrying them away from the smoke filled mosque. Fire crews blasted the building with water jets but it was futile against the raging smoke. The heat from the flames made Galbraith wince. There were twelve fire engines on scene, over thirty ambulances, and innumerable police officers. Everyone was running around darting between the vehicles lining the street. Passers-by held their phones out and filmed the carnage as they watched, in horror, the events unfolding.

Over the next few hours a structure to the disorder developed. Different tented areas were erected within the cordon zone. An area was created for the dead where officers busily tried to identify them, tagging their toes with identification badges poking out from the white sheets covering their bodies. There was an area for the wounded to be treated with an all-encompassing A&E working on site. Another tent was erected where officers were taking statements from those involved. Lastly, there was an area for the police from which to run the investigation.

Having spent sixteen hours working out of the bomb site, both Galbraith and Forrest were exhausted. Neither of them had eaten anything nor had any time to rest. Finally, when the bitter coldness of the night had seeped into their bones and their eyes could barely stay open, they were given the stand down by the senior investigating officer, otherwise known as Gold Crime. Forrest drove them back to the station to a background of classical music blowing soothingly out of the radio. He had the heater on full blast coupled with the window open to help him stay awake.

Just as they were saying goodbye to each other in the yard of the police station, Galbraith looked at Forrest and mumbled, "Why did he target a mosque?"

He turned around and shouted back as he walked away, cigarette in his mouth... "Chaos, Imogen! Chaos!"

*****

XXXI

CREEP

WITH arms outstretched she yawned loudly from her bed. *The best way to start the day*, she thought to herself. Then, she peered across to her fiancé and found him nestling under the duvet, his hair fluffy and soft across his forehead. Galbraith rolled out of the bed and on to the floor easing herself down gently.

She performed ten sun salutations before adopting her meditation position. She put her legs astride two round cushions lying atop one another. She rested her knees and shins on the floor with her sitting bones mounted firmly on the cushions. With her back straight up and her knees flat on the floor, she began her meditation – cleansing her mind of yesterday's atrocity.

They say there is a moment when one awakes from a long, deep sleep that one encounters pure bliss. One's problems are forgotten, the past is forgotten and the future becomes of no concern. One simply lies there, awake but asleep to thought, enjoying the moment. Then after a few seconds, your mind begins the oscillations of life, self, hunger, and misdirection, and you awaken.

It is in this somnolence that one is enlightened. The self is replaced by the now. When people awake from fainting, they often do not know who they are or where they are. The story we believe about ourselves is vacant in our minds.

Galbraith spent fifteen minutes in her posture without postulating. The thoughts of last night's endeavours were put behind her and she was able to begin the day cleansed of hurt. She put on her work clothes and stood in front of a mirror; she felt like an imposter. She was a character in a play of life, playing the part of a person destined to fight crime and to seep their soul in the salvo of society. It felt difficult today, easier following the meditation, but nonetheless difficult.

Following the bombing at the mosque, the officers seemed to share a collective hangover. Instead of drunken shame it was grief that lingered on the faces of the office dwellers. Galbraith did what most of the automatons did: she sat down at her desk, wiped away the mess of the last inhabitant, logged into the police system and looked at what crimes had been dished out by the sergeant.

It was only after an hour had passed that she actually concluded that Forrest might not turn up for work. His churlishness was usually eradicated by a good investigation or live incident and the bombing would normally have drawn him in like a worm to the rain.

Galbraith approached DS Brown who sat enveloped in a huddle of his male sycophants.

"Where's John today, Martin?" she asked.

"Annual. Not back in till next week darlin'," he hollered, barely looking at her face. His eyes fixated elsewhere.

The difference between uniform and suits in the police was autonomy. Uniform were driven by demand and the radio, whereas detectives could go as they pleased most often. Galbraith went back to her desk and finished off the statement she had written for a sexual assault investigation. She then calmly picked up her coat, booked out a car from the log and headed to the yard.

Eyes cut into her as she entered the vehicle hangar. A dozen uniformed men and women, the apotheosis of masculine culture, stared at the dainty Galbraith who now thought that tights would have probably been a good idea.

She got into the car and pulled a phone from her pocket. She looked up pizza restaurants in Camden. A man, who struggled to link his consonants, answered the phone. She ordered the cheapest pizza on the menu for delivery and was told it would be forty minutes.

Galbraith drove at a steady pace in the job vehicle. Rolling about in the passenger seat was her police radio. Listening in, praying no major crimes were reported otherwise she'd have to turn back, she followed the satnav on her phone to the address. Here she waited. It didn't take long.

A moped passed-by the block before turning back around and parking outside. As the delivery boy got off his bike, Galbraith wound the window down. She could hear his bike purr before he disengaged the engine.

The driver headed over to the intercom of a block of flats overlooking the street. He pressed the buttons and waited for a response. Galbraith could hear him talking to the occupant, explaining a pizza had been ordered. The driver didn't get far and returned to his bike, pizza in hand. He called back to the office to check the address once more. As he did so, Galbraith kept her eyes focused on the curtains of one of the flats above. She saw it, the twitch of the curtain, the face looking down. He was home. And the pizza boy drove away.

Galbraith took her phone out once more and made a call. She spoke only two words into the receiver before putting it back down. "He's here."

Two hours had passed when Forrest, clad in his usual black duster jacket and white shirt, surfaced from the building. He was already smoking a cigarette as he bounded towards his car. He got in and pulled off away from Galbraith. She started her engine and gave pursuit. He didn't venture far.

She followed him by staying on his right hand shoulder, so to speak. That is two car lengths back and one lane over to the right, when possible. She was aware that he would be anti-surveillance trained and was waiting for him to double back, take a roundabout twice, pull over unexpectedly or jump a red light, but he didn't. Instead he drove perfectly, almost like he was letting her follow him, but that thought hadn't crossed her mind.

Forrest pulled into a small side street and Galbraith angled herself on the main road to see where he'd gone. She saw his black 1998 Porsche come to a stop in a parking bay about half way up the sleepy road. She quickly pulled her phone from her pocket and typed the street name into Google. It gave her a list of businesses featured on the street with one more prominent than the rest... Camden Borough Council HQ.

Forrest casually strolled into the glassy building. Galbraith pulled her phone from her pocket again and made another call. She gave her location to the anonymous recipient and hung up just as fast. She waited some more.

Seven minutes had past when Forrest emerged carrying a brown envelope. She knew what that meant. She saw him pull away from the building and turn back in the direction from whence he came. She then pulled out and drove into the same spot he had taken in the side road and entered the council building.

A blast of energy struck her like an espresso after a heavy night of drinking – she was excited. She saw the signs pointing to the CCTV centre and made her way through the building to the basement. The entry log was outside the door and a sign said 'By Appointment Only.' She looked down the list of attendees and saw Forrest had signed at the bottom. She didn't sign the register and hit the intercom buzzer.

"Yes, can I help you?" said the speaker.

"My name is DC Galbraith. I need to speak to your manager at once."

She flashed her ID at the camera mounted above the speaker and the door clicked open.

Inside the CCTV hub was a smorgasbord of cameras and screens mounted over a concave wall that encircled the viewer. Three men who didn't appear to get out much sat in sumptuous black leather thrones and all three of them swivelled round to greet the bare legged detective.

"I'm the manager," stated the man in the middle.

"May we?" she said, pointing to an empty office at the side of the room.

"Of course," he said without hesitation, albeit the idea of his leaving his seat immiserated him almost as much as the happiness derived from the sight of a woman in the office.

Galbraith had a common tactic for dealing with civilians like this. The trick was to make them seem important, but all the while making them feel inferior to you.

"Hello sir. Might I say you run quite a fascinating operation here. I've never seen anything quite like it. My colleague DC Forrest and I are investigating some serious turpitude. I understand that this is not quite de rigueur and I don't mean to obfuscate you with my request but the CCTV you just copied for my colleague John, I need a copy too."

"Huh?" He grunted, clearly lost. "But he just left?" the man said, bewildered.

"Exactly, I knew you'd understand. A disc copy will be perfect." she said and then sat down in a chair by the door, immediately pulling out a pen and file as though she were extremely occupied.

The man was completely baffled. He didn't quite know what to do. He was standing there, his shirt untucked, his glasses slipping off his nose and his greasy brown hair hanging loosely about his face. He pushed his glasses back up, winced his eyes and swept the hair across his head without moving his feet.

"Yes, um, sure. Wait here officer and I'll get it for you."

It took him just a few minutes when he returned with the disc and a statement for Galbraith to sign.

"Ah, yes, what did you say your name was again officer?"

"DC Maybrooke... Maybrooke with an 'E' on the end."

"Thank you."

He handed her the disc.

Galbraith left the room full of screens and headed back out to her car. She unlocked the vehicle and threw the CCTV on to the passenger seat. She took out her phone and attached a small black box which she kept inside her jacket pocket. The phone immediately flashed up a new screen with the imperative to *'ENTER PASSWORD'*.

She typed in the code and the screen washed over with a map. She typed in a serial number and the map suddenly expanded showing two dots. The first dot blinked at the location where Galbraith was parked and indicated her location; the second dot blinked and revealed the location of Forrest's car. He was back at his home address.

Galbraith had positioned herself, out of sight, diagonally across from Forrest's building and kept one eye on the entrance. She pulled a laptop from her bag and logged in. She knew Forrest had no computer in his apartment and would have not been able to the view the footage yet. The CCTV went into the computer with a small whirl and an icon appeared on her desktop.

The footage began and showed a residential road in Camden at 22:17 hours. The footage was only 90 seconds long. It was a fixed street camera and the operator had not used the zoom controls so the camera simply faced the quiet residential street from a height of twenty feet. It seemed to show two men, one of whom was walking a dog. One of the men was walking towards the sight of the camera, and the other away. She knew instinctively that the man walking towards the camera was Forrest by his cigarette smoking sashay and the billowing of his coat in the wind.

The clip was innocuous enough: the pair of men walked towards one another, there wasn't an exchange, only a brief pause as they brushed into each another. Barely noticeable unless one was looking for it. *Why does he want this footage?*

She deduced two of the most plausible reasons for his request: firstly, this footage incriminated him in something and he needed to see what might be on there, or second, the whole thing was a trap and he had set up a rouse to draw her out and confirm his belief that she was on to him. Either way, he had some explaining to do.

Forrest sat in his chair as the words on the page began to grow more difficult to read. He was reading one of his favourite philosopher's books. Arthur Schopenhauer always had a way of making Forrest's misery seem more palatable, like it was some positive aspect to his character. He was drinking, again. The contents of the vodka bottle disappeared into his stomach churning alongside the burger he had bought on the way home. The curtains billowed in a brazen gust as rain tapped a melody on the glass windows. The moon crept behind a black cloud, as his eyes grew heavier, the whites being concealed behind the clouds of his eyelids. A radio in the background crackled out BBC Radio 4 as the hourly news update came on. He dropped his book to the floor and closed his eyes.

"Major Jim Rafferty is the 146th British officer to die this year in the conflict, and the highest ranking of them all. His death comes at a time when the government are in final talks about a withdrawal from the territory. His family were informed last night and his body is due to be flown back for a memorial service. The Prime Minister today said…"

Forrest muttered as he lay there listening… 'Poor bastard'. His eyes grew heavier and his breathing more shallow. He nestled deeper into his arm chair and tried to adjust his head and neck into the cushion. It was then that his eye-lids shot open and he sprung up from his seat. He got up so quickly that he had to balance himself. He trotted over to the door and reached for the black coat hanging on a hook. He put his hand inside and ferreted around the coat pocket. The notepad from the briefing was still there. He looked down at the notes he had made – *retired army police terrorists*. He knew then at that moment, that they had missed something, something major. *What about the dead?*

*****

XXXII

MUSE

FORREST awoke earlier than usual, convinced that he had had enough sleep to get him under the drink drive limit. Wearing the same shirt as the day before, he set off for work in his car. He smelt of stale cigarettes and regret.

He walked briskly and with purpose into the office. The other detectives looked at him curiously. He was three hours early for work, but no one enquired as to why. He sat at his usual desk and fired up the computer. It seemed to run even slower than normal.

He analysed the intelligence reports submitted into those 14 names linked to the bomb. He was right, they weren't looking into dead soldiers. He then reached for his telephone and punched in a number. The man on the end was a friend of his.

"Yes, the entire list. All dead personnel dating back three years… Can you check them against people from London… Can that somehow be narrowed to dead soldiers from Newham?... And someone with knowledge of bomb-making - keep the search to Royal Engineers, the Grenadiers, and so on… Okay, thanks, speak soon," Forrest said, as he hung up the phone.

An hour had passed before his email flashed up from the MoD contact. It contained within it a spreadsheet of all those dead army personnel within the last three years connected to London and from an explosives background. The spreadsheet was not necessary. It contained only one name. John Jackson.

Forrest punched in a Google search for the dead soldier. A number of news reports flashed up documenting the soldier's death. A service had been held for him in Newham, his home town. The detective read almost all the stories he could find to eliminate bias from the journalists. He then called his friend back.

"I need his full file, names, addresses, autopsy reports, the lot... I know it's classified... I don't need you to email me it, I can meet you... Oh for fuck's sake, just give me his family's address... Ah, that's good news, I'll pay this friend a visit... I appreciate it Warren, take care."

Forrest then ran a credit check on the dead soldier. As he predicted, the man's bank cards had not been used since his reported death. However, just a week before his death, the entire contents of his savings were transferred to his sister's account. With this in mind, he walked out of the office as close to happy as anyone could be without smiling.

*****

XXXIII

RENDEZVOUS

NIGHT had fallen by the time the leathery faced detective emerged from his monochrome tower, just as colourless. The officer had a large holdall in his right hand as he strode across the pavement with a definite frisson that added extra length to his strides. His counterpart had lunged deeper into her seat as she kept watch on him, secretly decoding his every move. The lights of his car blinked thrice as he plunged the bag in the back and climbed inside the coupe. Galbraith heard the engine start up and the car pull off away from her. The tracking device was still fitted so she was able to bide her time before giving chase.

Forrest's vehicle rolled to a halt outside a dingy bar. Inside his car, he fidgeted through his pocket and retrieved a photo of two men printed on the page of a newspaper. He rolled the paper up and exited the vehicle. The bar was dim and cold inside. Used cigarette ends littered the paving stones at the entrance and a weather-beaten sign advertised food for sale within.

The bar had an aroma of wet shoes and musty beer. A barman nodded at him as he approached; he was drying glasses with a dirty cloth and his countenance, his manner, everything about him suggested total apathy towards his job.

"Hey, gimme one more" stated the only man drinking at the bar.

The barman didn't respond verbally but poured out a whiskey and coke under the drinker's nose.

"One for the road," he slurred, knocking it back.

As he reached for his wallet, Forrest put his hand out and interrupted him, "I'll get this one old friend."

The man turned his head to look at Forrest. He winced in the dark, trying to remember. His brain was slow, muddled and muffled by the booze.

"What, you me friends?" he slurred.

His voice was coarse. It was the voice of someone who had smoked too much and drank too often.

"Yes. A long time ago."

The man scratched his matted brown hair.

"Army days?"

"Before. Look at me Danny. Look harder."

Forrest pulled on a hanging bar light and shone the bulb over his face, forcing long shadows to flex over his features. The barman went back to cleaning glasses.

"Do I know you?" he said, quizzically examining the face in the lightbulb.

"Yes, I was in your unit. You called me the Forrester. Don't you remember Danny?

"The Forrester! Hmm, yes of course I remember you," he said scratching his head, "How did you find me? How long has it been?"

He rambled on and then swigged his drink some more. Forrest stood beside him leaning on the bar. He had never seen the man before, but compared to the photo in the newspaper, he looked much older, worn out, his hair had gone, his eyes were lower and his beard had greyed prematurely.

"It's good to see you old friend. Tell me, how are you coping?" said Forrest.

"Ha! Life is shit mate. Yeah, there's no place in society for people like us mate. You did the right thing getting out when you did. Too long in the fire burns you black inside and out, I say."

"You did a brave thing for your country, friend," said Forrest.

"I once believed that," he was still slurring, "but then I realised we were the fireman *and* the arsonist. Our jobs look great from afar but in reality it's far from great, eh."

"It's so dark in here I think we could do with a fire!" Forrest said smiling. "People like drinking at night, their true colours show up better against a dark background."

"Forrester, I'll drink morning, noon, Sunday, Monday, any time you call me!" he laughed and bounced about in his chair, his hand on the whiskey drink.

Forrest could easily search a dead body, he could tell a family they had lost their child in a car crash, he would see criminals get sent down for years, but he felt more emotion now than he had for months. He saw that this man was simply a reflection of himself. That he too, had fallen by the wayside. Both of them products of a hegemony that ate them when they were at their prime and shat them out when they had become of no use.

"Old friend, I plan on seeing you again. It's been too long. But I've come here to ask you about John Jackson. Have you seen or heard from him?"

The drunk man's face filled with consternation, so much so his whole countenance mulched up into a centrifugal ball and then pushed back out again.

"Forrester, he died two years ago. You must have heard?"

"I left before then. Tell me about what happened, if you can."

He gulped his drink.

"Not much to say. We were serving in Iraq. Me, John, all the lads were up on the stanchions of a bridge in the desert. The order was to rig it to blow by detonator – pretty straight forward stuff really. The whole squad were up there mate. We'd been told to expect a sand storm that day. The brass were aware but sent us up regardless. Maybe they thought it would provide extra cover or thought the enemy were crossing and couldn't hold on. Anyway, I was up there, and John was my number two. When the sand kicked in, it got bloody everywhere. I couldn't hear for shit let alone see. The next thing, there was an explosion. My line went slack below and I knew it was Jackson. Never saw the bugger again. We searched for a couple of days but only found bits of charred equipment and clothing. Blast took out another lad too, such a waste of life."

"What about the body?"

"Didn't find it. Best guess was something else got to it before us."

"Did you attend the funeral?"

"Yeah, they had a memorial service back at home for all the boys we lost when we returned."

"Tell me about it please, I want to know."

"A small service, gun salutes and the like. His sister came but he didn't have much family. He used to talk about his mother being unwell and I think she must have either died or been too sick to make the service. You don't really ask that sort of thing."

"So how many of you got killed, from your troop?"

"Well, John as you know. There was Richie Stiles before him, good guy too, loyal, larger than life. And Scotty Bowman, fitness freak type, family man, died some months later. Singh, Denning, Hawkins, I could go on for ages. In some ways, I wish I were them. They get the pay out, the feature on the news, the page in the paper and the widow's pension. What do I get? I'm all alone mate with only the drink for company."

"Danny, don't you think it strange that he died the way he did? The way I knew him, he wouldn't have made mistakes."

"Yeah, if I'm honest it did bother me at the time," Danny said, "but I try not to think on it too much these days. Jackson wasn't like the rest of us. He went to a good uni, got a First in Engineering. He joined the army on the graduate scheme and had all the talent one could hope for. He was generally a really nice and calm bloke. But, eh, once you got a few beers in him he would change. He'd start going on about how much he enjoyed killing the Muslims, and how the country had fucked his family over. He was a terrible drinker, but thankfully he didn't drink very often."

Danny sipped his drink before continuing, "At other times he'd go on about how poor his family were and that he couldn't have ever gone to such a prestigious university without the support of the army. He also talked about having a disabled brother living with his mother who was battling breast cancer and that he wasn't too sure he should be leaving them. Everyone was mortified when John died. He was an expert, he never made mistakes. Life is like that sometimes."

"I know. It's hard." He patted him on the shoulder. "Do you know how I might reach the sister you met at the funeral? I'd like to pay my respects."

The drunk thought for a while and stroked his chin.

"Nah. Don't remember much. I know she was called Trisha. We went back to hers after the service to some flat in Forest Gate. Can't remember where exactly but it was in a tower block."

"Y'know, John didn't speak much about her. Is she doing okay since he went? Does she have a husband, family, or even a dog for company? Poor woman."

"Urgh, no I don't think so. She didn't have anyone back when I met her. She was pretty much on her own. I know she is in contact with their disabled brother but he wasn't at the funeral for very long. Come to think of it, their mother must have died shortly before John did or she would have been at the funeral. But I didn't pry into it."

"Thanks Danny. I'll see you again soon old friend."

Forrest threw a twenty pound note at the barman and shouted, 'Whatever he wants', before walking out.

Galbraith saw Forrest emerge from the dank bar and shield his eyes from the sun. *Was he drinking in the day?* She noted down the address of the pub in a notebook that she pulled from her inside pocket. His car started up once more, and he drove off in the direction of his home.

It was some hours later before Forrest emerged once again from his apartment. The sudden movement of his coat billowing in the wind caused Galbraith to jump up in her seat and to check that the keys were still in the ignition. As before, she gave him adequate room before pursuing his vehicle using her tracker. The Machiavellian sleuth's car was tracked to a rundown suburb of outer London. And there, she waited.

*****

XXXIV

HAIR OF THE DOG

HE paused before exiting the car and looked in the mirror of the sun visor at his worn looks; what a handsome man he once was, many years ago. He reached over to collect the envelope and his phone, and then he alighted from the vehicle. The walkway to the block of flats was poorly lit, and the concrete slabs were uneven. A washing line ran across the patchy lawn outside the estate and an old pair of shoes dangled on a wire in the wind.

The front door had an intercom system entry panel numbered 1 to 38. Forrest looked at the fire-keyhole but it had been vandalised beyond use and his vain attempt to turn the lock failed. He decided to buzz a neighbour who answered the call with a distinct lack of enthusiasm. Over the intercom, Forrest explained he was a police officer and without a reply from the voice in the speaker the entrance clicked open.

Upon examination of the door which used a simple lock mechanism featuring magnetic blocks to secure it, he let it close. After making a mental note, he climbed the stairs to the top floor. His ear felt warm as he pressed it against the wooden door of Number 36. Low vibrations of a voice tickled his ear drum. Someone was home. He knocked three times loudly. Below the door lay a doormat which read *Lord make me a channel of your peace.*

She answered the door just as Forrest's somaticized heart raced in his chest. She really looked like her brother.

"Can I help you?"

"Yes, I'm hoping this is the right address. I'm trying to find the family of John Jackson." His voice was taciturn and he bowed his head low like a dog surrendering. "I'm an old friend of his, we served together. I just wanted to give you a card. I didn't mean to disturb you. I'm sorry."

He turned on his heel to walk away and made sure to flash the white envelope as he did so.

"No, no, it's okay. Um, please do come in" she said, widening the door.

The flat was very dark as Forrest entered the corridor. Not what he wanted. He hit the light switch to his right and excused himself, "Sorry, bad eyes," and began nursing an imaginary ostentatious limp as he scuttled down the aisle of the flat carefully gleaning all and sundry about him.

"Your leg; is it okay?" she asked.

She seemed genuinely concerned.

"Yes, yes, it's fine. It takes me a bit longer to get about but I'm used to it now."

"What did you say your name was again?" she asked.

"I'm Arnold, Arnie Mann. I was based with him in Germany."

"Oh, yes of course."

She didn't remember having heard his name.

The pair exchanged a few pleasantries as Forrest sat there meekly picking lint from his clothing. She seemed to enjoy the company. He spoke of platitudinous exploits, the kind any sister would forget. All the while his eyes searched her for clues, searched the flat for answers.

The two strangers were sat down on opposing sofas in the low ceilinged flat. The sofas were black but worn away exposing a creamy foam underbelly beneath the cracks of the surface. On the walls hung old photos of her and her brother, the family dog, and the parents that had passed on. A balcony whistled high in the wind of the tower block. Above the television sat a large photo of Jesus Christ. And the woman in front of him looked just as tired as the furnishings with which she chose to surround herself. The flat said one word to him: comfort. She was surrounded by comfort. An old worn comfort, which whispered to him the word *nostalgia*.

He needed more. In the background the television was on quietly. Arnold Mann reached for the remote control: "Oh I love this show!" he said ebulliently and turned the volume up to a pitchy plateau. The sound bellowed about the small flat. He had to quickly excuse himself.

"Excuse me, can I use your bathroom before I go?" he asked politely.

His cumbersome limp bought him the extra time he needed and the loud television would mask his movements. He looked for anything, everything that would show Jackson had been here. There were no men's clothes in the corridor, no jacket on the wall, no shoes on the floor. In the bathroom, there was one toothbrush in the holder, only female hair products and body lotions around the bath and one towel draping over a radiator. The wily sleuth scratched his head and continued. He checked the bin in the bathroom and found nothing. He checked the plughole and found only the long hair of a woman. He checked for tiny hairs around the sink from a recent shave but came up empty. Silently, he slipped into the kitchen at the end of the corridor, but despite his efforts, there was nothing leading to the conclusion that another man had been there. Nothing in the sink, nothing in the fridge, and nothing strewn around. He felt defeated. He was sure.

As he made his way back to the living room he saw the door to the bedroom was ajar. He pushed it gently open and peered inside, listening to whether it creaked and at what point. Having scanned the room he closed the door fully before opening it again, leaving it ajar once more.

He went into the living room and found the sister had moved to the chair he was on. The television set was now quieter and he assumed she moved over to reach the remote. Arnold Mann lowered himself on to the second sofa and leaned back.

"Thank you for your time. I'm truly sorry I never got to say goodbye to him. When he was alive, he asked me to do him one huge favour. He said it meant the world to him. Well, let's just say I did it. If only he knew how hard it was but I did it." Forrest sobbed. "I should go. Please pass on my condolences."

With that, he reached over for his jacket and pulled out the envelope from his pocket. "Put this on his grave for me won't you; it says it all."

"Oh, thank you."

"Hey, do you mind if we open it? There's a song that plays from the card, it was his favourite. It might be a nice moment to listen to it together."

"Yes, please go ahead," she replied warmly.

Forrest slipped open the envelope and held the card open. A song rang out from a speaker in the card. It chimed a simple melody of *Swing Low Sweet Chariot*. Once the tune had played out, Forrest left the card atop the television.

To his left, he noticed more photographs. The dog in the photo was different to the previous one, white and black with shorter hair.

"Is this your dog?" he asked.

"It was John's. I looked after it whilst he was away, but when he died, it wasn't fair to keep him in such a small flat so I gave him away," she said.

"I see. This photo looks very recent. I gather it was taken close to the time he left us."

"Um, yes I believe so."

As the detective descended in the lift he felt the cold outside coming closer. He pulled his jacket tightly to his body creating a gloomy adumbrated figure in the lift mirror. He stared at himself, at the coruscant flashes ahead of him. As he looked down, he saw the hairs on his coat. The hairs from the second sofa. A dog had sat on that sofa at some point. He could see a mix of short white and black hairs dotted about his torso. The same dog in the photo. As he left the block, he put a pound coin between the magnetic strips of the door.

Forrest climbed into his vehicle and pulled out his phone. He then reached into the glovebox and pulled out a beige box which he attached to the base of the phone. An application booted up on the box and Forrest listened intently. He could hear the voice of the sister coming through the microphone in the card now on her television.

"A cop was here... Yes, of course I'm sure, he was definitely a cop, they're on to you, John, you need to move, do it now... Yes... Okay... Do you need me to put more money into the account?... I'll do it now... I love you too. Be safe Johnny."

Forrest returned to the station to see Galbraith sat at her desk. She was watching him, he knew, and she knew he knew it, but neither broke character. He was so excited about the find that he kept his jacket on as he logged on to the terminal. The officer typed in *Patricia Jackson, aged 39* and ran checks across police indices. There was nothing on her, not a trace. He then ran a credit check across all her bank accounts. She lived well within her means, had just the one credit card, no debts and relatively small savings. The activity on all of her accounts was nothing extraordinary. She spent money every Sunday on a Tesco shop. She bought clothing sporadically, items from Amazon.com around once a month, and clearly didn't possess a car.

Forrest wasn't able to see the individual purchases she was making, such as dog food or petrol, but he could see where she was spending her money, at what times, and in what amount, along with the withdrawals she was making.

It was then that he noticed the error the bomber had made; his belief reified in an instant. One of her bank accounts revealed a large deposit which had been made approximately six weeks ago. Following on from this, the owner of the account withdrew cash on a daily basis, in large sums only, and via cash points and never over the bank counter. Someone was clearly using her card to take the money out in person.

It made Forrest wonder. *Why give him a card? Why not just hand him a bundle of cash? Perhaps she would claim that the bank card was stolen and used without her permission? Or maybe the bomber didn't want to risk carrying large sums of cash in case he was found out?* But what Forrest did know for certain was that all the withdrawals were made in East London, and the vast majority at a cash point in Mile End, some distance from where the sister lived. That's where he would find the bomber. He smiled through crooked teeth.

*****

XXXV

NASCENT

THE shady detective put it into first gear and glided out of the police yard. He began the jaunt over to Mile End Park in the morning light, when he pulled over at the side of the road to find a smoke. He was about to light the cigarette when Galbraith sprung up from the back seat and pointed the gun to the back of his head.

"Don't fucking move. This is a Glock 9mm semi-automatic pistol capable of blowing the eyes out of the front of your head from this position. Now throw the fucking car keys towards me and keep your hands on the roof of the car."

"No," he said bluntly.

"John Forrest, I am arresting you for the bombing of the Newham Council building on November 16th. You do not have to say anything but it may harm-"

"Cut the crap kid and put that gun away."

"Back up is already is on its way," she exclaimed.

"Firstly, no they're not. And secondly, I'm glad you finally decided to show yourself having followed me for the last two days. If you want to track someone then lose the perfume. I smelt you the second I got into the car."

"Stop talking!" she shouted.

Galbraith went into her jacket for her radio. Forrest span round and Galbraith's fingers leaned into the trigger.

"Now you listen to me Imogen. If you broadcast on that radio, I'll walk away and then you'll have to shoot me. If you keep the gun trained on my head, I'll lead you to our man."

Galbraith said, "I know it was you. I saw you. I saw you go into that building and take the CCTV and purposefully put your prints inside the crime scene. I know you've been taking footage from previous nights and looking at other locations. You've got a working knowledge of bomb-making, you served in the Forces, and you no doubt broke into that block of flats and did God knows what to the occupier, but I'll find out."

"Imogen, I'm not going to hand you the car keys. I'm going to continue my journey to Mile End Park. Once I get there, I'm going to look for the bomber and you can either come with me or you can wait in the car. Either way, you ain't going to shoot me, and I'm not going to surrender."

He put the car into first gear and the wheels began rolling. Galbraith was incensed.

"You mother fucker. I'm calling for back up."

"Why? It's just you and me. I'm unarmed. You want that big arrest, kid. If you wanna be famous, then this is your chance. You'll ruin your career if you arrest me. You'll be the laughing stock at the station, arresting a colleague whilst on duty for terrorism. I'll tell them you've gone mad. You'll be restricted pending psychiatric assessment, all the while this guy is continuing to kill innocent civilians."

Galbraith depressed the radio transmit button, "Met Control receiving DS Kline."

A voice responded. "Go ahead DS Kline."

DS huh? Thought Forrest. There was a long pause from Kline.

"Is my radio transmitting clearly, control?" she prevaricated.

"R5," said the voice back.

She put the radio down.

"Okay, explain, but you only get one chance, John."

Forrest took a deep breath.

"The bomb was made by a bomb expert. It doesn't fit any current terrorist factions. It's too small for Al-Qaeda and international terrorists wouldn't target a council building. It has to be domestic. The bomber acted alone, or at most, with one other. He was highly skilled in making bombs himself and had to have belonged to a unit of some description, like Bomb Disposal, Royal Engineers, and so on.

"He's targeted Newham Council for a specific reason. It's personal; there's a grudge. He must have lived here or had someone close to him that did so. Over the past week, something was bugging me. I came across a guy on my way home who looked familiar but I couldn't see him in the light. He said he didn't have time 'for this right now'. I didn't know what that meant. That CCTV footage is from that incident. I thought there was something in it but it was a red herring.

"Then the DCI said that they were looking into retired or serving personnel only. They didn't factor in the dead. I've found someone that is wearing the right shoes, kid. From Newham. He has a hatred for Muslims. He has a disabled brother living in the borough and his mother died from cancer about the time he supposedly was killed in Iraq.

"Some things still perplex me for sure. Like why did he send the bomb to our office? There are many things we can speculate upon but it has to be the guy. I've seen one his friends who confirms John Jackson died suspiciously with no body found. I've also got a recording of his sister talking to someone I believe is her dead brother."

Kline wasn't buying it.

"I've seen how happy you've been since the bombs started going off. At that party, the other night, you were a new you!"

"Listen, kid. I choose to lead my life on a miserable plane; I've accepted that that is who I am. But happiness is temporal, like the first bite of a meal, or an orgasm, or any fleeting moment of joy, and I enjoy the company of old friends, and the nostalgia of fond histories. And I'm happiest when I'm investigating something truly wicked, like this bomber."

"C'mon, you think I'm an idiot, John. You're just equivocating in order to buy time. I must admit, it's a nice story you've twined out of your ball of lies."

"I like you more now that you've finally grown a back bone. Now shut up and listen." The car continued through Whitechapel and towards Mile End, past the university and a boarded up pub. "I've discovered the bomber is using his sister's bank account and making almost daily withdrawals from a cash point in Mile End. He has to be here. We can find him."

DS Kline began to believe him. "How can you be so sure?"

"John Jackson, despite his racism and general homicidal tendencies, was a quite brilliant engineering student. I looked him up. He topped all the exams and was highly commended by his peers. If it were not for his subversive views, he could probably have been a phenomenal success in any area of engineering he set his sights upon. I'm sure he was the most proficient and adroit explosive expert the army could call upon."

"Time's ticking Forrest," said Galbraith.

"He faked his death in Iraq. He would never have allowed a faulty to bomb to go off. If anything, it was the perfect mask for his death. He could take out a colleague with a powerful bomb and the body parts of neither would ever be discovered. His family would get the usual pay out and access to his pension, all the while he is building a plot for revenge. The money from his sister is simply her returning the money rewarded for his dying."

"Okay, but why? Why bother going through all the trouble just to blow up a council building? What's his angle?" she asked.

"I know how he feels from personal experience. I know what it's like to lose a loved one and feel that the state, the state for which you've given your blood, has badly let you down. Jackson's mother was terribly sick. She had breast cancer that metastasised through her body and killed her. She lived in Newham. Perhaps he blames them for her lack of care, for her death, for his brother being disabled. And I now know that she died from her illness in The Royal London hospital: his next target."

"Forrest, then why are we going to Mile End?" she barked.

"His sister warned him he had to move location. He'll be packing up his things and moving, we have to act quickly. Furthermore, at his sister's place, I noticed a recent photo of him with a black and white dog. She must have given it back to him when he returned as there were dog hairs all over her flat but no sign of a dog living there. Mile End Park is the largest park in the area and a good place to stay for someone with a big dog to walk."

"We need to let someone know John! He might be trying to bomb the hospital as we speak!" she said.

"He won't be. Like any other institution, the hospital is busiest on a Saturday night. Thus, he'll wait until tomorrow evening before acting. And in terms of us bringing the entire Firearms Command down here, he's too clever for that. He'll have some kind of plan for that. It'll end worse for everyone and we could be responsible for many deaths. It needs to be just me and him. You can wait outside if you like, I don't really care... Sergeant," he said.

"So you know where he is?" she asked.

"I will in about five minutes," he replied, pulling into a parking bay beside Mile End Park.

*****

XXXVI

SLEEP

FORREST began walking off. DS Kline shouted after him but he simply ignored her and headed over to a group of drunks and began conversing with them. It took some minutes. Kline checked her phone and paced back and forth beside the unmarked police car. It wasn't a wise move to get involved with Forrest's street contacts as they could seize up.

The detective handed a shady-looking drunk a cigarette; the pair seemed to know one another quite well. There was some banter between the two men and Kline was sure that Forrest even smiled. After a short while, the pair walked off and they stood away from the group of drunks with whom the man was sitting. It was still early in the morning and the group looked cold, huddled quite closely, wearing beer jackets to keep warm.

Forrest's countenance changed. He nodded away while the drunk spoke in urgent tones to him. Then the pair returned to the group. At this point, Forrest addressed them all. Kline kept watch from a distance. The detective was briefing them all like a commander gearing his troops up for a siege.

A lone female from the group, small in stature, slim, with greasy brown hair and a spotty face stood up. Forrest gave her a smoke and pair walked off together away from the others. Forrest then stopped and handed her a wad of notes. She seemed taken aback by the amount of money. He then pulled out his phone and handed it to the female. They spent the length of time smoking their respective cigarettes looking at his phone as she appeared to be explaining some intricate detail to him. After that, he took his phone back and returned to Kline.

"Well?" she asked.

"We've got our man. They've seen him on a daily basis walking his dog. Sometimes he apparently just sits there for hours looking out at seemingly nothing. One of them, the female, has been in Mehmet's Shop just on the corner, at the same time as our man."

"Wait, that isn't finding him? And why are you listening to a bunch of drunks? They'll tell you anything for the amount of money you handed her."

"These people are here 24/7, they walk all the night and beg all day. These are their streets. They see all. The number of times our undercover cops have tried to infiltrate their society makes them more suspicious. A guy like our bomber would pique their interest."

Kline was still unsure to trust him.

"What did you show her on your phone?"

"A photo of our man. I found it on the news article covering his death. Granted, he looks different now, but not unrecognizable. The girl-"

"You mean that crack head woman over there."

"Drug addiction is a disease Imogen, if that is your name. And she's a beautiful person underneath the façade of emaciation. She said that it was definitely him, but he always wears a hat, and has a beard now."

"So how do we find him?" she asked.

"We may be in for a long wait..."

Forrest put the car into drive once more and drove along the edge of the park to a shop on the corner. Above the window was signage which read *Mehmet's Food and Wine*. The detectives were parked on the other side of the street facing the store. Forrest got out of the car and walked into the shop leaving the nervous Kline on her own again.

Forrest pushed the door open which triggered the sounding of a bell behind the cashier's till. Immediately, he was hit by a blast of blinding, shimmering light from enough fluorescent tubes to light up an airport runway. He grimaced as his eyes adjusted. Looking about, he discovered a convenience store which was typical for the area. Rows of stale fruit and veg in unremarkable boxes lined the wall to his left; above were rows of tinned goods and packaged dry food then along the wall opposite stood open-faced refrigeration units. Forrest quietly browsed each vista checking that no customers were present in the store.

Forrest saw a man with tanned skin of middle-eastern origin standing behind the counter. The man had a round, friendly face, jet black hair, wore a casual shirt, and had spectacles on a neck strap. This had to be Mehmet.

"Good evening," said Forrest, producing his badge and placing it on the counter. "I've something very important to ask you. This information is confidential and must not be passed on to anyone else. Do you understand?"

The man nodded, quizzically.

"I said do you understand?"

"Yeah, yes," he mumbled. At which Forrest made the deduction that he was Turkish.

"I'm going to show you a photo of a man now. This man shops in here. When he visits, he most likely buys dog food amongst other items. He now has a beard and wears a hat. Do you understand? Is that clear?"

"Yes, but what's this to do with me? I'm just a shop keeper, I-"

"Just take a look."

He opened the article on his phone containing the photograph and slid it across the counter. The shopkeeper put on the glasses hanging from his neck and stared at the image. His head arched up as he did so in battle with the overbearing lighting. His eyes winced as he focused.

"Yes, yes I know him. This man, he comes here. He ties his dog outside because I don't allow   dogs inside."

"How often does he visit the shop?"

"Um, I'd say most days."

"At what time?"

"Mornings generally, he's a real early bird. Comes in around 7am," said the shopkeeper, who chuckled a little as he answered the detective, pleased he could assist.

"That would be the dog's morning walk. What about evenings?"

"No, I don't think so. He buys milk, a paper, dog food... the usual stuff."

Forrest continued to press him, "I need to know what he shops for. Whether he buys anything you need to store in a freezer? Think carefully."

The friendly faced shopkeeper was pensive and spoke slowly, "Hmm, now you mention it, today, he bought only bread... peanut butter... dog food... and... milk. Hang on, I may be able to get the receipt."

He started pressing various buttons on his till. A long receipt trail began to run from the top of the machine. It was now 6pm and a day's takings were being shown on the audit trail.

"While you're doing that, show me to your CCTV system. I need to see him."

The shopkeeper handed Forrest the receipt for the purchases the man had made. He read them silently to himself: *a tin of fruit, orange juice, milk, bread, dog biscuits, peanut butter, rolling tobacco with papers, and two newspapers.*

The shopkeeper then led Forrest to his CCTV system behind the door at the rear of the shop. He looked at the receipt for the time and punched in 07:14 hours. The footage was clear and Forrest watched with marvel at the bomber entering the shop. The strange gait, the bushy beard, it was him.

The detective picked up an A-Z road map and paid the shopkeeper in change. He returned to the car.

"I was worried you weren't going to come back," said Kline.

Forrest didn't acknowledge her comment.

"Come and sit in the front with me," he said to her.

She listened, just as Galbraith would have done. Forrest pulled out his A-Z and found their current location. He drew a large circle around the park with a pencil.

"This is the local area on a road map. The park has six entrances on foot. The north and south side are surrounded by shops akin to Mehmet's. They all sell the same sort of thing and there's nothing special about this shop. The only reason he would use it over the others is for convenience; it'll be on his route to and from the park to where he's staying. So we can eliminate all the other areas around the park where he may live."

He then drew a second large circle around Mehmet's shop.

"Now he clearly needs to use the park to walk the dog. That suggests there isn't another one closer which is suitable."

The circle around Mehmet's shop included a smaller green area than Mile End Park.

"We can therefore discount this small park as being closer to him. The dog described by the shopkeeper is a young Wolfhound. They're big but they're not running dogs. They don't necessarily need a huge park and could use the smaller one. That means again he travels here because it's closer. I discovered he doesn't buy anything that needs to be frozen: this suggests he doesn't have a freezer or anything to cook with, perhaps not even electricity. He is most likely squatting in a disused flat. We will locate him by finding any mothballed flats within this circle."

He drew a final circle completing a Venn diagram containing the first large park, the second small park, and Mehmet's shop.

"This area, just a few hundred feet square, is where he'll be. It's time."

*****

SWAN

XXXVII

THE rain began to pour across the windshield. The glistening street lights highlighted the falling tears as the waning sun disappeared behind a cloud. The moon whispered in the distance, and nocturnal beasts were on the verge of awakening from their slumbers. The car pulled out from the parking space across from Mehmet's shop and into a narrow vista behind the park. They circled the bleak streets of Tower Hamlets perusing the local buildings, noting down all the different possibilities of where their suspect could reside. Each building, no matter how new, how modern, or how rustic, all gave a false sense of tradition. Each building was decorated with falsity in the form of hollow columns, Victorian bay windows, the pointy facades and irascible doors: a sophism. The drive was silent, no small talk ensued, no nervous energy was built nor any anxiety assuaged.

Having driven the area of the Venn diagram several times, Forrest pulled over beside a warehouse that had once been a textile factory. The deep brown, dusty, monolithic edifice peered out across the park. The factory's windows, dark and stained, seemed lifeless. There was a metal door over the entrance of what was once a place of employment for unskilled local workers wanting to make an honest living.

"This is it. He's here," said Forrest, solemnly.

"Can you be sure?"

"I'm sure. Look at the corrugated fence over the door, it's recently been pulled open."

He didn't move in his seat but closed his eyes. His arms by his side, he seemed to be at peace. Kline had a question boiling over.

"How long have you known I wasn't Imogen Galbraith?"

He took his time to answer.

"The second day you worked with me." He sensed she'd only ask him to explain so he went ahead. "You were very convincing. Your naivety at the lorry crime scene, your lack of knowledge and inexperience was made apparent. But you didn't cover all the bases. When you first arrived, I noticed you wearing a relatively old suit, which I dated at roughly three years old. On the second day, you wore a two year old suit jacket, on the third a five year old outfit, and so on and so forth. The average age of your smart outfits for work is 2.5 years. If you truly came from a uniform background, as you proposed, then why own so many suits with that lifeline. I'm guessing you went into the CID environment some four years ago, became a DS, and then went into internal affairs. Women outside of employment don't particularly wear suits for leisure or socializing, it's strictly a work garment. Anyone female from uniform always buys lots of suits to celebrate their new role.

He was calmer than she was used to.

"Five years actually. I went into CID pretty soon after I started the job," she conceded. "Something worries me, Forrest. I've lied to you about my identity for the past fortnight and you seem to be unbothered by this. It's a terrible act on my part and I'm sorry for my actions; I'm sorry for not totally being the real me, but I promise that when we have shared intimate moments, I've given you my all, more of who I am than what anyone else sees."

Forrest spoke slowly and his voice dropped an octave.

"That is the point, kid. The question I ask myself every day. Who are you? Answer me, who are you, Imogen?"

"Imogen Kline. I work for-"

"No!" he barked, "I asked who you are, not what you're named."

"Okay, I'm a twenty-eight year old woman, engaged, no kids, living in London, a liberal, who likes fitness and reading-"

"No! It's not a dating website. Who are you? What is your character? What's in here," he said, tapping repeatedly on the side of his own head.

"Um, I'm confident, I believe in doing what's right, I dislike bad people, I'm brave, kind, John I don't know what you want me to say."

"Exactly! You don't know who you are. You're as much Galbraith as you are Kline. You're as much a DS as you are a fiancé. Everything that you think you are is totally a construct of your mind. A narrative that spins in the darkness of your hopes and fears, masticating everything that your sensory perceptions glean. You're simply the product of what you, and others, tell you. You believe you're these things because you've told yourself this for years, because others have repeatedly told you this. They'll tell you you're smart, attractive, good at your job, and you think because of this that it becomes you. But you see, this story traps you in a cycle. It traps you in the belief that you have to now always be attractive, intelligent and good at your job, or you fear losing the person you've become. You fear the death of the self. It's why the same reaction to running from a lion creeps in when we have to put our constructed selves on the line – our reputations. Both of these events trigger our flight or fight response and cause panic because it's the same fear of death. I don't hate you for being Kline any more than I hate you for being Galbraith, for being anything. Remember that you are only ever the product of the narrative in your mind. The story you've been told. You can change this story of being this person whenever you like. I have never judged you for this because we're all liars in this respect."

276

Galbraith took her time to reply.

"John, it's okay to hate me. I betrayed you. You don't have to be so aloof all the time."

"I'm afraid I do," he replied. "Well Imogen Kline, are you ready to die?"

She squeezed the gun held between her hands: "What do you mean?"

Forrest turned around in his chair slowly and stared deeply into her hazel eyes.

"This world. This pit of suffering that we call home. Unless God's aim was for all living things to suffer whilst they breathe, then he has failed. The world is a nightmarish land full of disease, injustice, repression and hate. All around you is unimaginable evil. Hospitals full of those suffering unbelievable torment; prisons filled to the brim with hate-filled carcasses, empty of souls awaiting God's approval just to die. In nature, thousands of species of animals at any moment right now are tearing the flesh, scales or shell off another just to survive one more day. Think about that... Descartes was wrong. It should be, *I suffer, therefore, I am*."

He paused and seemed to want to say something else but stopped before the words could come out. Kline looked at him and noticed a solitary tear creep slowly out the corner of his eye, almost like something being said.

"John, to combat that you must reject this version of reality. You must find that behind everything is an undying force of love that holds us all together, connects us and can never die. That we can never die as our energy will pass on forever. We are quite literally made of stardust. If time is truly a circle, then we will go on forever and can never be killed. If you live with such pessimistic lenses, you won't grasp at the value of life, and that way, you will die more than once. You die every day. Is there nothing that you care about? Is it really that worthless; life?"

He looked at her, "I've a daughter. Her name's Annabel; she's three years old. She's all I care about. I know how best to look after her now."

Forrest stepped out of the vehicle and lit a cigarette. Kline followed. He stood at the side of the car and looked at her.

"This is the end of the road for you Imogen. I'm a mudslide, I take everything down with me. It's best you stay here," he said.

She laughed. "You must be crazy. I'm not letting you go in there unarmed. I can get back up here. We can surround the premises, force him out. You don't have to play the hero on this one Forrest."

She checked herself for truncating his name.

"Imogen, if you do that, many will die. This man is a trained killer, a bomb expert, a soldier who faked his own death in order to cause pain and misery to all and sundry. No amount of backup will prevent many of our colleagues from dying today. If I go in unarmed, just me, then people's lives can continue merrily along blissfully ignorant of our heroic deeds. *Dulce et decorum est pro patria mori*. I'm asking you to trust me one more time to stay here and let me deal with this."

"How will you stop him?" she asked.

"How I always do, by pure rational reasoning of it out."

She hesitated. *This was insanity, surely*. She leaned in to the car and reached for the radio receiver in the glove box and held it to her chest.

"Back up will be here in less than ten minutes. Good luck, John."

Forrest took off his jacket and tie revealing a white shirt tucked loosely into his black trousers and tossed his beloved coat on the floor. He turned and as the rain fell on his face , he walked towards the building with his arms raised in the air. Bedraggled, the detective vacillated through his melancholia; the louche Sisyphus had only wanton revenge on his mind. Creeping towards the precipice of Death's parapet, he suddenly felt awakened. A frisson of boundless joy entered his heart centre and fired blood into his muscles - like a bolt into Frankenstein's monster, he became human again. The walk was assuaged by the temporal glare of the falling sun on the textile factory's gloomy windows. Then the rain fell harder. The ablutions absolved him of tiredness and with every step his fear dissipated. Kline followed him with her eyes only.

He peeled back the corrugated iron door and swung through a small gap and inside the old factory. It smelt of damp. Dust particles danced in beams of light that cut through the old air playing a melody for them to jive to. The room was huge. Bricks and rubble coated a cracked, concrete floor. The ceiling was high and baron with holes from whence lighting once hung. Columns were flecked about the room but seemed strained under years of abuse. The detective kept his hands in the air as he moved slowly forwards.

"Jackson!" He shouted. "Jackson, I know you're here. It's John Forrest. Your mother died, your brother was abandoned by the state, and you've witnessed more death than you can bear. I'm unarmed. Don't shoot me; I just want to talk to you!"

There was only silence that echoed back. Forrest quietened his breath as he waited for a reply. Out from behind him came a stone bouncing across the concrete floor. It skipped along like a jolly surfer riding the waves. Dust flew into the air before the stone crashed into a mound of debris at the far end. He watched it with curiosity. Turning slowly, he saw him for the first time.

The solider was dressed in only boots, green combat trousers and a grey vest; his hairy chest was exposed and dog tags hung round his neck. In his hand, he cradled an assault rifle with the sight carefully pointed at Forrest's chest. He was running towards Forrest with the gun pointed straight at the detective. His footsteps were loud and clopped heavily on the hard floor. As he got closer, Forrest could hear the soldier's heavy breathing. He charged at the detective but Forrest didn't flinch, and with the butt of his gun, he thrust the heavy weapon down upon Forrest's nose, breaking it instantly.

"Get on the fucking floor, face down, hands apart, palms facing the air, look away from me." He shouted the commands in a clear and concise fashion. Like a dance class, the detective followed his orders in mechanical step-by-step order. The soldier patted Forrest down to find no weapons on his person.

"Where's your colleague, the woman?" he shouted.

"She's not coming in."

The soldier looked out of a window and glanced left to right. He then seemed to relax briefly before walking over to a red padded chair, which looked as though it had been harvested from the side of the road. It was worn and beaten, but he sat upon it like a king taking his throne. His rifle was placed by his side like a seeing-eye dog positioning itself by its owner.

"You may rise to your feet," said the man.

Forrest slowly crept up to a standing position and dusted himself down wiping away the grime from his black trousers.

"You mind if I smoke?" asked the detective.

The man nodded watching him closely.

Forrest reached slowly into his pocket and retrieved his smokes, lit one and blew out a long, fluffy puff in the air.

"What are you?" asked the detective, using his hand to rub his nose.

"I'm the epitome of a pugnacious prick. A parasite! A bubo on society's armpit. One might even say a palindrome, for I intend to end this as I began."

Forrest was struck by his verbosity. The soldier carried a deep voice hinged on a cockney accent that sang a sweet charm of polysyllabic words. He was educated and esteemed, with no falsity, as his accent prevailed over the cleverness of his words.

"You seem taken aback by my speech, Mr...?" asked the man.

"Forrest, John Forrest."

"John Forrest. Hmm, that does have a ring to it."

He thought for a moment. The pause was awkward. The seated king had him in his chamber now, unarmed, interrogating him almost sadistically. But Forrest wasn't scared, and it showed. He didn't stutter his words.

"I didn't expect a boy from Newham to be so articulate."

The soldier sat forward in his chair.

"But you don't know me Mr Forrest."

Forrest felt obliged to answer the implied question. He made sure to break the formality and keep it to first name terms.

"You read Engineering at Leeds, as well as being quite a brilliant orator and featured in many of the university's newspapers as a debating champion. You are proud of your heritage and accent, and eschew those who tried to dampen your working-class soul."

"Bravo!" he said, clapping slowly, mockingly. "Now, tell me Mr Forrest, why shouldn't I shoot you in the face?"

Forrest was frozen solid. His mind raced ahead, picturing him raising his gun, the barrel staring down at him. His mouth was so dry, his heart beating rapidly in his chest, his body shaking with adrenaline. Tunnel vision was setting in, his hearing became astute; he was panicking for the first time. Forrest began pacing back and forth but no nearer to the man in an effort to burn off the extra fuel in his veins.

"Well, there are a number of reasons why you shouldn't shoot me, John. I'd personally use a knife; it's quieter and won't raise suspicion. But I agree, it seems to you I probably have to die, or may have even come here to do so. However, killing me now really won't benefit you. Our colleagues know we're here and it'll create a situation for you. If you spare me, for now, and make your escape, you will live to kill another day."

"Oh Mr Forrest, you're beginning to appear diffident. What if I want you here my dear brother? What if I want a '*situation*'? I mean, I have to die at some time, I may as well take as many cops with me as possible?"

Forrest regained his calm. "You don't mean that, John. You're not a cop killer. You know as well as I do that you like the police. You feel the same as me: the police, army, nurses, we all got shat on when the government cuts began. We all got fucked over by the pompous parliament when those responsible for screwing the country carried on unceasingly. And you know, like I do, that inherently, we're the same pieces of meat, we've just been braised in different gravy, ready for serving up to the highest bidder."

"Give me a smoke," said the soldier.

Forrest threw the pack of cigarettes in his hand at the man, who caught them. He then took out his lighter and threw that at the bomber, who caught it, and lit one.

"Good choice of cigarette." said the soldier. "Y'know, I've reminisced about life quite a bit recently. You and I, we both chose to live outside the box. I guess the umbilical cord of a 9-to-5 keeps others attached to the main stream, but we've never been part of the pageant. I often feel I'm a visitor to an aquarium of idiots telling me *'there's plenty more fish in the sea'*. I joined the army, you the police. I wish to die, and so do you it seems."

Forrest retreated a step or two as his balance recovered. Forrest battled through his panic, fighting the demon choking him at the throat, shaking his core and engulfing his mind. The adrenaline rush had passed and he felt tired, with tingling pains now engulfing the base of his back.

Forrest spoke softly, "I know I want to die. I've faced it many times. I'm not afraid. If anything, I'm tired of living. This suffering we call existence. Now, throw me my cigarettes, I'd like a smoke."

The bomber threw the cigarettes at Forrest, and then the lighter. He caught the packet and opened the top. His hands were shaking and as he pulled a cigarette from the pack four others fell to the floor. He lit the fag and it tasted smooth. He closed his eyes and treasured that pull of the cigarette.

"Why? Why did you kill all those people?! A council building? A mosque? They had nothing to do with your gripe against the world!" he blurted out.

"Ah, at last, the man has grown a spine. Have you not worked it out yet? My mother was diagnosed with cancer before I joined the army. I requested that they postpone my incumbency so that I may set the wheels of care in motion for her. But they refused. I swallowed it. Then over the years, time and time again, my leave was cancelled as new wars were dreamt up by a group of posh men who all went to the same school. The final straw came when I received news that she was terminal. My leave was once again cancelled. I'd discovered that the council had then evicted my brother from his property due to cuts to his disability living allowance, his spare room tax, his care package was shrunk and the medicine that was seemingly working became too expensive to cure people. Newham were a part of that."

"I understood that element, but why the parcel bomb to our police station? It doesn't make sense," asked Forrest.

He laughed so hard his head rocked back. "What does make sense you fool? I killed twenty people in a council building and blew up a mosque, yet you question me about sense. Not everything has to be cold, calculating logic. I underestimated you, if I'm truly honest. I wanted to be caught eventually, but this is a little too premature. Thankfully, the O.K Corral stand-off awaits me still. The parcel bomb was a ploy to see how you'd react, and whether my council bomb idea of luring people into the car park for a secondary device to explode would work sufficiently. I remember seeing you that day, standing on your plinth and addressing the crowd. I could have killed you all if I chose. And thanks to you my little guinea-pig, the council workers of Newham have never looked better."

Forrest's face devoid of emotion gave nothing away.

"Well, I don't feel I have much time left now. Can I ask John, that you not shoot my face. For my mother. I don't want her to see me like that. I've already got a black heart and fucked lungs, put the bullet in my chest."

"And what about her outside?" said the bomber, still sat down in his throne. He'd finished his cigarette at this point.

"Do whatever you like. She's a snitch after all. Dying like this will ensure my family get the pay-out they deserve. Unlike suicide, I can die on duty and go out a hero, and my kid will be fine. You carry on doing what you're doing old friend. Show these fuckers what life is really about," said Forrest.

"You have a child? Then why risk yourself so foolishly?"

"I'm sad because I brought a child into this world, this farce. Two old men may sit and dwell on their lives only to see it for the mosaic of putridness that connects all the sufferings in our life together, on this futile journey governed by decay."

The bomber stood up once more, gun in hand, and ambulated over to the window. He looked out to see a mélange of neon lights, police caps poking up from police cars, armoured vans and pointing guns. He slipped back, away from the light. And there, from the wincing crack of the window, he saw the sun reappear, greeting him. From behind the nimbus cloud.

"You know what I'll miss most Mr Forrest – the seasons. I'll never see another summer sunset, or smell the fresh grass in spring, or feel the cool breeze and bustle of a winter gale on my face. But I live only to complete my dream of an unholy death, don't ruin my death, or you ruin my dream," said the bomber.

"What is your plan then?" asked Forrest.

"I'm surprised you haven't deciphered it as yet, seeing how keenly you found me."

The bomber leaned against the wall by the window, out of sight.

"May I proffer a deduction," said Forrest, as the soldier nodded, "some of the debris in this room appears newly formed. The stanchions holding up the ceiling initially appeared worn over time, but I've since realized that this has been done purposefully. I would surmise that you've rigged the building with explosives and now await the inevitable response by the armed units to rescue me before blowing the building apart."

He sniggered, which fulminated into a snorted laugh.

"Ha! Yes! You're quite the perspicacious one aren't you?" said the bomber.

"How do you intend to deal with the flash grenades and snipers?" asked Forrest.

"They won't pose a problem. I chose the textile factory as the walls of these old buildings are thick enough to prevent your cohorts from shooting me through the bricks. And you've clearly missed the deadman's switch in my left hand. Should the fun begin, I'll trigger it, and if I get killed or laid unconscious, the switch will be released and everyone will die. After all, a man's game charges a man's price."

"Freeze! Hands up! Don't move or I'll blow your fucking head off!"

The bomber slowly rotated on the spot, first turning his head towards the voice, then his shoulders, and his body steadily twisted round like a snake uncoiling. He seemed pleased to have another player at the party. His smile, malignant and wide, made his eyes narrow at the edges. He sniffed the air like a man who'd just been freed from prison.

"I can smell you from here. You stink of cheap perfume, fear and naivety. Tell me young lady, what will you do once you shoot me and I drop my detonator?"

He flashed open his left hand to reveal a silver metal claw like a knuckle duster, wrapped in his fingers. His gun remained in his right palm.

"Drop the gun. Do it or we all die," hollered Imogen.

"Then we all die," said the bomber.

Forrest looked at her. He saw in her, at that moment, the truth of her nature. All the fuss, the bravado, the fitness regime, the pretty hair, the engagement ring, it was all pomp and ceremony up to this point. She had courage and the soul of an officer. He was there for his pessimism and apathy towards living, but she was there with the optimistic will to carry on.

"Imogen, don't shoot. He has us at checkmate. He wants you to call in the firearms team, he wants to be shot. Call them off."

"It's just me Forrest!" she said in a breathy, rapid voice.

The bomber was still grinning. Imogen held the gun with two hands pointed directly forwards, the barrel aimed at his head, finger on the trigger.

"Well, in that case, I think I'll have a cigarette. Mr Forrest, please?" he said, looking over at him.

"Sure," said the detective. He pulled a cigarette out from the pack and the lighter, and calmly walked over to the bomber. At first, Jackson seemed unsure whether to let the detective approach him, but in seeing their relationship, trusted the male detective wouldn't risk the life of his friend. "Here you are," said Forrest, handing him the smoke. The bomber slipped the gun in his hand to the floor behind him.

The bomber placed the cigarette in his mouth and Forrest lit it for him. Forrest's eyes stared into his; his countenance took a defined shape, like concrete. "These things will kill you, you know," said the detective, grabbing the bomber's left hand. He squeezed the soldier's fist crushing it into the device.

"You fucking cretin! The switch is already engaged. Didn't you think I'd have prepared for visitors? Don't you know there is no escape," said the bomber. "Even if you shoot me you can't stop this going off!"

Forrest carried a halcyon gift of calm in his words as Imogen listened to him speak.

"In fact, that's exactly what I'd hoped for. I didn't come here to survive. When I said you and I were the same, I lied. I'm not like you. You're a killer, but you can't handle your own death. I've never killed anyone, but I welcome mine." He turned to Kline. "Imogen, it's time for you to leave kid. I don't blame you. I never have. I believe in the right to choose to die, especially for your country."

The bomber began struggling but being one handed, trapped in a vicelike grip of the heavier Forrest, his plight was useless.

She spoke with zeal only dampened by the tears in her throat; "Don't do it, Forrest. Please, please, don't do it. What about your daughter Annabel?"

"This is for her. Goodbye, kid. Run! Run away!"

Forrest's right hand squeezed the throat of the bomber who was swinging his fists into the face of the detective. A pain rang through the muscles of Forrest's cheek, but to no avail. Forrest squeezed harder and pulled the bomber from the wall and lowered him to the floor, almost with ease. The adrenalin rush took over his body and gave him the strength to proceed. He mounted the bomber, laying his bulk over the slender soldier's body. Like a bear, he pulled at the bomber's cloistering fingers, prising out the steely gem inside. The man clung on, futilely, hopelessly, as Kline bolted out of the corrugated fence. She screamed for the police to retreat. The switch flopped out of the bomber's hand and rolled slightly across the floor, like the first stone that was cast upon them entering the scene.

Upon leaving the factory, the sound of the bomb punched her ears. It was a dull thud, quieter than she anticipated. The shattering of glass followed the sound as rubble tumbled into a cloud of dust, debris flew through the air and the police ducked for cover, but there were no screams, no cries. And after a few seconds, the birdsong from the nearby park chorused out across the road and bounced about her.

It is said that a swan sings when death is nigh. The song of the damned heard across the ripple of the waves. A final call from the manifestation of the living. There was no song on this occasion, only the ripple of life ebbing away and an aftershock of blood coating a room red. The moribund Forrest lay in the stillness and listened to the last beats of his heart, the last whisper of his soul. And it was there, in the quiet, that he felt, at last, connectivity with the world. He had long seen people die, and he was now, no longer afraid of death. He welcomed it. He was home.

*****

LETTERS

XXXVIII

KLINE crossed the road and countered the numbers of each building. Gravity pulled her head down, and loathing held it there. The building wasn't cool and didn't try to be. It hung there, like a computer technician at the Christmas do wearing an edgy tie, but remaining ever so banal - a white collar factory. She passed Ernie on the front desk one final time and gave him a forced crooked smile, the smile of a persona non grata, and indubitably not the last one of the day. She climbed the stairwell up to the third floor. The smell was familiar but the climb was more laborious than usual. It reminded her of her final walk around her school as a sixteen year old girl: the feel of the bannister, the light in the windows, the hard concrete steps painted red, and the memories of leaving the building, forever.

A pause, a deep breath, her eyes fixated on her hand, she pushed the office door open. The scene resembled an outlaw gate-crashing a local saloon attracting everyone's fearful faces. Inspector Walsh played the barmaid gently wiping a glass behind the bar, and she half-expected her to say, 'Now we don't want any trouble in here.'

They knew she was internal affairs; it had to come out at the inquest. Some things can't be kept secret, and the death of a colleague meant the whole internal department suffered. Some thought he died because of her involvement, some thought she had abandoned him in that factory, whilst others just hated the Professional Standards Unit no matter what their involvement. Her future as an undercover agent was surely over.

She walked the frosty path across thin ice to her desk, avoiding the cracks of faces around her so she may stay afloat. Reaching her desk, she calmly opened out her holdall and began filling it with Galbraith's possessions. Her files on Forrest were first, followed by her patrol equipment, radio, vest, and then her personal effects: shoes, makeup and perfume. She heard a voice in her ear and looked up to see Martin Brown stood over her. His tongue was visibly pushing his cheek out like he was eating a large cherry.

"They found this on him when he died, it looks like it was meant for you but he never got around to posting it," said DS Brown.

He threw the object on her desk and retreated back to the baying mob circling her.

She looked at it carefully. A white envelope marked *Imogen*. She slid it off the table and into her pocket. This was not the time. A brief moment of anger nearly spurned her to stand and address the crowd in defiance of her motives but grace and dignity overcame emotion. She stood up, bag in hand, and walked out the door without verse or venture.

A window left open allowed a cold breeze to escort her from the premises. She burst through the front door and met the welcoming street, like an old friend reunited, an unshackled playmate. The sun winked at her in knowledge the winter solstice had gone by and days would become longer.

She headed back to her base station in Islington for a debrief with her inspector. In front of her sat the reports that she'd written along the way. Those reports documenting Forrest as an irascible and dangerous man, volatile like a pan full of oil spitting at the naked flesh.

She remembered the investigations that the pair had covered. She began researching their jobs to see how they had resulted. The cargo hold full of dead immigrants led to both the survivors being arrested for criminal damage to the cargo hold of tyres. However, in light of the deaths of their fellow travellers, both survivors were freed without charge by the police. Regardless of this, immigration held them in custody and they were deported within a week. The bodies of those who died were taken to the morgue for identification and return to their home country. It never made the local press.

The young black boy who was shot ended up withdrawing from the prosecution and refused to assist the police. As Forrest had predicted, the Harrington Boys had committed the shooting, and on the very evening after they had visited the shisha lounge, the gang tried to move the gun and were caught by the surveillance team monitoring them. The two men carrying the gun were both held in prison on remand to await trial. The shooter of the boy was never discovered.

The man Carlos Ramon who reported being raped did turn out to be a prostitute. Kline researched the intelligence conducted on the case and the detective in charge had found Ramon on various websites offering his services as a prostitute at the very address where the offence had allegedly taken place. Through Ramon's email account, they uncovered all the messages between him and the accused. The man who was arrested was called Stephen White: he was a married man, with three children, and worked in the City. He had used Ramon's services for over two years. In interview, he claimed that Ramon had wanted him to leave his wife for him and had stopped taking payment from him some time ago. They'd even gone on holiday together and he could prove this. When he came by on that night, he brought over some wine and they discussed their affair. When he told Ramon he was not going to leave his family, they had sex, and then Ramon asked him to leave. Before he knew it, the police were knocking on his family home arresting him for rape. He later claimed it ruined his marriage.

The husband Eric Barnes who was arrested for the murder of Cassandra Pinto-Barnes confessed in interview to her murder and pleaded guilty at the first hearing. He had discovered she was stealing money from him and sending the proceeds to her family in Portugal, where she already had children with another man. He admitted being in the kitchen with her and stabbing her through the neck in a fit of rage. He was deeply remorseful and broke down in his cell.

Kline opened the file marked John Forrest and began deleting her previous reports. She reopened a new file; it was brief in earnest and stated that Forrest was an exemplary officer who died defending his country. She recommended him for the Queen's Police Medal in recognition of his talents and service and sent the report to her seniors.

She returned to her lonely apartment wondering whether it was likely she would still have a job with internal affairs; in the debrief the DI was unclear; a decision would be made soon. Sat in her kitchen, she stared at Forrest's letter. The steely glass table clinked as it met with her coffee cup. She picked up the letter.

Nightmarish thoughts seeped into her consciousness. She re-called the past week's events since he'd died: that they had conducted DNA tests on the bodies in the warehouse, that someone had mentioned seeing a limb, tattooed with a British guard carrying a musket, and how she walked away from the discussion. She preferred the other story, the one where Forrest had disappeared, having all along staged his death like the bomber had once done. Perhaps the pair had worked on disappearing together and used her as a stooge to front the story. Maybe he had escaped shortly before the explosive had gone off and disappeared into the sunset like a cliché. Perhaps it was just a dream.

Thoughts of a life less ordinary cleansed her brain of the enigmatic interrogator. The feeling of loss, once again, bubbled up to the surface, uncontrollably jetting out like a shaken can of fizzy drink. Such a meaningless and preventable loss was his untimely death, like a dead bird at the feet of a domestic cat, prone and torn on the kitchen floor.

She breathed deeply in and out, and began to process the events of the past fortnight.. *How would John have seen it: Isn't life all an illusion? Isn't it just a spectacle propagated by fears, imagery, advertisements and dreams? Who was he? An idea constructed in my mind or a concept dreamt up by my own feelings. Did I ever really know him?*

Or perhaps, there's something wrong with the world if it cannot accommodate such a fine detective. Why does a deficit have to live in him for the genius to thrive, like Icarus, who fell because he flew too close to the sun?

She opened the letter tearing carefully along the seam of its white envelope as though it itself were a part of her old friend. Inside was a note. It was very much like Forrest, written in poor handwriting on cheap paper, the method of delivery was unimportant; it was the message that was special. So many of us get lost in the aesthetics of a person, or how they appear, or speak, or act, without truly listening to what they're actually saying. Despite the explosion, the letter remained untarnished. *Taken from his body at the scene?* She wondered. And then she remembered her conversation with him about writing a letter to someone but never posting it, and Forrest's good friendship with the Scenes of Crime Officer.

She read the note:

Dear Imogen,

Firstly, I'm sorry if I've caused you upset. I hope by the end of my letter you feel some degree of pleasure resulting from my death, but before that, I want to ensure that you don't follow in my footsteps.

The only way knowledge can be acquired is if there's something to be grasped and something grasping it. In this world today, we grasp at everything and know nothing. None of us takes time to truly grasp at nature, or people, or knowledge. I used to look at something and imagine that the scene was actually a painting. That someone had sat down and created this event from their mind, and taken their time to paint all the little faces, bricks, cars, steps, and so on, in the finest detail. And when you realise that everything is sculpted that way, it becomes quite beautiful. Even the saddest situations can give rise to joy, for when the sadness in me is allowed to meet the sadness in you, I feel ever so free.

The problem for me was the realisation that the world is a happy place at an unhappy time. My problem wasn't an addiction of any sorts, just reality. I wish I could have lived at a time in the past where technology didn't exist as it does today – from a land where people were simpler. I've always felt like a misfit living in the wrong epoch.

So in the end the question on my mind was whether my life had meaning. Behind the scrim of loss that was left with others, was there anything of note implanted in time; or was I, like the fading head of fire at the end of my cigarette, just dust in the wind at God's fingertips. I'll leave you to judge that.

What we must remember is the first rule of thermodynamics: that no energy is created in the universe and none can ever be destroyed. Every single part of me remains in this universe for eternity and can never die. You realise, that all we are and ever will be is simply debris from the Big Bang. Think about that. Debris from an explosion that is now able to understand how it became debris. I'm happier being outside of the human form, being returned to the cosmos. Being stardust.

Thou wast that all to me, love,
For which my soul did pine—
A green isle in the sea, love,
A fountain and a shrine,
All wreathed with fairy fruits and flowers,
And all the flowers were mine.

And all my days are trances,
And all my nightly dreams
Are where thy grey eye glances,
And where thy footstep gleams—
In what ethereal dances,
By what eternal streams.

Have the conviction to grasp at life Imogen. Nothing is more important.

John.

Printed in Poland
by Amazon Fulfillment
Poland Sp. z o.o., Wrocław